The Tale of a Transplanted Heart

Novels by Beverly Hurwitz MD

Who Has Your Back?
WAR in the OR
Is the Cat Lady Crazy?
Nobody Else's Business

Also By Beverly Hurwitz MD

Park City Hiking Guide
A Walker's Guide to Park City

The Tale of a Transplanted Heart

Beverly Hurwitz MD

Surrogate Press®

Published in the United States by
Surrogate Press®
an imprint of Faceted Press®
Surrogate Press, LLC
Park City, Utah

SurrogatePress.com

ISBN: 978-1-964245-06-5

Library of Congress Control Number: 2024913072

Book Cover and Interior design by:
Katie Mullaly, Surrogate Press®

This book is dedicated to all of those connected
to the world of organ transplantation,
to all of those who are protecting bats,
and to all who have suffered from and been lost to viruses.

The people and places in this story are fictitious with the exception
of a few cultural icons. Any resemblance to other real people,
places or other entities is purely coincidental.

Doctor Melinda Villarose suppressed a scream after slamming the door to her new windowless office. In the unforgiving fluorescent light, she focused on the one thing in the room that wasn't institutional ivory. Behind the diminutive desk hung a haunting landscape of a storm approaching a quaint old barn. A lone horse grazed in the pastoral background. A sinister looking cloud was hurling a lightning bolt through the blackened sky.

Melinda focused on the lightning bolt and tried to project her anger into it. But then, she worried about the horse. *Why did the artist leave this animal there? Why wasn't it running toward the barn?* Melinda wanted to scream at the horse too. Instead, she inhaled deeply and shuddered. She was so disturbed by the meeting she had just had with her new boss that she sat down at the computer and furiously typed a letter of resignation.

After that, Melinda was able to stop shaking. She turned her chair around and again looked at the painting in its antiquated oak frame. Her eyes kept getting drawn to the small image of the horse. It was honey colored with a flowing white mane and tail. Against the shadowy greens of the trees and the dark sky, the horse appeared as a spot of sunshine.

Was that why Doctor Carmichael left this painting behind when he took everything else with him? Did that spot of sunshine help him get through the storms when he occupied this office? Did he think the next occupant of this office would find this picture comforting? Or did he just not like the painting?

Melinda got out of her chair to look at the picture more closely. Feathery, impressionistic brush strokes created the stark white barn, the foreboding clouds, and the deep summer greens. The horse, in contrast, was painted with solid color, as though another artist had added it. The horse also looked pregnant; actually, very pregnant. *Twins?* Exceedingly rare in horses. Hard to even imagine.

Once again, Melinda felt like screaming. *Pregnant beings aren't going to be allowed around here anymore, Mrs. Horse. You better gallop out of here right now. Our new hospital owners believe that pregnancy is not compatible with training to be a physician.*

Melinda returned to her desktop and opened up the file of candidates for family practice internships. From a field of potentially ninety-two, all vying for nine positions, they'd outright rejected sixteen. They'd ranked the remaining seventy-four in order of favorability. All of the top candidates would probably end up going to more prestigious programs.

In the complicated system of matching medical school graduates with clinical training programs, only the best hospitals and the best candidates could hope to get their priority choices. There are some hospitals that don't get enough graduates to fill their programs, and there are some doctors, especially in the case of international medical school graduates, who don't get selected by any hospital. As soon as the match results become known, there's a scramble for the leftovers. Melinda's hospital would be happy to get any of the candidates in the middle of their rankings.

Doctor Melinda Villarose had spent the past nine years co-managing the residency program at Bandore County Hospital, along with the now absent Doctor Stuart Carmichael. Her old colleague had just taken leave to continue his battle with cancer, and it seemed unlikely that he'd be back. Melinda knew of no prospects for another physician being assigned to assist her in the selection and training of tomorrow's primary care doctors. It appeared that she'd now be alone in this task that was challenging for even two people.

Except for the years that she'd served as an army psychiatrist, evaluating prisoners and military lunatics, Melinda Villarose had worked for Bandore Hospital in one capacity or another for more than two decades. She had watched it grow from a small rural facility into one of the largest hospitals in the state. With more than three hundred beds, it currently served the entire northern tier of the region and a population that would have to otherwise travel three or more hours for medical assistance.

However, Bandore County Hospital was now being considered a money loser for the Tazodan Health Corporation that had just purchased it. The immediate plan was to close down all of its services that weren't profitable, starting with the department of psychiatry which Melinda had formerly chaired.

2

Melinda had just come from her first meeting with the new management team. They appreciated the cheap labor provided by the family practice residents, but the costs of overtime pay and substitute physicians when these residents took maternity leave was a problem. There were currently two senior residents, one junior resident and one intern off the schedule for maternity leave, and another was out for illness. That was equivalent to almost a quarter of the staff. If Melinda couldn't adjust the profile of the incoming interns to reduce these costs, the residency program would have to be reduced or eliminated.

"But half of all family practice applicants are female," she argued. "Are you telling me to only select males?"

"You're the profiler here, Doctor Villarose. Surely, with your psychiatric and military expertise, you will be able to select physicians whose first priority is their medical career. Men make their careers their first priority all the time," said Ingrid Smythe, senior vice president of the Tazodan Corporation and the new chief executive of Bandore Hospital. "Physicians who are getting paid to train for three years should prioritize such a generous opportunity. Family is important too, but as the verse goes, 'to everything there is a season.'"

"What about the chapter and verse of state and federal laws against discrimination? What about reproductive rights?" Melinda countered. Her arguments got so twisted around by a forked-tongued Tazodan attorney, that she could feel her blood pressure rising. Her extensive knowledge of human relations policies and employment law was apparently just an inconvenient impediment to the goals of this corporate wolf pack.

"You have your assignment, Doctor Villarose. Please submit your list of acceptable candidates to Ms. Smythe for approval by Friday morning."

With that statement, the three executives who had called her to their conference table, dismissed her. She was so shaken, she didn't even remember to walk to the new office she had just been transferred to, until she got to her old office and found it occupied by a stranger.

Melinda turned her attention back to the sunshine horse with the bulging belly. The mare was going to stand right there and weather the storm. *Is that what I'm supposed to do? Is that why Doctor Carmichael left this painting behind?*

Melinda started pouring over her file of candidates for the family practice residency program. She and Doctor Carmichael had spent months reviewing the applicants' records, interviewing them, consulting with their references, and trying to dig up whatever other scraps of information they could find about these students' potential for satisfactory performance as physicians. Of the seventy-four they hoped would be good choices, forty-four, almost sixty percent, were female.

After spending an agonizing five hours reranking the candidates to come up with a different male to female ratio, Melinda added another paragraph to her resignation later.

She was particularly worried about one specific candidate, a medical student who had requested acceptance into the Bandore training program outside of the National Resident Matching Program. Medical student Thea Baccay, who would be the pride of any training program, wanted to train in this no-name hospital in nowhere USA, for very personal reasons. She should have been a shoo-in, but now, she could be the highest pregnancy risk on the whole roster of family doctor wannabes. Young, recently married, and childless, Thea could be exactly the type of candidate that Tazodan would reject.

It was almost eight o'clock when Melinda finally dragged herself out of the hospital, but she couldn't stop stewing about the outrageous injustice to her cherished hospital programs.

"We have a report of a one-car accident on Ninth Street," the police dispatcher told Officers Harris and Siddoway on a foggy Sunday morning. "A witness says a speeding black SUV crashed into the concrete pillar of the Lincoln Avenue overpass. The caller thought the overpass could be compromised and she might have seen a body in the rubble. We need emergency traffic control."

Bystanders were gathering around the wreck when the police arrived. A black-clad pair of legs could be seen amidst chunks of broken concrete on top of the car's mangled front end. A big burly man was trying to remove a piece of concrete, only for another piece to come crumbling down. He quickly backed away as Officer Siddoway ripped open a leg of the skinny black jeans and searched for a pulse behind the victim's knee. It was faint, but there was definitely a pulse.

Officer Harris called for an ambulance and back-up, and reported the car's license plate number to dispatch. Another police cruiser arrived to divert traffic until the engineers could determine the stability of the overpass. More drivers on Ninth Street stopped at the scene of the accident, and with help from bystanders, they were able to lift a large piece of concrete off of the shoulders of the victim who'd apparently been thrown face down onto the hood of the car. Everyone gasped when the crushed skull became visible. An ambulance crew arrived to extricate and transport the victim.

As Officer Harris directed traffic, there was another call from dispatch. They'd just received a call from a frantic woman who reported that her fifteen-year-old daughter had left home in a rage, stealing her mother's car keys and SUV. The license plate number confirmed the accident victim's identity as that fifteen-year-old girl. Another policeman took over the accident scene while Officer Bree Siddoway was dispatched to the victim's home.

Once there, Bree Siddoway was confronted by a hysterical young woman with a toddler in her arms. No one else was home.

"I knew something like this would happen," Deidra Collins repeatedly wailed. "Oh my God! I didn't know what to do anymore. Zoey was so out of control. I tried everything: punishment, bribes, counseling, changing her school, medication. Oh my God! She was so smart. She had so much potential. Please tell me this is all a nightmare and my daughter's coming home."

While this devastated mother tried to comfort her crying toddler and compose herself, Officer Bree Siddoway looked around the modest suburban residence. It was all very ordinary, well maintained and except for strewn about toddler toys, quite tidy. There were no ashtrays. There were no liquor bottles or pill vials sitting on counters.

Deidra Collins was tall and curvy. Her long copper-colored hair was pulled back into a ponytail. She wore sweats, sneakers, and no makeup. She had no noticeable piercings or tattoos. There was no alcohol on her breath. What worried Officer Bree Siddoway was that Deidra Collins looked entirely too young to be the mother of a fifteen-year-old.

Bree didn't know if she would be transporting this distraught young woman to the I.C.U. to comfort her daughter, or to the morgue to identify her remains, but she told Deidra that she was there to take her to the hospital that her daughter was being taken to. Since Deidra no longer had a car, she was appreciative. She gathered up her little boy and some of Zoey's favorite things that she hoped would be comforting to her seriously injured daughter. As the police cruiser pulled away, Bree inquired about Zoey's father.

"My husband Jon is Zoey's stepfather. He adopted her after we got married when Zoey was twelve." Deidra burst into tears again before telling Bree that Jon was traveling, and she wouldn't even be able to tell him about the accident until later in the day. She said he travels all over the world photographing sporting events for news networks. "He's gone about sixty percent of the time."

Rather defensively, Deidra said that her husband Jon and Zoey had a great relationship because of their shared passion for sports, though certainly not for their favorite teams. "Jon's a lifelong Green Bay Packers fan. Somewhere around second grade, my daughter developed a thing for the Dallas Cowboys. My father watches football but not consistently. He likes the Kansas City Chiefs, and my mother's father likes the Buffalo Bills, but no one in our home was ever fanatical about watching sports except for my daughter. Maybe she got the Cowboy thing from another kid in her class. Just about everything in her closet has the Cowboys logo on it. She also likes the New York Yankees, while Jon's a fan of the Minnesota Twins. But they both like the Chicago Bulls."

Deidra's tears continued to flow, as she freely rambled on as if forgetting where they were going. Bree passed her a packet of tissues and asked her if Zoey had a biologic father who should be notified. Deidra started to cry harder, and the conversation abruptly ended.

At the hospital, they were directed to the I.C.U. Bree held the crying toddler while a physician explained to Deidra that her daughter was brain-dead, and that they could maintain her on a ventilator only long enough for her to be an organ donor if that's what the family would choose. He briefly explained how organ donation works. He advised Deidra that they were having trouble maintaining Zoey's blood pressure and that in a few hours, her organs might not be salvageable. Deidra was asked if she would like to talk to a counselor or someone else about the decision.

Deidra sobbed quietly as she sat next to her brain-dead daughter. Twice she picked her phone up, but it appeared that she put it down without calling anyone. After about twenty minutes, she signed the papers for organ donation. She was certain her husband would approve. Though she wasn't sure if Zoey had been suicidal, or if she had just had a horrific accident, Deidra said that she believed that it would have been her daughter's wish to have someone else benefit from her death.

Only when they were several miles away from the hospital did Deidra calm down enough to reveal to police office Siddoway that Zoey's biologic father was an unknown. One winter evening, in her unsuspecting suburban neighborhood, thirteen-year-old Deidra Martin was returning home from a friend's house. From behind a bush, a man jumped out, grabbed her from behind, threw her jacket over her head, threw her into the bushes, raped her, and then fled. She was able to run home, and her parents immediately took her to the E.R. for forensic evidence, but the rapist was never caught. When it was realized that Deidra was pregnant, her parents chose to raise the child as their own. Deidra wasn't given any say in the matter.

Deidra and Zoey lived with Deidra's parents until Jon Collins came into their lives. Deidra had met Jon at a college basketball game that she took Zoey to for her tenth birthday. Deidra emphasized that Jon was a very good stepfather. For Zoey's thirteenth birthday, he scored tickets for a Cowboys game that might have been the highlight of Zoey's short life. But Deidra admitted to Bree that Jon was also frustrated by Zoey's behavioral issues. Puberty had morphed their daughter into an angry, irrational, untrustworthy hooligan.

Bree dropped Deidra and her son Todd off at her parents' home. Grandma and Grandpa Martin hadn't yet received the tragic news. Zoey had been a daughter to them too.

Officer Bree Siddoway immediately informed the morgue that there was no biologic father to protest organ donation.

Bree had a personal stake in the matter. Her stepbrother Gavin was in desperate need of a kidney and none of the willing relatives had proved to be a good match.

4

octor Melinda Villarose hadn't had a good night's sleep since her meeting with the Tazodan execs. When she did sleep, she repeatedly dreamt about the sunshine horse. She could see it facing away from the blackened skies and soaking up the retreating sun rays, while leisurely dining on dandelions. "Horse lettuce," her grandfather used to call dandelion leaves. Melinda's best memories in life were her childhood summers on her grandparents' farm.

In her dream, a tremendous bolt of lightning struck behind the horse. The mare raised her head high and flared her nostrils, as if smelling the electricity. Heavy raindrops pelted her, and her tail was blowing straight out at a ninety-degree angle. She'd only have to take a few steps to be sheltered by a nearby canopy of trees, but she put her head down and went back to grazing.

Maybe the horse knew she was safer from the lightning if she stayed away from the trees. Maybe the wind and rain washed away her summer dander and refreshed her senses. Maybe, she was driven less by fear of the storm than by the biologic imperative to procreate and nurture the next generation. The soon-to-be-a-mother mare stood her ground.

Then, the yellow horse blurred out of Melinda's dream and the ferocious dark clouds came into focus. One of the clouds looked like an angry face. Melinda's dream turned to a yearbook page of faces, mostly of those female medical students she had moved to the bottom of her rankings.

She awoke from the dream and languished in bed, consumed with the thoughts of those faces which undoubtedly belonged to wonderful women. It was usually the very best people who chose to be family doctors.

While four out of five medical students opt to work in specialties that only take care of one stage of life, or one body part, it's a steadily shrinking minority of doctors who are inclined to take care of whole people and their whole families for their whole lives. Especially in a for-profit health care system that prioritizes procedures, family doctors aren't valued by the corporations that have hijacked health care.

Moreover, unlike specialists like oncologists, who only have to be well-informed about advances in the management of cancer, family practice doctors have to keep up with rapidly changing knowledge about all kinds of human maladies, from headaches to heart attacks to hemorrhoids. The speed at which treatments keep changing makes a lot of medical knowledge obsolete almost as soon as it's acquired. It was far more demanding to be an up-to-date generalist than to be an expert specialist.

Do these Tazodan execs who talk about cutting the family practice program know any of that? And who else are they going to get to work in these back woods? Is their ultimate plan to close the hospital, or will they just replace all of the doctors with lower-level providers?

Melinda popped out of bed and went to the Internet to see what she could learn about Ingrid Smythe and the other new administrators that Tazodan had assigned to manage her hospital.

There was little information about most of the administrators, but Ingrid Smythe's web presence suggested that she was a financial genius, if not a goddess. She held prestigious degrees in economics and law. She had worked on international trade agreements for almost a decade as a member of a globally prominent law firm that provided legal services to governments.

Sixteen years previously, at the age of forty-three, Ingrid and her third husband, an infamous venture capitalist, created a corporation that now owns multiple companies. Most of the web information was about Ingrid's husband. Some of the companies listed under his name produce components for medical equipment. Some extract natural elements used by pharmaceutical and manufacturing partners. One of the companies owns seven mines. Another produces biologic products for laboratories. Another company is a financial partner for vaccine research. One company manufactures jewelry made from lithium crystals. *No wonder Ingrid wears such exotic necklaces.*

Apparently, Ingrid Smythe had become a financial consultant to Tazodan in its early development and the corporation was now paying her a king's ransom to analyze and improve the revenue cycle of newly acquired hospitals. Melinda would later learn that Ingrid liked to hang out in hospitals because it helped her to keep abreast of medical science developments that were relevant to the operation of her companies.

Some of the websites that reveal personal data indicated that Ingrid had two adult children and some grandchildren. So surely, this extraordinarily successful woman could be made to understand the inherent procreativity of women who would choose to be family doctors.

Melinda spent the rest of her day thinking about her presentation to Tazodan Vice President Ingrid Smythe. Even if she wound up resigning, she still felt compelled to fight for the family practice program.

5

When she arrived on Friday morning, Doctor Melinda Villarose was surprised to find that Ingrid Smythe's office had been expediently renovated out of the offices of two former administrators. An impeccably groomed man sat at a sleek front desk.

"Ms. Smythe won't be in today," the man said to Melinda's consternation. "She did tell me to expect you and that you would be bringing a presentation for her. She asked me to ensure you submitted the presentation to me in her absence."

After all the time she'd spent getting ready for this encounter, Melinda was enraged. "I hope Ms. Smythe isn't ill," she said, trying to mask her anger, as she tightened her grip on the disk she had hand-carried to the meeting.

Ingrid Smythe's receptionist gave her a reassuring smile. "Not that I know of. I think she had to attend an emergency meeting over at the mother ship. She'll be back on Monday."

"Then maybe I should reschedule," Melinda said, as she turned around to leave.

'Mr. Receptionist' leapt to his feet and stepped into Melinda's path with his hand out. "I believe Ms. Smythe intended to review that disk before her scheduled meetings on Monday, but I'll see where there's an opening in the schedule for you to meet with her after that."

Melinda felt trapped. She hesitated to hand over the disk. In the abrupt hospital takeover that had only just begun, she hadn't yet been informed about how the new administration processed confidential information. If Tazodan was so willing to overlook employment regulations, how could she be sure the personal files of seventy-four future physicians wouldn't be used inappropriately.

Melinda asked the receptionist if he had security clearance. He reached for his badge which dangled from a lanyard under his tailored vest. "James C. Dzobak," Melinda read his badge aloud. "Thank you, James." She input his hospital ID number into her phone. "There's highly confidential information on this disk. I need to know who I'm delivering it to."

James made a humble little head bow. He started to return to his desk without asking Melinda for the password to the disk, without which it couldn't be opened. Melinda seized an opportunity. "Are you new around here, James? I know of someone local named Dzobak, a former patient; but of course, that's confidential."

James cocked his head as if interested.

"Have you been with Ms. Smythe wherever Tazodan sends her, or are you her local support staff?"

James seemed receptive to small talk and admitted that he'd been with Ms. Smythe for just six months. He'd trained with her at Tazodan's flagship hospital, but Bandore County was his home. His career had kept him away for a decade and he was glad to be back. His folks were getting on in years and needed more assistance. That's the real reason he'd taken this job, or so he said.

Like old-timers, Melinda and James talked about the closure of the local factory, the selling off of the big farms, and the expansive, expensive development around the lake. They shared their concern about the antiquity of the infrastructure, especially the schools.

Melinda came to understand that although he was performing the duties of a receptionist and secretary, James Dzobak was actually Ingrid Smythe's chief data analyst. Melinda was now really stunned that 'Mr. Data Analyst' hadn't asked for a password to the disk, but she decided to try to further exploit the local connection. Thea Baccay was also from Bandore County. Maybe Ingrid Smythe could be influenced by this assistant of hers. Melinda got the feeling that James was a smooth operator.

Melinda told James that the disk was all about the potential new doctors that the hospital hoped would be willing to serve in their community. She told him how Bandore County was too rural to attract most doctors, and that many of the doctors who would come to train in this hospital were seeking better training than was available in their less developed countries. She told him it was hard for this hospital to attract top people, but that there was a top candidate who actually wanted to train here, but wanted an early acceptance to the program which required administrative approval.

Then, Melinda told James about Thea Baccay: How local kid Thea had started winning science fair awards when she was in fourth grade. How Thea had discovered a fungus that was infecting local gardens when she was in seventh grade. How she'd published a paper in the *Journal of Cellular Biology* before she graduated high school. How she induced an ivy league university to start a graduate program in neuro-psycho-immunology when she was a college junior majoring in biochemistry. How she published multiple research papers while a graduate student and as a medical student.

Melinda also told James how Thea got swept off her feet by one of her medical school professors, Darius Amari, a rising star in virology. How just a few months after Thea and Darius married, COVID came along and ravaged her new husband's heart. How Darius was now on a waiting list for a heart transplant. How Thea expected to be a widow by the time she starts her residency if a suitable donor heart didn't materialize. Melinda also told James that Thea was rooted in Bandore County, and that she had a strong family network here to support her.

Melinda hoped she'd garnered some sympathy for a hometown girl.

She also wondered if the problem of the missing password would fall on James's head or her own.

What Melinda didn't tell James, was that Thea Baccay planned to have children with her husband, and to do it here while doing her family practice residency, so that her family could help out. Darius's sperm had been preserved in case he doesn't make it, or in case he gets a new heart and is then on anti-rejection drugs that could impact his fertility. Cyclosporine, the anti-rejection drug that organ recipients have to take, is known to impair sperm counts, but Thea Baccay had let Melinda know that it was definitely in her plans to have children.

Darius Amari got the standby call at 8:33 Sunday morning. Zoey Collins's tissue samples had been sent to the lab even before Deidra Collins had signed the consent forms, and results would come back shortly.

The transplant center where Darius received care was the closest for the heart, though it was still an hour away by helicopter. Transplant surgeons preferred hearts that were less than four hours old, so Darius's center had a good chance of being first in line. Livers could be viable for eight or more hours, and kidneys could survive twelve hours, even longer in some cases.

After Deidra Collins signed the consent forms, surgical teams from each of the potential recipient's transplant centers were also put on standby. Zoey's heart, liver, kidneys, pancreas, and intestines appeared to all be salvageable, and her skin could be used for burn victims. Some of her ligaments could also be transplanted into people with busted up joints.

Thea and Darius lived in his university-owned townhouse right next to the hospital campus where the transplant center was located. Of the seven critical heart transplant candidates that lived within commuting distance of this center, they were the closest. But it wouldn't matter who could get there first. The heart would go to the patient who was the closest biologic match, assuming there was one.

The transplant coordinator, Julie Jacobs, informed Darius that the donor was very young and healthy and a good match for height and weight. Although male recipients did better with male hearts, Julie did advise Darius of the donor's female gender. Better than most patients, Darius and Thea would understand that transplants mostly depended on the donor and recipient having good chemistry, rather than being of the same gender. Besides, Darius couldn't wait any longer for a male heart. He was just days away from death.

The wait time to see if Darius won the tissue compatibility lottery was agonizing. His suitcase was always packed. Since becoming so sick that he had risen to the top of the waiting list, he'd spent every hour of every day just hoping for this moment. For the past three months, he had been confined to a wheelchair. He was on oxygen, and he'd quickly turn blue if there was any interruption of the oxygen flow, like the tubing getting caught under the wheelchair.

Darius was also more or less drowning in the bodily fluids his weak heart could no longer push around, even though a surgeon had installed a VAD, Ventricular Assistive Device, into his heart to help it pump. The fluids backed up in his lungs and made it hard to breathe. Fluid also backed up in his tissues and settled in his lower legs which had become so swollen that he could hardly stand, let alone walk. The fluid also made his abdomen swell and it was getting increasingly difficult for this normally skinny man to eat more than a few bites of even his favorite foods.

Thirty months previously, Darius Amari had been a healthy forty-year-old who played pickleball three times a week and ran on a treadmill every other day. When Darius was growing up in the communities of British embassies, he had become an accomplished table tennis player. When he first landed in America, he was disappointed to realize that ping pong was valued more as recreation than as sport, so he was thrilled to transfer his skills to pickleball. He strongly believed that scientists' minds were kept sharp by keeping physically fit, but now, neither his mind nor his body seemed to be functioning. He'd turned most of his research responsibilities over to his lab director and best friend, Sullivan Dietz, who he hoped would take over for him if he died. Sullivan shared Darius's research goals and he was a great asset to the operation of the lab.

Darius and Thea wondered if transplant coordinator Julie Jacobs would even tell them if no one was a close enough match and the heart was going to waste. They knew transplant coordinators never give out information about donors and recipients. They also knew that only twenty percent of potential donor hearts actually get to a recipient on time, and only about ten percent of patients waiting for a new heart are lucky enough to get one in time. Darius was already on borrowed time.

Thea tried to distract herself by reading a medical journal. Darius tried to digest the enormity of the decision the young victim's loved ones had made in favor of donation. Hard as they each tried to calmly pass the time, neither of them could focus on much of anything but Darius's phone. The next ring could change their lives in one of two drastically different directions.

One hour and thirty-three minutes after the first call, the phone rang again. Darius Amari's and the donor's tissues matched as well as any unrelated persons could.

7

James Dzobak called Melinda Villarose on Monday morning. Ms. Smythe wanted to meet with her on Tuesday afternoon. He said nothing about the missing password and Melinda didn't ask.

Melinda immediately put a call in to Thea Baccay, but didn't reach her. She needed to present this young physician in person. Thea looked like a skinny girl on her way to junior high, but the resonance of her deep voice surprises the hell out of people and draws them in. She also has a somewhat unique way of gesturing with her hands that makes others feel connected. And then, there's her little upturned mouth that make people want to smile back at her.

When Thea Baccay requested early acceptance into Bandore's residency program, she was brought in for a more extensive interview with Doctors Villarose and Carmichael. When the interview concluded, Melinda was so enchanted with Thea, that she invited the medical student to dinner. That's when she learned that Thea had driven almost four hours from her medical school to Bandore Hospital by herself because her husband was too incapacitated to come with her. That's when she first heard about Thea's husband's critical heart problem.

Melinda was concerned about Thea's drive back and invited her to stay overnight in her townhouse. Thea accepted and the two women made a strong connection during their evening together, despite their thirty-year age difference. Melinda had lost her husband to coronary heart disease a few years previously, and learning that a young bride like Thea was facing widowhood at this momentous time in her life, touched her deeply.

Thea called Melinda back an hour after Melinda left her a message. She told her that Darius got a new heart the day before, and the surgery had gone well. He was now in the cardiac intensive care unit and there was no way she could drive up to Bandore.

Melinda explained that securing Thea her residency spot had become less certain since the hospital takeover. They needed to make a more personal connection to try to cement Thea's position. The hospital had to submit its list of ranked medical students by the end of the week, so there wasn't much time. Thea however, insisted that she didn't think she could make the trip.

Twenty minutes later, Thea called Melinda back. Darius was doing well, but Thea's presence was of no consequence to the critical care he needed for his first few days with a new heart. For the next day or two, he would be maintained in a medically induced coma. She might as well use the time to come to Bandore. A friend would drive her up.

Melinda explained about the potential issue of maternity leave. She and Thea discussed how they'd approach Ingrid Smythe.

"Thea Baccay, this is James Dzobak," Melinda announced as they entered Smythe's outer office. "James, I hope it's okay if I park Thea here momentarily while I meet with Ms. Smythe. Thea is in town to see her family and you two can share your local connection."

James showed Melinda into the inner office where Ingrid Smythe sat at her keep-your-distance desk. Smythe didn't greet her but continued to focus on her computer screen as if Melinda wasn't there. After half a minute, still looking at the screen, she spoke.

"It's a good thing my assistant James knows how to get around passwords, Doctor Villarose, or I wouldn't have been able to review this file. I need to ask you about some of these applicants."

"I'm so sorry, Ms. Smythe. James and I got to talking about our roots here, and I forgot to give him the password. Are passwords now obsolete? That file contains such confidential information that I worry about it."

Smythe still didn't look up and she didn't answer the question.

"Which of the candidates do you have questions about?" Melinda finally asked.

Ingrid Smythe looked Melinda up and down. The soft silver curls that framed Melinda's smooth skin made her look like a youthful grandmother. Her oversized white coat concealed her fit figure. Ingrid didn't like it that under that white coat, this physician leader wore skinny jeans and running shoes.

"Leona Bryant, for starters. She's already got three kids and she's only twenty-six. My guess is she'll have another one on our company's dime."

Melinda was prepared. She had carefully reexamined the parenthood status of the female applicants and she knew the records of the ones that she wanted to keep on the top of the list.

"Leona Bryant's husband is a full-time childcare provider. Her family structure is no different than that of any male physician. She seems sincerely committed to being a family doctor. When she delivered her last baby in her third year of medical school, she was only off of the schedule for a few days. Leona comes with stellar recommendations. Our hospital would be lucky to get her."

Smythe continued to look at her computer screen. "Ilene McQuaid looks like she's fighting the biologic clock. I see she had a ten-year career as a flight attendant before she went to medical school, and she also recently married. She could be thinking it's baby time."

"Ilene seems truly dedicated to a medical career after living her life in airplane cabins. She's in the top tenth of her class and her wisdom, wit, and worldly experience are well beyond that of most of our potential residents. I believe the new husband has adult children and I doubt they're going to start a new family. He was a pilot and after traipsing around the world for years, they both want to settle down. Ilene is a great fit for our program and maybe she'll even stay in Bandore County, if we're fortunate enough to match with her."

Ingrid Smythe typed some notes as Melinda spoke. They sparred over the maternity potential of two other women before Ingrid finally made eye contact.

"So, tell me about this early acceptance candidate, Thea Baccay. James informed me that there are extenuating circumstances."

"Very extenuating, Ms. Smythe. Thea Baccay's husband underwent a heart transplant the day before yesterday, but as her family is here in Bandore, she's actually here right now. Please excuse me for a second while I check on her."

Without waiting for Smythe's approval, Melinda sprung from her chair, stuck her head into the outer office, and beckoned Thea to come in. Before Ingrid Smythe knew what was happening, a very young-looking women tiptoed into the room as though there was a lion lurking there.

 **8**

"This is Doctor Thea Baccay, Ms. Smythe. I invited Thea to join me so you could meet her. She's here very briefly. She'll be traveling back to the transplant center shortly."

Only momentarily did it appear that Ingrid Smythe was caught off guard. She quickly regained her balance with a very direct inquiry about Thea's ethnicity. "Are you Hawaiian, Doctor Baccay? I spent some time in Honolulu and came to envy the complexion of the locals."

Melinda was stunned. *What a brazen exhibit of racism! Does she not know that our resident physicians represent a full palette of skin tones?* Melinda became anxious about having arranged this encounter, but Thea seem unfazed.

"My parents are Filipino. We joke that my husband looks more South Pacific than I do. We know little about his origins."

Ingrid Smythe furrowed her brow with curiosity. Thea dove right in with a story that she knew always fascinates.

"My husband Darius was an orphan in India when he was adopted by Yasmin and Farid Tabibi, who were originally from Persia. The Tabibis fled Tehran in 1979 when there was a revolution that turned Persia into the Islamic state of Iran. Farid Tabibi had a cousin in Switzerland who sponsored their immigration to Europe where Farid was able to advance his education. He became a top-tier computer whiz, and he was eventually hired by the government of Great Britain to develop connectivity in embassies around the globe."

"Talk about being well-connected," Ingrid sniped, but she let Thea continue.

"Darius's adoptive mother, Yasmin, was a seamstress. She was also gifted with a remarkable sense of style. Her appearance was always so artful that people noticed. On her husband's first assignment, she rescued a diplomat's wife from a wardrobe malfunction just before an important state dinner. Thereafter, she got called upon for her sewing skills by many other people in the embassy.

"On assignment to another embassy, a diplomat's wife was awed by Yasmin's talent for using clothes and accessories in exceptionally creative ways. Yasmin became the family's personal stylist, and she was able to enter into the inner circles of diplomatic society. After that, the computer whiz's wife was in demand wherever Farid was sent.

"In 1983, Yasmin accompanied a diplomat's wife on a visit to an orphanage in India. The visiting dignitaries found themselves completely surrounded by a mini mob of scrawny toddlers when the face of one particular child pierced Yasmin's consciousness. She couldn't stop thinking about the little boy. He had spectacular pale blue eyes.

"The Tabibis never planned to have children. Moving around so frequently would be an impediment to a child's education. But Yasmin was fascinated by this little boy, and she visited the orphanage again just to see him. The orphanage director had assumed the child was about thirty months old, but Yasmin observed him playing constructively, more like a three-year old. He was also exceptionally observant of what was going on around him.

"Yasmin insisted that her husband come see this child. They watched the little guy pick up a bug, study it, and then gently put it back down. Yasmin also noticed surprising advances in his vocabulary compared to her previous visit. Both of the Tabibis were smitten. Even with the help of a British diplomat, it took more than eight months of cutting through reams of red tape before they were able to bring this orphan home.

"Home at the time was Kenya. Then, the Tabibis got transferred to Turkey where their adopted son's lack of a birth certificate became a problem. Yasmin had served as a style consultant for another diplomat's wife, a woman who always seemed to be able to obtain whatever she wanted. She asked this woman for help in getting a birth certificate for her son.

"Since globally, one out of five people's births are never officially recorded, depriving them of citizenship and rights, the sale of birth certificates is a big business. That's how their adopted son, Nathan Tabibi, became Darius Amari, a natural-born citizen of Iraq. The Tabibi's never knew if the real Darius Amari was living or not, but that birth certificate enabled them to continue Farid's employment and international travels along with his wife and child.

"Although Darius had an Iraqi birth certificate, he never spent any time in Iraq. His father's work did take him to New Zealand, Egypt, Sudan, Syria, Bulgaria, Rhodesia, New Caledonia, Nigeria, and numerous other places as the world rapidly computerized. Darius's only education option was home schooling, and he learned to read so quickly in Farsi and English, that no education system would have been able to keep up with him.

"The Tabibis considered Switzerland home, and the family lived there between assignments. This enabled Darius to learn German, French, and Italian, all of which are spoken in Switzerland. By the time he was seven, Darius had also mastered use of his dad's old IBM desktop computer. When the Internet came along, he started to become a self-educated wizard. He was accepted into a prestigious university program around the age of sixteen to pursue his research interests in microbiology."

"Where are Darius's parents now?" Ingrid asked. *It must have been their diplomatic connections that interested her. Or was it Yasmin's styling talent that caught Ingrid's attention?* Melinda noticed Ingrid fiddling with her necklace as Thea spoke of her mother-in-law's artistry.

Thea lowered and shook her head. "Deceased. I never met them. They were on an assignment in Israel in 2000 when a suicide bomber blew up the bus they were riding on. Yasmin was killed instantly. Her husband died from his injuries a few weeks later. Darius was about nineteen then."

"So now, you're Darius's only family," Ingrid remarked. Then she casually added, "Are you two planning on having a family?"

Thea knew the question was coming, "That's hard to answer when less than two days ago, I was planning on being a widow. But if Darius survives, and if his health will allow it, we hope to someday have a family. That's sometime in the distant future. Right now, we just need him to not reject his new heart.

"I'm a fortunate person, Ms. Smythe. My mother, aunts, sisters, and cousins all live around here. We're very close and they're willing to help take care of Darius while I complete my training. We have three nurses in my family. My entire family will pitch in to support us in any way needed. That's why I want to train in Bandore. I was offered a position in the residency program at the university, but I want to be close to my family and my family is here."

"So how did your Iraqi husband get into medical school in the United States?" *Ingrid was clearly more interested in Darius than in Thea.*

"Darius teaches microbiology and immunology in the medical school, but he is not a medical doctor. He was able to get to America and get a green card because of his credentials as a published scientist, and because of his mother's connections. One of the diplomatic core people who Yasmin had befriended, and who was bereaved by her senseless death, was able to get Darius a host family, a lab job, and a path to U.S. citizenship.

"From there, Darius pursued his education and goals. He lived frugally for years, taking low-paying lab jobs while furthering his education. His research earned him a professorship in the medical school and his grant writing skills enabled him to get funding for his research. He teaches a few classes and spends most of his time in his lab. We just pray he can get well enough to resume his research. In his current state, he can't do much of anything."

"What kind of research does your husband do?"

"He studies viral immunity in bats."

Melinda saw Ingrid's eyes widen. "Who's funding him?" Ingrid demanded to know.

"I don't actually know the specifics, but the funds came from multiple entities and some private donors. Darius spent several years getting it all worked out."

At that moment, Thea's phone signaled. She looked at the screen and abruptly said. "I have to go now." With tears in her eyes, she literally ran out of the room. Melinda tried to run after her, but wasn't quick enough. Just when she thought she'd caught up, the elevator door closed. Thea was on her way, presumably, to the transplant center.

Melinda returned to Smythe's office. She was going to apologize to the boss for running out like that, but James said Ingrid left immediately after she did. Defeated again, Melinda thanked James for his assistance in facilitating the meeting. Then, she finally got up the nerve to ask him how he obtained the password to the disk she had delivered.

James just sheepishly smiled.

 **1**

Ingrid Smythe returned just after Melinda Villarose left. She immediately summoned James Dzobak into her inner office.

"I need you to find out whatever you can about Thea Baccay's husband Darius Amari and his research. It's got something to do with bat viruses. One of my companies is working on a vaccine for the Dengue virus and they might be interested. Global warming is bringing Dengue fever from the tropics to North America. It's an awful disease."

"How ironic, Ms. Smythe. Actually, I just had a fascinating conversation with the lab director for Darius Amari. He's the friend who drove Thea Baccay to Bandore Hospital today. Right after Doctor Villarose beckoned Thea into your office, this guy showed up looking for her. I told him she was in a meeting. He asked if I could direct him to the cafeteria."

A weird smile spread across James Dzobak's face. "I was explaining to him how to get there when he took out his phone and there was a Batman insignia on his phone case."

"Batman insignia?" Ingrid wrinkled her nose.

James blushed. "Well, I have to admit that I'm actually an old Batman fan. My grandfather read Batman comic books in the 1940s. My dad grew up on the 1960s TV Batman series, and I grew up on Batman reruns in the 1980s. My dad still has my grandfather's old comic books and they've become quite valuable. The Batman brand has been a thriving industry for a long time. But for all the affection I grew up with for Batman, I never actually gave any thought to bats. That changed drastically for me today. This guy, his name is

Sullivan Dietz, is passionate about bats. I was intrigued by him, so I escorted him to the cafeteria."

"So, do you know what this Darius Amari is doing in his lab?"

"As I understand it, bats have been around much longer than humans, and they've apparently developed much more effective immune defenses than is seen in any other mammal.

Most bats are immune to hundreds of viruses, but a tiny percentage of them succumb to rabies. Untreated humans who contract rabies invariably die. This lab is trying to understand why some bats get sick from rabies while most bats have developed immunity to this virus.

"After we guffawed over some Batman jokes, this Sullivan Dietz told me stuff about bats that blew me away. Did you know that bats are highly intelligent, social, and vocally communicative? I had no idea. Bats from different regions speak with local dialects. Baby bats babble like human infants and their mother's talk babytalk to them. Bat mothers maintain close relationships with their children even after they mature. Bat friends groom each other, share food, help each other with maternity duties, and mourn when their friends die. In some bat species, the males court females by singing them love songs. The vocal apparatus of some bats enables them to produce seven octaves of sound. Most human voices can go three to four octaves and just a few people, like Mariah Carey, can manage five octaves.

"Besides being the only mammals that have mastered flight, bats have many unique traits that make them one of the most successful species on the planet. They are also absolutely essential to agriculture. Insect eating bats can devour a thousand bugs an hour. Nectar eating bats pollinate crops, disperse seeds, and propagate forests. It's also amazing how immunologically competent they are considering that they live in extremely cramped quarters.

James was getting more enthusiastic as he spoke, so Ingrid gave him a stop sign. "So, this Sullivan Dietz is also a bat researcher?"

"I asked him about his connection to bats, beyond our Batman superhero. He told me that when he was twelve, he and a friend explored an abandoned old barn. When he climbed up into the loft, he startled a colony of bats that were roosting on the rafters. The terrified bats flew all around him as they attempted to flee, but not one of them bit or scratched him. As a kid who wanted to be a veterinarian, he decided in that moment that bats were very cool creatures."

"So, is he a veterinarian? What does he do in this lab?"

"I'm not sure. He really didn't talk about the research. He just likes to talk about bats and how they get blamed for carrying disease when in reality, they can teach humanity how to conquer disease."

"Did he tell you anything about this Darius Amari?"

"Just that it was his dream job to work with such a brilliant researcher in a bat lab. I only spent a few minutes with the man, and half that time we told each other Batman jokes."

"So, James, you got yourself quite an education about the eccentricities of Batman worshipers and bat researchers. It does sound intriguing, but what I need you to do, is to find out is who is funding Darius Amari's research and what is he studying."

Doctor Melinda Villarose was distressed that she couldn't reach Thea Baccay after the med student's tearful departure from the interview. Thea had left Bandore at about two-thirty, so by seven o'clock she should have been home. There were no reports of highway problems.

Perhaps Thea was reserving her phone for messages from her husband's surgical team. After several unanswered texts, Melinda left the message that she hoped Thea had made it back safely and that everything was okay with Darius. It was after nine o'clock when Thea finally returned her call.

"Thanks for your concern, Doctor Villarose. This afternoon, while I was with you and Ms. Smythe, Darius scared the bejabbers out of his doctors with a precipitous drop in blood pressure. They were just about ready to take him back to the O.R. to make sure there wasn't a bleed when his pressure finally came back up.

"Then, he started to have some rapid heart rhythms. That's supposedly common just after heart transplant. The heart can be irritable in its new environment. They're watching him very closely. At the moment he appears to be stable; I guess that means about as stable as someone who was almost dead three days ago can be."

"What a trauma today has to have been for you, Thea. I'm sorry I suggested you come all the way here when you're under such stress. I'm glad you're both alright, whatever alright means in these circumstances."

"Thanks for your concern. I so appreciate your trying to help get me into the Bandore program, Doctor Villarose. Darius will still need twenty-four-hour care when he gets through the immediate post-op stuff. One of my sister's was a nurse in a cardiac care unit, but she's taking a respite from nursing until her kids are a little older. Darius made me promise I would not give up my career to be his caretaker, so he has accepted the willingness and the expertise of my family to support us until we can get through this.

"I apologize for not getting back to you sooner. Everyone we know has been checking up on Darius. The calls and messages have been more than I can manage. My battery went dead on the ride home and I was using Sully's phone to communicate with the hospital."

"Sully? Is that the friend who drove you here? He must be a very good friend."

"Sully is the best. He started working with Darius before they even opened the lab and he's been continuing the research and managing everything else while Darius has been incapacitated. I don't know what we'd do if we didn't have Sully in our lives. He's fantastic in the lab and he's just a great person.

"By the way, Sully connected with the guy who sits at Ingrid Smythe's reception desk, a James somebody. They really hit it off in their brief time together. Sully has a way of winning people over. Perhaps James does too.

"How do you think I did on the interview? Did you get any feedback from Ms. Smythe after I left? Maybe Sully can get some feedback from her assistant, James."

"You were great, Thea. I've only had two prior encounters with this new administrator, but she showed more interest in your situation than I anticipated. Hopefully, your big trip up here will prove to have been worthwhile. I would love to have you in our program. I'm sending wishes for Darius's speedy and complete recovery. Thanks for getting back to me."

"Thank you, Doctor Villarose. Your personal interest in my situation has been like a spot of sunshine in a storm. I hope I get to have you as a mentor."

Melinda Villarose's anxiety about Thea and Darius finally dissipated enough for her to try to go to sleep. In her dreams, the yellow horse was galloping away from the storm.

James Dzobak used an artificial intelligence app to try to learn about Darius Amari. Within seconds, his computer gave him summaries of articles Darius had written for a variety of scientific journals. AI had even translated an article Darius had written in German. However, to James, it was all a foreign language. The information was so technical that he couldn't comprehend any of it.

James sent one of the articles to a physician friend for an interpretation; an internist with fifteen years of clinical experience. "Immunology isn't my strong suit," the doctor responded. "I don't really know what Amari is up to, but it must be important for such a prestigious journal to have featured this article. I suspect immunology has advanced way beyond the basics I learned back in medical school."

James got similar responses from two other doctors he'd shown the article to. All anyone could say was that Darius was studying how viruses interact with the immune, metabolic, and neural systems that their hosts use to fight disease.

James couldn't find Darius Amari on any social media platforms. Other than his academic profile and links to his research papers on the medical school website, Darius did not have an Internet presence.

James turned his attention to investigating who was funding this research. That led to information about who's regulating such research. James was astounded by what he discovered.

The study of dangerous germs is loosely controlled by regulations from numerous overlapping government agencies. In the

U.S., there's extensive federal oversight of researchers working with the deadliest pathogens like Ebola and Anthrax. The CDC (Center for Disease Control and Prevention) is mostly involved.

The Department of Health and Human Services (HHS) oversees the importation of infectious biologic agents from foreign countries. The U.S. Department of Agriculture, the Department of Defense, the National Institutes of Allergy and Infectious Disease, state and local health departments, and other official entities all impose regulations on labs, but no single government agency is actually responsible for tracking or regulating all of the labs that legally handle dangerous germs.

The CDC designates five levels of safety requirements for laboratories, depending on what they handle. A biosafety level one (BSL-1) lab can study bacteria like Staph and E. Coli, which are not easily spread.

A biosafety level two (BLS-2) lab can handle germs that cause disease in humans but are unlikely to be spread by aerosols. Still, there is some risk to the lab workers. In the United States, BSL-2 labs can study organisms that cause infections like rabies, hepatitis, AIDS, and malaria. Some countries have stricter controls and require these germs to be studied in more secure labs.

Biosafety level three (BSL-3) labs work with germs that can easily be aerosolized and can cause severe disease in humans like yellow fever, West Nile virus, tuberculosis, and SARS-COVID. BSL-3 labs have to be built with stringent air flow controls and workers do their jobs in hazmat suits.

The germs that cause contagious, deadly diseases for which there are no effective vaccines, like Ebola and Anthrax, are studied in biosafety level four (BSL-4) labs. Such labs must have multiple safety systems including advanced technology to decontaminate air, water, trash, and the people who work there.

A biosafety level five (BLS-5) lab would be where scientists could study organisms brought back from outer space, and other germs whose potential for causing disease is unknown, like ancient organisms that might be released as the polar permafrost melts.

The U.S. is home to an estimated two hundred BSL-3 and BSL-4 labs. Some are close to population centers. In 2021, there were forty-two BSL-4 labs known to be operating globally, with another seventeen under construction. There were nine BSL-4s in the U.S. and twenty-four scattered around Europe, especially in Great Britain. At least fifteen other countries had one or two BSL-4 labs.

James couldn't find much information about who was overseeing these high-level labs in some of these countries. Some labs were being developed expediently in response to the COVID-19 pandemic. Ultimately, all of these labs would have to compete for research funding when politicians in countries like the U.S.A. turned to other issues to spend taxpayer money on.

James quickly came to realize that this data only applied to legal labs. There are no reliable statistics about how many illegal labs there are. James had found numerous articles about an illegal lab that was incidentally discovered in 2023 in the town of Reedling, California, when a green hose was noticed sticking out the back of an old warehouse.

Inside, investigators came upon an unlicensed lab owned by a foreign criminal fugitive where foreign workers were illegally and improperly handling thousands of animals in deplorable conditions. There was also inappropriate storage of multiple samples of infectious organisms with labels such as rubella, malaria, Dengue, COVID-19, chlamydia, hepatitis, HIV, (the virus that causes AIDS), and others. There were also many unlabeled specimens.

This lab was also buying fake COVID-19 test kits in China and reselling them in the U.S. What this lab was actually doing with all of these germs and animals was unclear. Fortunately, the operation was shut down before a biohazard emergency occurred, but James was left to wonder how many such illegal labs might be operating all over the globe.

James found out that Darius Amari's lab was certified as BSL-3, but that didn't make sense if he was primarily working with rabies virus which could be studied in a BSL-2 lab. Rabies doesn't spread through the air, and it's not contagious from person to person. You can only get it from the saliva of an infected animal that bites or scratches, and if you do, there's a vaccine that can protect an exposed individual. Rabies is only dangerous because if it is contracted by a human, cat, dog, or other mammal that does not get promptly treated, then it's almost always fatal. Untreated, the rabies virus destroys the brain and the spinal cord.

James was starting to get the creeps from all this information when he stumbled on even more disturbing data. A Wikipedia webpage titled, "List of laboratory biosecurity incidents," reported dozens of dangerous lab accidents that have been documented to occur in legitimate labs around the world. Accidental exposures to Zika, Anthrax, Dengue, swine flu, polio, and other lethal germs have occurred even in the best run labs.

James shuddered to imagine what the risks from illegal, unregulated labs could be. He also wondered how many accidents at legitimate labs never get reported or accounted for.

James also learned that universities are required by law to disclose who funds their research, especially in the case of foreign sources. Apparently, Darius Amari's grant came from an international scientific organization that's supported by unlisted private equity firms and anonymous donors. The organization is legitimate, but it's developed itself to be able to legally fund research while simultaneously obscuring who is so interested in the research that they'd pay a fortune to sponsor it.

That got James thinking about Ingrid Smythe's interest in who was funding Darius Amari. James didn't know about Darius's connection to people in international diplomatic circles, but he did know about Ingrid Smythe's interest in foreign money.

From the first day that James had worked with Ingrid Smythe, he had secretly penetrated the security of her personal laptop. He just wanted to see if he could do it. He had no evil intentions, although he did copy her business records. He opened up a file about the corporations and companies that she owned. One of them was a privately funded lab in Argentina that was working on a vaccine for the Dengue virus. It was registered as a BSL-2 lab.

That left James wondering. Dengue is transmitted by mosquitos, not bats, so what was Ingrid Smythe's interest in bat viruses?

12

The Friday morning after Thea's visit to Bandore Hospital, James Dzobak informed Doctor Melinda Villarose that Thea's early admittance into the residency program had been granted. Her position would be secured as soon as she signed a contract. Melinda immediately sent Thea a text to give her the good news and tell her she didn't have to go into the match. She also used the opportunity to inquire about how Darius was doing.

Thea didn't get back to Melinda until eight o'clock that night. She was doing her clinical rotation in surgery and if there was any place that cell phones were unwelcome, it was the O.R. As it turned out, the case that had kept her late in the hospital that day was a heart transplant case. Medical students normally didn't scrub in on such procedures, but Thea had been granted special permission. She understood so much more than the average student.

Thea seemed to want to talk about the transplant she had witnessed. The recipient was a fifty-seven-year-old fireman with severe coronary artery disease. The donor was a twenty-four-year-old overdose victim. Apparently, the current scourge of fatal drug overdoses was boosting the availability of organs from young, otherwise healthy donors, the kind of organs that were prized by the people who were waiting for a transplant to save them.

Thea wondered out loud If her husband's donor was an overdose victim and what drugs Darius's donor might have been taking. He was still having heart rhythm issues, so they kept adjusting his medications.

"Then he's still in the hospital," Melinda realized. She also realized how anxious organ recipients must become about the qualities of their donor; one more psychologic load to carry in their fight for life.

"What happens when they discharge him?" Melinda had no clinical experience with transplant medicine.

"They've already started physical therapy, but he'll need intensive rehab once he's stable enough to leave the hospital. He was so debilitated before he got to the transplant, that he's lost all of his muscle mass. Add the trauma of a such a major surgery and he's now physically, psychologically, and immunologically weakened.

"They'll probably keep him in the hospital until his vital signs stay stable for a few days," Thea lamented. "After discharge, he'll be in an intensive rehab facility for a few weeks. Also, for the first four weeks after transplant, he'll need a biopsy of his heart every week. Examining a tiny piece of the heart is the only way to determine if the organ is being rejected. After the first month, he'll need heart biopsies every other week, and then it will be once a month for six months. Then, it's every other month for the rest of the year and then they'll decide the thereafter. If rejection is going to occur, it typically does so in the first year. By the five-year mark, sixty percent of transplanted hearts are rejected."

"Oh my! I had no idea how much is involved after the surgery," Melinda confessed. "So, he might not be able to come with you when you move to Bandore to start your internship in July. What will you do then?"

"Don't worry about that, Doctor Villarose. I'll start whether Darius is able to move or not. If he can't, we'll make arrangements for him to have assistance there. He's hanging on to his university housing in case. We were going to keep that townhouse anyway because we knew that if Darius did get a heart, we would be returning to the transplant center with some regularity. But I'm optimistic he'll be able to move with me. Darius has a very strong will and enormous self-discipline. He'll follow every one of the heart transplant guidelines and make a good recovery. I know this man. He's going to turn his personal tragedy into triumph."

As Thea's optimism oozed from her words, Melinda detected a trace of doubt in her tone. "So, how is Darius doing now with this issue of cardiac irritability?"

Thea paused momentarily. "Well of course, he's frustrated. He's so anxious and determined to get back to his research and a normal life that he's kind of angry at the heart for misbehaving. But Julie the transplant coordinator said this is normal for a person as driven and successful as Darius. He's actually the kind of person that transplant teams favor, as he's most likely to be compliant with all the aftercare that's required to make the transplant a success. No transplant team wants to waste an organ on a recipient who won't take their medicine and who lacks the motivation to get back to a productive life. Donor organs are just too scarce."

"I wouldn't want to be on that selection committee," Melinda mumbled. "I'm thrilled you'll be in our intern class, Thea, and sending best wishes to both of you. See you in a few months."

 **13**

Whenever her schedule would allow it, Police Officer Bree Siddoway would accompany her thirty-year-old stepbrother to his appointments with the transplant coordinator. Gavin wouldn't give Bree the whole story if she didn't go with him. He'd been battling kidney disease since he was sixteen. He'd been on dialysis for the past two years and he hadn't moved up any higher on the transplant waiting list. Bree knew that her brother's lower ranking on the list was only because other kidney failure patients were sicker.

Bree Siddoway was nine years old when her mother went to work at the World Trade Center in Manhattan one day and never came home. Bree's dad moved their family out of New York after 9/11. The following year, he started dating a single woman with a seven-year-old son.

Bree's grief over her mother's death started to heal when their families blended, and Bree took on the role of second mother to Gavin. He was an agreeable child and in a short time, she came to love him. In even less time, Gavin came to adore Bree.

When Gavin was a high school sophomore, he was determined to make the football team. He hurt his ankle the week before try-outs and kept it a secret while taking huge quantities of ibuprofen. Then, he started taking naprosyn and ibuprofen together and the ankle was hardly hurting, so the day before the tryout, he tried to run some laps. It was hot and he wound up passing out. He admitted to the paramedics that came to rescue him, that he also hadn't been peeing for the past day or two.

In the E.R., Gavin was diagnosed with acute renal failure. Due to a toxic reaction to the excessive dosing of the two non-steroidal anti-inflammatory drugs together, his kidneys had totally shut down. With aggressive treatment, most patients recover from this life-threatening condition, but not all kidneys recover. After acute recovery, Gavin's renal function started to slowly decline.

Since starting on dialysis, Gavin got to periodically meet with a transplant coordinator to review whether or not his place on the waiting list had changed. Carlos Mackenzy, the counselor/coordinator, was himself a transplant recipient. Congenital heart disease had stolen his entire youth, but a well-matched heart came his way just as was turning twenty-two.

Carlos Mackenzy understood what it was like to live in despair year after year, wishing and waiting, while watching a continuous barrage of reports of others dying and turning their organs over to worms. This was such a morbid concept that you wouldn't even want to discuss it with someone who wasn't waiting for a transplant.

Carlos also understood a post-transplant phenomenon that was impossible to explain to someone who had never experienced it. Shortly after he got his new heart, he started to have episodes of feeling like he wasn't himself. He would be overwhelmed by alien emotions in response to things that he would never have even paid attention to before his transplant. One time, he found himself in tears in response to a dog food commercial. Another time, he started hyperventilating when he couldn't find one of his shoes for a few minutes. Little things like that never used to bother him.

When Carlos tried to tell his doctors what he was experiencing, he was advised that it was normal to have new feelings after such a major operation and after such a profound lifestyle change. They said his anxiety was a response to being able to become an active person for the first time in his life. They said his depression came from survivor's guilt over the loss of the donor's life. They said it was the medications that had him feeling out of sorts with himself.

Carlos didn't believe it was any of those things. He thought these sensations were coming from his new heart. He stopped trying to tell anyone else about it and after a few years, the sensations no longer felt quite so alien. His emotions had evened out or he had taken ownership of them. He wasn't sure which.

Carlos had been working as a transplant coordinator for almost two years when another heart transplant recipient told him that she was having feelings that she didn't recognize or understand. Carlos knew exactly what she meant.

Over the next eight years that Carlos was working as a transplant coordinator, only two other patients ever brought up this issue. One had received a liver and the other a heart. He never heard about these strange sensations from kidney recipients, though there were so many more of them. Carlos even started to ask patients about it when he'd see them for their post-transplant follow-ups, but most didn't relate to what he was talking about. He wondered if some did relate, but didn't want to admit it. It was kind of like saying you were possessed.

Carlos had poured through the records of the recipients who reported sharing his sense of alien feelings. When he compared them with his own profile, the only thing they had in common with each other was that their tissue matching was more compatible with that of the donor's, than was the average recipient's. Carlos hoped he would someday have enough data to prove that the changes he experienced really did come from the donor's heart.

By coincidence, Gavin's transplant appointment came up a week after the death of Zoey Collins. Carlos never shared information about what was going on with other kidney patients. It was all very confidential. However, Bree Siddoway was a policeperson who made extra effort to facilitate organ donations, and she was responsible for some recent successes, so Carlos confided in Gavin and Bree a little about the case. He told them that a young donor's heart, liver, pancreas, intestines, and kidneys had all found matches. The skin went to a burn patient. He also told them that on preliminary testing, the heart had matched a recipient better than any case this transplant center had ever seen.

Gavin left the appointment with the consolation prize: there were now two less kidney failure patients ahead of him on the waiting list.

Bree left the appointment wondering if the information about Zoey Collins's organs would bring any comfort to Deidra Collins. Her deceased daughter had saved seven lives.

14

Shortly after Bandore County General Hospital got its match results for their family practice residency program, Doctor Stuart Carmichael dropped in on Doctor Melinda Villarose. He looked paler and frailer than when Melinda had last seen him, but he still had twinkly eyes and some spring in his step. They left the hospital together to go to lunch.

Doctor Carmichael refused to discuss his battle with cancer other than to say he was holding his own. "So, tell me about the next class of interns. And what happened with the early acceptance candidate? She was so exceptional."

Melinda beamed. "Thea Baccay. We got her. I would have thought she'd bring our whole class up to a higher level, but her personal life is so chaotic right now that I worry that we didn't get her at her best."

"Did her husband ever get a donor heart? He had moved to the top of the waiting list just before her second interview." Stuart Carmichael winced. "Please don't tell me he died."

Melinda smiled again. "He got a new heart in February, right before we had to submit our rankings. I've kept in contact with Thea. Her husband's recovery was up and down at first, but the donor heart is starting to beat regularly and there's no signs of rejection. What an ordeal! I've been boning up on what transplant recipients have to contend with and as a psychiatrist, it gives me angst."

"How so?" Stuart asked.

"Because" Melinda answered, "on a cellular level, organs may preserve personal characteristics that scientists have long believed can only be maintained in the brain. I've learned that after heart transplant, some recipients are reporting changes in preferences, emotionality, temperament, and their sense of identity. In some cases, memories from the donor's life have emerged.

Until recently, these phenomena were being reported by only a tiny percentage of heart recipients, so there's been quite a bit of controversy about their validity. Now however, maybe because of more publicity about cellular memory, increasing numbers of transplant patients are reporting such experiences."

Stuart Carmichael was intrigued. "Really? I have to tell you, about two decades ago, I had a patient whose husband was on the waiting list for a liver. Hepatitis had destroyed the one he was born with. They'd been married about fifteen years when he got saved by a transplant. But according to his wife, he had a major personality change afterwards. He went from being a nice, rational guy to being a temperamental hothead. I tried to research this issue, but there was really nothing about it back then. Is Thea's husband showing something like that?"

"I don't know, but Thea made a comment that made me wonder. She said that Darius's new heart seems to have suppressed his sense of humor. Before his transplant, he could joke about any of the miserable aspects of having a failing heart. But since he's been awake and alert, he's just expressed anger about having an irritable heart."

"But wouldn't that be a normal reaction?" Stuart countered. "He's had such a horrific existence waiting for a new heart, he's gone through a terrifically traumatic surgery, and now the new heart is giving him trouble. Wouldn't that put a dent in anyone's sense of humor?"

"You're right," Melinda conceded.

"And you can live without a sense of humor if it comes to that," Stuart added. "So, tell me about the rest of the incoming family practice class."

"Most of our matches came from the bottom third of our rankings." Melinda then explained to Stuart how Tazodan's bias against pregnant residents altered their ranking of candidates. Stuart wasn't shocked, but he was incensed. "How can a family practice program not honor the priority of family?" he lamented.

Melinda shook her head in solidarity. "Our top pick that we got besides Thea Baccay was Suzie Nguyen. Remember her? Studious Texas woman who hopes to serve the Vietnamese population in Houston. She's unmarried, but I think she has a partner who she didn't talk about. She did keep saying 'we' when we discussed where she'd live if she did her residency here. She was at the top of our rankings at number fifteen.

"Our lowest ranked pick that we got was Sam Hornan, number seventy-two of seventy-four."

"No way I'd forget Sam," Stuart chuckled. "He just about sang his way through his interview."

"Oh yeah! He could be the most personable guy that's ever applied here, but academically, he's the bottom of the barrel. I suspect he's gotten by on his charm and good looks. Hopefully, he's educable enough to be turned into a decent doctor. I think his heart is in the right place. That's why we kept him in the rankings."

Stuart leaned back. "Heart in the right place seems like a phrase we might want to drop around here."

Melinda groaned. "You're right again. It has a whole new meaning, doesn't it?

"The other most remarkable of our matches besides, Thea, Suzie and Sam, is Dayo Igwe, the older guy who was a surgeon in Nigeria. He has a wealth of clinical experience, and he seems very dedicated. He also likes to teach."

"Yup, I remember him well. It's amazing how some of these foreigners give up so much to try to get into the U.S."

"The match I have the most concern about is Vance Kenner. He's academically solid but he seems to be depressed, maybe vulnerable. I could see him in radiology or pathology, but not taking care of crying babies and cranky grandpas."

"I wondered if he was having marital problems," Doctor Carmichael's recalled. "Something he said made me think he was in a break-up situation."

"Do you remember Kioni Ouma, from Minnesota? I would have ranked her higher, but I suspect she's a maternity risk. Anyway, she matched us."

"I do remember her. She wore a fashionable hijab. But I got the feeling she could win over the local yokels. She was very friendly and exceptionally pretty."

"You'll probably also remember Nabil Al-Katib, the ophthalmologist from Yemen who couldn't get credentialed in his specialty by U.S. standards. He seems willing to reinvent himself.

"Also, from the bottom of our rankings, we got Kerry Williams. She went to medical school after raising five children and working as a nurse for sixteen years. She still has two kids at home and I'm worried that she's overextended. She had several bouts of prolonged illness as a medical student."

"I'd forgotten about her, but now I'm reminded. And the ninth?"

"We didn't match a ninth, but I now have five candidates for that slot, three females, one male, and one nonbinary. I wish you could be here with me for the interviews. I've got three to go. One of them is pregnant right now, but won't be by the start of the program. Then she'll be the new mother of a newborn. One of them has a very hard to understand accent. Don't yet know about them all, but Bandore will be lucky to get any of them."

15

Ten days after the new family practice residents started their internship, Ingrid Smythe called Melinda Villarose into her office. "So, I hear your class got off to a rough start with one of the interns out with COVID."

"We managed to fill the gap, Ms. Smythe, even though we're short one person already. Our senior residents took on extra night shifts, and the other interns also covered for Doctor Hornan and took on more patients. We've reworked the call schedule, and we expect Sam Hornan to start next week."

Ingrid Smythe looked at her computer screen. "We've had some patient complaints, Doctor Villarose. Nobody can understand this Doctor Dayo Igwe."

"I know, and Doctor Igwe knows too. It's really not his diction so much as he's just very soft-spoken. It's not hard to understand him at all if there's no background noise, which is hardly ever. He's working on projecting his voice more. He's really a great fit for our program. He's very skilled at physical diagnosis."

Ingrid Smythe was going down her list. "I also see a complaint about not being able to understand Doctor Nguyen."

Melinda threw her hands in the air. "You've got to be kidding me. Suzie Nguyen was born and raised in Texas. Other than having a tiny bit of a Texas drawl, she speaks better English than most of the people who live in Bandore County.

"I'll bet that complaint came from an old white guy who didn't like being attended to by a young Asian woman. I've seen that kind of complaint before regarding our Asian residents. You know, we have a second-year resident from France here, who even I can't

53

understand half the time, but no one complains about her because she's white.

"And let me tell you something about Doctor Dayo Igwe. One of our E.R. docs was about to send a headache patient home last week and he told Doctor Igwe, who's interning in the E.R., to discharge the patient. As the patient walked down the corridor, Dayo asked the woman to walk back towards him, and he asked the E.R. doctor to watch. He pointed out that her feet were wide apart, and her arm swing was out of synch with her leg motion. The E.R. doctor agreed to get an MRI and found a brain tumor,

"I've since learned that Dayo Igwe trained where doctors didn't have access to brain scans, so they had to use their knowledge and power of observation to identify neurologic problems. Until just two generations ago, neurosurgeons had to operate on the brain based on their guesses as to where a brain tumor was. Doctor Igwe is a definite asset to our staff, and he may have just saved this hospital from a lawsuit over an undiagnosed brain tumor in addition to saving a patient's life."

"Who else are you hearing complaints about?" Melinda asked, while Ingrid Smythe stayed silent.

Ingrid was feeling like she'd poked a mama bear trying to protect its cubs. This Doctor Villarose seemed excessively involved and protective of these doctors-in-training. Maybe she could be a source of information about Darius Amari. Ingrid's assistant James sure hadn't come up with anything useful. Now, James was trying to learn more about bat science so he could better understand Amari's research papers. Still, Ingrid wondered if James wasn't just out of his mind over bats.

Ingrid gave Melinda a few moments to cool down before asking her how Doctor Baccay and her husband were doing.

"Thea's doing great. For all she's been through, she manages to keep an upbeat demeanor. She's also very efficient. She can make patients feel really cared for even with brief contact. Other than she looks so young, I'd be surprised if you ever get a complaint about her. But, then again, even our best doctors get complaints from patients with unrealistic expectations, like 'that stupid doctor said my son's strep throat was contagious even if we gave him a shot, and we'd have to cancel his birthday party.' I could give you numerous examples of the idiotic complaints our staff has had to endure.

"Thea's husband is still being monitored at the transplant center, but so far, after four months, there's been no sign of rejection. They finally feel optimistic about his survival. I understand the physical rehab is intense. I'm meeting with Thea next week, so maybe I'll know more then.

"Did you know, I try to meet with at least two or three of the residents every week, so it takes me three months to evaluate all of them. Their workloads are so demanding that it's difficult to schedule meetings with them. These people work really hard."

"What do you do at these meetings?"

"Give them feedback from the attending physicians, the senior residents, and the nurses. Tell them about complaints that you or others have passed on to me. Listen to their concerns about hospital issues. Listen to their complaints about the infamous Doctor Rhea. You do know about Doctor Ezra Rhea? Don't you?"

Ingrid knew that the Chief of Surgery of Bandore County Hospital, Ezra Rhea, had been esteemed in the community for many years, but his patients had recently shown a high rate of infection. "Doctor Rhea's tenure here is under review." Ingrid responded. *And so is yours, Doctor Villarose*, she thought.

Ingrid Smythe was irritated by this mama bear, but Melinda Villarose's emotional connection to Thea Baccay could still prove useful. Other sources Ingrid had consulted in the university's business and administrative offices would only repeat what she already knew. Darius Amari was one of a number of researchers who was studying the immunologic supremacy of bats.

"Well, our residents are tired of covering up and compensating for Doctor Rhea's mistakes. I'm very glad to know the new administration will be addressing this issue," was Melinda's last comment, as Smythe took a phone call and motioned for Melinda to depart.

16

Melinda Villarose had set aside extra time to meet with Doctor Thea Baccay. She'd been disturbed to learn that Thea had moved up to Bandore by herself, while her husband stayed connected to the transplant center. It spoiled Thea's reason for coming to Bandore, and not accepting a residency position at University Hospital.

Of course, Thea and Darius had no way of knowing that a new heart would arrive in February. Now in July, four months out from surgery, Darius no longer needed the skilled nursing care that Thea's family could provide. He was functioning independently. Thea and Darius also couldn't have known that Thea was not going to wind up a widow who needed the support of her family.

Melinda also wondered how Darius was going to work in his lab if he was living in Bandore. It seemed like they planned for his demise more than his survival. Melinda worried that after internship, they'd lose Thea to residency in a more prestigious program.

Melinda met with Thea for breakfast at the end of her night call. The intern had obviously had very little sleep as there'd been four admissions from the E.R., and two patients on the wards were having unexpected problems. One was a cancer patient in whom Doctor Rhea had implanted an intravenous pump. Thea had that haggard look that Melinda often saw in interns who'd been up all night.

Melinda advised Thea that she was leaving positive impressions with everyone she interacted with. The nurses were thrilled with how well she managed difficult patients.

When asked about how Darius was doing, Thea smiled. "He's making amazing progress. He's working out for twenty minutes three times a day. His transplant team thinks he'll be back to pickleball in a couple of weeks." Her smile quickly vanished, and she offered nothing more.

Melinda refrained from asking her what was really going on, but she sensed that things weren't all that great. As a diversion, she asked Thea how Darius came to be a bat researcher. The question brought a big smile to the intern's tired face.

Thea explained that she'd learned some of Darius's history when they traveled to Switzerland to visit his adoptive cousins. These people were the only ones in the world who Darius thought of as family, though they weren't actually related to him. Whenever Darius's adoptive parents weren't on assignment, they usually returned to the home of their Swiss cousins whose kids Darius shared childhood memories with. He wanted these people to meet his bride.

Thea learned from an older cousin that when Darius was around eight, he found a baby bat trying to nurse from the breast of its dead mother. "Probably because he had been an orphan, Darius became distraught about the motherless baby. His adoptive parents learned of a woman in a local village who ran an informal sanctuary for injured bats.

"The 'bat lady' came wearing gloves. She examined the dead mother but couldn't find injuries. It was probably sick, and she didn't want anyone to touch it. She put the carcass in a special bag so it could be transported to a lab to check for rabies. She wrapped the tiny baby bat in a blanket, and gave him bat formula through a small syringe. He eagerly drank. Then she gave him a makeshift pacifier to suck on."

Thea explained that mother bats have only one pup at a time. The baby clings to the mother's fur and except when she's flying, she hugs it with her wings. To survive with human caretakers, baby bats need a lot of physical affection until they're mature enough to fly off and find their own families.

"Darius took his bicycle from the embassy housing complex to the bat sanctuary to check on the baby every day. It was a sweet-natured flying fox that bonded with its caregivers. It always sought belly rubs from young Darius. After the baby learned to fly, it was released into the wild where bats can live to be thirty or forty years old. In captivity, even with excellent care, most won't survive unless they have other bats as companions, though it has to be other bats that they like. Bats can be selective in their friendships.

"Darius was heartbroken to have to part with the bat, but he turned his distress into an obsession about what killed the baby's mother. You could say that was the start of his career."

Like most people who've only heard about bats' bad reputations, Melinda had always been reviled by them. She was curious if Thea was also interested in these animals. "You seem to know a lot about bats, Thea. Do you work in the lab too?"

Melinda learned that Thea had never worked with bats. It turned out that her interest in bats was driven by tragedy. Her father had lived in the U.S. since college. When Thea was in graduate school, her father went back to the Philippines by himself to visit some older relatives he worried he might not see again. While visiting, he enjoyed a classic Filipino dish, adobo. Made from the meat of megabats, it's something between a soup and a stew. Apparently, bat adobo is a prized delicacy in many countries of the eastern hemisphere.

Shortly after returning from his trip, Mr. Baccay developed symptoms he attributed to catching a cold on the airplane. It wasn't until he developed hallucinations and started frothing at the mouth, seven weeks after returning from his trip, that his doctor realized he had rabies. By then, it was too late to treat him with the preventive vaccine and immunoglobins. He died three days after his diagnosis was recognized.

Thea said that transmission of rabies from contaminated bat meat is exceedingly rare and no one else who ate the adobo was affected. Some experts believe that rabies cannot be transmitted this way at all. Her father had no other known contact with bats or any animals, and his death from rabies had become a nagging mystery for Thea. In her second year of medical school, in Professor Amari's immunology class, Thea asked some challenging questions about rabies. It was the start of a relationship.

You could almost say it was love at first bite, Melinda thought. "So sorry about your father, Thea. Is the rest of your family okay?"

"Oh yeah! My dad was an architect who developed a building firm. He did a lot of commercial and municipal projects. My mother always did the business management and most of the same contractors that worked for my dad now work for my mother. One of my sisters now does the architecture, and my mother has projects lined up for the next two years."

Finally, Melinda asked the question she dreaded the answer to. "Thea, if Darius is living up here with you and his lab is at the medical school campus, how can he do his research?"

"Oh. Darius can only work remotely. His transplant doctors would be furious if he was hanging out with dangerous germs while he's on immunosuppressive drugs. This was the bargain Darius had to make to even get a heart, but because of Sully, it's okay.

"Back when Darius got COVID, Sully had to take over everything and he had the experience and the skills to do it. He can execute the procedures that produce the data and Darius evaluates the data and decides what to look at next. Sullivan's hands paired with Darius's brain has boosted the productivity of the research for both of them."

"So how often are you now getting to be with Darius?"

"My cousin and I drove there for my weekend off because she had stuff to do in the city. It was fantastic to be with Darius and not be adjusting his oxygen mask. He can walk around. He can make a sandwich. He could do nothing in the weeks before the transplant. He'd turn blue when he brushed his teeth."

"Did he get his sense of humor back?" Melinda ventured to ask.

Thea looked away before answering. "He's having trouble finding the humor in having a dead person's heart in his body. Because like me, Darius is barely adult size, and because size is important for transplant success, he worries that his donor might have been a kid. It seems to be weighing on him. But his transplant coordinator Julie says this is normal. Over time, organ recipients become more accepting of the sacrifices of their donors."

17

As soon as she hung up with Sullivan Dietz, transplant coordinator Julie Jacobs tried to reach Thea Baccay, but she didn't get a response. She then looked up the number of Carlos Mackenzy, a transplant coordinator for another center. She was familiar with Carlos because he'd given a presentation at a North American conference for transplant coordinators.

Julie had learned that in early adulthood, Carlos Mackenzy had been the recipient of a donor heart, and he believed that the new heart had changed him in inexplicable ways. As a transplant coordinator, he'd met some other organ recipients who reported having a similar experience. Carlos was calling it "Donor Organ Transference Syndrome," DOTS for short. Traditionally, if this controversial phenomenon is discussed at all, it's usually referred to as "cellular memory."

Many transplant coordinators have encountered patients who have claimed that their new organ changed them, especially since Claire Sylvia, the recipient of a donor's heart and lungs, wrote a book* about changes in her preferences and personality after her transplant. Claire Sylvia ultimately learned from contacting the donor's family, that her new tastes and traits were essentially those of her donor.

Many in the transplant community believe that there are other explanations for changes that the recipient thinks came from the donor.

Occasionally, an organ recipient reads a story of an accident victim who died on the day they were transplanted, and they become influenced by what they learn of that person's identity, even when the deceased proves not to be their donor. One of Julie's young kidney recipients believed that the soul of a deceased person had been reincarnated in her, though the only connection between them was the date of the transplant and the date of death.

Organ failure patients who have spent their lives fighting for their lives, sometimes resort to fantasy to gain some relief from the chronic psychologic distress.

Julie Jacobs also had quite a few patients waiting for new organs who had expressed anxiety about the possibility that the memories from someone else's body parts could impact their lives. After receiving an organ, some wanted to know more about their donors, but transplant medicine maintains strict privacy rules about donor and recipient identities. If organ failure patients want their lives saved, they have to accept the risks.

Donors' families also have to accept the risk that their loved one's harvested organs might not be suitable for transplant. There are no guarantees in this or any other field of medicine. The time between a donor's death, organ harvesting, and the recipient's surgical salvation is far too brief for deliberation. Only if both parties formally agree, can any information about donors or recipients ever be shared, and that can only happen after the transplant, when it's too late for anyone to change their mind.

Julie had also cared for a couple of patients who thought that their new hearts had changed them, but in their cases, their symptoms seemed more likely the result of taking steroids along with cyclosporine, the anti-rejection medicine that organ recipients take for the rest of their lives, amidst a slew of other drugs.

Cyclosporine has numerous nasty side effects. Mood swings are just one of them. This drug also predisposes patients to infections and cancer, which for many patients, provokes anxiety and fear of participating in social activities. And that's really frustrating for heart recipients after they're finally able to get up out of their wheelchairs, take off their oxygen masks, and join in; but only if they stay away from anyone's who is coughing or sniffling.

Julie Jacobs was intimately familiar with the side effects of anti-rejection treatment. When she was a twenty-year-old nursing student, she donated one of her kidneys to her twenty-five-year-old sister. Her sister's kidneys were destroyed by eclampsia, a complication of pregnancy that in her sister's case, wasn't treated in time. Her sister's immune system rejected the kidney, resulting in her having to take very high doses of cyclosporine. Unable to fight off even relatively benign germs, she ultimately died from overwhelming infection.

Julie wound up raising the little boy that her sister had left behind. As much as anyone could, Julie Jacobs knew the impact of transplantation from the perspectives of both a donor and a recipient, and she had more than twenty years' experience as a transplant coordinator. Still, she didn't have any serious experience with DOTS, what Carlos was calling donor organ transference syndrome. She was familiar with many of the stories circulating about people who reported personality changes after receiving a donor's heart, but she wasn't sure she believed them. However, the story Carlos had told in his presentation about his own experience seemed credible enough that she couldn't altogether dismiss it.

Carlos Mackenzy was eager to hear about a case of potential DOTS, so Julie filled him in on the background of Patient X. "He was a forty-two-year-old research scientist. He was active and healthy and had no risk factors for severe COVID when the virus knocked the breath out of him, back at the beginning of the pandemic when little was known about how to manage severely affected patients. He had been feverish and coughing for twelve days when his wife, a medical student, arranged to get him on home oxygen. A few hours later, no matter how high she turned up the flow, X's blood oxygen level dropped. He turned blue and he was ambulanced away. His wife wouldn't see him again for six weeks.

"X spent a month on a ventilator. About a week after his doctors started life support, they asked his wife for a do not resuscitate (D.N.R.) order. In addition to profound lung failure, his heart and kidneys were also shutting down. The I.C.U. physicians didn't want to have to shock an arrested heart back to beating if its owner was going to be revived in a state of complete debilitation for the rest of his existence. The wife agreed and X had no other family to protest.

"A few days after they posted the D.N.R. sign over X's bed, miraculously, his lung function took a turn for the better. After weeks of having to turn the ventilator pressures up, they were able to start to wean him off of respiratory support. His kidneys also recovered, but his heart, not so much.

"The D.N.R. order was rescinded, and X's heart continued to beat, but it remained sluggish. After he got discharged to home care, and he finally weaned off of supplemental oxygen, he had a few decent months. But then, he started showing signs of heart failure. His downward spiral persisted for more than two years. He probably wouldn't have lasted another two weeks if a matching heart hadn't come along when it did.

"X got his transplant in February. The donor was registered into the system through Carlos's transplant center. The new heart was an excellent match in size and tissue compatibility. X's surgeon had no problems connecting it, and they got him off the heart-lung machine quickly. His blood pressure and heart rhythm gave the doctors fits for the first few weeks after transplant, but once they fine-tuned his meds, he stabilized. So far, there were no signs of rejection and he'd been dedicated to his rehab program.

"However, according to the close associate who had called Julie, X was showing unexpected changes in his demeanor and his behavior. X's friend and research partner seemed alarmed. He said that X always liked to joke around but in a good-natured way. Now, he was making cutting remarks to people that his friend says are very much out of character.

"The friend also said that X's food preferences have drastically changed. The two had gone to lunch together at least a hundred times in recent years, often in the university cafeteria. X didn't like to eat four-legged animals. Cows, pigs, and sheep were never on his menu. He always ordered fish or something vegetarian. Once in a great while, he'd eat chicken. Recently, they'd gone to lunch and X ordered a hamburger with bacon. When his friend asked him how come, he flippantly said, "you only live twice." He's also smothering his food with ketchup which he never previously used."

"Interesting case. But if this X is a jokester, maybe he's spoofing his friend," Carlos suggested. "With his background, I'd be willing to bet that he knows all about the reports of cellular memory in transplant patients."

Julie confirmed that X and his wife had devoured everything that has ever been published in the field of transplant medicine. "Maybe," she suggested, "they know as much as people in the field. They're both very scholarly; I'd say scary scholarly.

"It's also apparent that this friend is also knowledgeable about cellular memory. However, the friend sounded like he was genuinely concerned about these changes in X. He's also a scientist, and I really didn't get the impression that he would joke around about something like this. And from what I know of the heart recipient, I can't imagine he'd joke about it either.

"The food preference change does seem weird, but what does it actually mean if the donor did love hamburgers and ketchup?" Julie questioned. "Don't most people? Maybe X's second chance at life just makes him want to have new experiences. Maybe he's just rebounding from the restrictive heart failure diet that he had to live on for the past few years."

"Well, I'd be happy to talk to X if you think that could help clarify what's going on. I know what it's like to feel out of sorts with yourself," Carlos offered.

"I don't think that's the problem, Carlos. X's friend said that he and X are very close, and he's asked him about having alien feelings. X absolutely denies having what you're calling DOTS. This friend also spoke to X's wife about it, but she hardly even sees her husband. She's an intern in a hospital that's hours away from the transplant center, so she and X are only together every other weekend. She doesn't get to observe him as much as his friend does, but she reportedly agreed with the friend that X seems different."

"Did you get to speak to the wife?" Carlos asked.

"I haven't reached her yet, I'll try again. As a physician just starting internship, I know her availability is limited. Between long hours in the hospital and the never-ending pursuit of having up-to-date medical knowledge, these people barely get to eat and sleep."

"I'll be glad to speak to either X or his wife or the friend, if any of them is inclined," Carols offered. "I don't know if I can be of help to them, but it would be helpful to me in my efforts to understand a phenomenon that the transplant community struggles with. Since I gave that talk at the conference last year about my personal experience, several other transplant coordinators and patients have been reaching out to me. Every case is challenging.

"The case I most recently was consulted on is a great example of how little any of us know. The heart recipient was a ten-year-old boy with congenital heart disease. The donor was an eleven-year-old girl who went to her gymnastics class with a giant wad of chewing gum in her mouth. She was doing a handspring when it lodged in her trachea and couldn't be dislodged, no matter how many times they did the Heimlich maneuver. Supplemental oxygen just barely got her to transplant status.

"Per request by their pediatrician, the family of the recipient did not know of the donor's gender, but after recovery, the boy began to claim that he was female. The father thinks it's an excuse because his son is afraid of playing sports with other boys, which he could never do when he had a bad heart. The mother thinks her son really has transformed his gender identity.

"Both parents agree that their son's gender was never questionable beforehand. Except for his cardiac limitations, he was always very much a boy with different interests than his sister. Meanwhile, the whole family is at war while this kid is really suffering. I have no idea if this is a case of DOTS or not. Family dynamics are so complex and so are current concepts about gender."

"Well good luck with that one, Carlos. I hope the family's getting some counseling.

"I'll try to get X to tell me what's going on with him. I have an appointment with him next week and I'm anxious to meet with him myself. If I suspect DOTS, I will put him in touch with you, maybe in the interest of disproving DOTS."

"How do you mean, Julie?"

"I have to tell you, Carlos, I've been afraid of the concept of cellular memory being validated, because it's frightening to both donors and recipients. Who's going to want to give their heart away if they think it holds their secrets? And who would want to receive a heart that harbors hate or pain, if it's true that the cells can remember? I don't doubt your personal experience, Carlos, but I do have a vested interest in protecting my dying patients from misconceptions that can only add to the heavy burdens that are already threatening their existence and their sanity.

"Thanks for your offer to help, Carlos. I hope this isn't a case of DOTS, because it wouldn't be good news for the transplant world if it was. But if this family does need help for that sort of issue, I believe you're their guy."

*In 1997, Harper Books published *A Change of Heart, A Memoir*, written by Claire Sylvia and William Novak about Claire's experience as the recipient of a donor's heart and lungs.

 **18**

James Dzobak knew that Ingrid Smythe was checking out the browsing history on his desktop when she thought he wasn't around. Whenever he could, he'd spend spare minutes entertaining himself by learning about bats.

James didn't intend for his relationship with his boss to become a game of cat and mouse when he set up his computer to capture her intrusions. He just wanted to know more about her connection to bats. Sullivan Dietz had sparked something in James that had been repressed for a long time.

As his mother told the story, James was about seven when his parents put Grandma Dzobak in charge for a long Memorial Day weekend. Granny was warned that James was likely to come in from playing outdoors with a frog in one hand and a snake in the other. His pockets also needed to be checked for ladybugs and lizards. Then, he needed to be firmly directed to take all of his new friends back outside and return them to their own homes.

However, a few years later, James's interest in animals was supplanted by his fervent interest in technology. It happened when he got his first computer, just after his beloved Labrador retriever had died. The computer hijacked his brain, his priorities, and his spirit. Ultimately, he turned into the geek of geeks.

Now, here he was, thirty-nine, freshly divorced and living with his parents back on the lake. Some of the wildlife had been pushed out by housing, but the deer were doing well by dining on landscapes. Newcomers were planting all the wrong flowers.

James was also amazed by the resilience of the Canada geese. They did a much better job than the ducks when it came to protecting their babies from cats, foxes, raccoons, owls, ospreys, and other predators. There were almost always at least three adult geese guarding the goslings, while lone mother mallards lost a duckling most every day.

If James arose early enough, he could watch some deer come down to the lake for a drink. If he went out after dark and threw an old sneaker high up into the air, a bat might come to investigate. Maybe it was a little brown bat. He had just bought night vision glasses, but being able to focus on a swift flying bat was a skill he hadn't yet acquired.

James was dumbfounded as to how he had grown up loving animals and not loving bats. How had the stereotype of blood sucking vampires become so dominant, when out of more than fourteen hundred species of bats, only three are known to consume blood? South American cow blood to be specific. All the rest of the bats just eat bugs or nectar, and they go out of their way to avoid humans. There are no blood sucking bats in North America, and unless they're defending themselves or sick with rabies, bats are exceptionally gentle creatures.

The repressed biologist in James had been awakened. How could humans not admire bats for their mastery of flight, their ability to navigate in the dark by sonar, their ability to migrate far and wide, to hibernate, to overcome reproductive risks by storing sperm and extending the duration of pregnancy, to live in close quarters with thousands of other bats, to be able to make love for hours, to be able to resist hundreds of infectious diseases, and to have the greatest longevity of any mammal relative to size? Bats could be the most advanced species on the planet. They are one of the oldest and most diversified. They are one of the most successful. One out of every four mammals on planet Earth is a bat. James was completely captivated.

Finally, after leaving links to websites about Dengue vaccines on his computer, Ingrid came around to asking James why he was so interested in bats. James started to give her an earful about how fantastic bats are when Ingrid interrupted him to ask if he knew that bats could be carriers of the Dengue virus, which was an up-and-coming scourge for humanity.

From what James had read, bats were being investigated as a possible carrier of Dengue. But since humans get Dengue from mosquito bites, and since bats are prolific eaters of mosquitos, they are probably not a major reservoir for this virus.

Once more, Ingrid commented about how horrible Dengue is. James asked her if she ever had Dengue. She said yes, so he asked her what it was like.

Ingrid revealed that decades ago, her family had vacationed in the Caribbean. Ingrid and her son both came home with mosquito bites. A few days later, they both had headaches that felt like their eyes were being pulled out of their sockets. Ingrid became nauseous. Her son started to vomit. The next day, they both had high fevers and pain all over their bodies. Dengue is often called "breakbone fever" because it feels like one's bones are all broken. After about a week of intermitting high fevers, terrible pain, and complete loss of appetite, they both erupted in rashes. Their livers became inflamed and poured out bilirubin, a chemical in the blood that causes intense itching of the skin. Ingrid said that both she and her son spent several days rubbing the palms of their hands and the soles of their feet against a rough cement wall on their patio. Fortunately, after about two weeks of abject misery, they started to recover.

Ingrid said they were lucky because some forms of Dengue cause internal bleeding that's usually fatal. About one out of every twenty people infected by the Dengue virus doesn't survive.

When Ingrid and her son had Dengue, their local physicians were unfamiliar with what was then, a tropical disease. Their symptoms were called "flu", "and "some kind of virus," and they didn't learn about the risk of reinfection until it was too late. If a person with antibodies to Dengue gets it again, there's a significant risk of lethal hemorrhaging.

Four years after Ingrid's son recovered from his bout with Dengue, he took a college break in the tropics. He didn't use insect repellant as stringently as he should have, and he incurred some mosquito bites. Eight days after arriving on the island, he died from hemorrhagic Dengue fever. He had been a healthy, athletic nineteen-year-old before this vicious virus took his life. There is no cure for Dengue.

James thanked his boss for sharing her story. He told her she might have propelled his research in a new direction. He was consoled to learn that Ingrid had a personal vendetta against Dengue. This virus had been in the news of late. Its incidence was rapidly increasing globally, and it had recently become epidemic in Brazil and Puerto Rico.

James had also learned that one of the only currently licensed vaccines for Dengue was unsafe for people who didn't already have antibodies to the virus. The Dengue virus is endemic in the Philippines, and most young children there have been exposed. However, the vaccine caused severe reactions in some children whose immune systems were unfamiliar with this virus. During previous attempts to create a Dengue vaccine, recipients got sicker if they caught Dengue after vaccination. James was learning that this was a really tricky virus, though Brazil was starting to use a Japanese Dengue vaccine that seemed promising.

James also learned that the mosquito that transmits the Dengue virus is starting to become resistant to insect repellants. Ingrid's business records indicated that she also had a chemical company on an Indonesian island that was trying to develop a more effective bug spray. Wouldn't that become a competitive endeavor with mosquitos and ticks on the rise?

James came to believe that Ingrid's curiosity about the research funding of Darius Amari was maybe more noble than nefarious. It was fortunate if wealthy people had such strong personal interests in viral research and disease prevention that they were willing to donate to the cause. It seemed obvious that government couldn't finance it all, especially in an anti-science and anti-vaccine environment. James felt some new respect for Ingrid Smythe.

Simultaneously, James was disheartened to realize that in spite of all of the adorable baby bat videos that he had left links to on his browser, Ingrid viewed bats as nothing more than lab rats. She'd be willing to sacrifice them if she could get a Dengue vaccine on the market the fastest. After all, as of 2023, Dengue had already shown up in Florida, Texas, Arizona, and Hawaii. The number of Florida cases had more than doubled in a year, and in 2024, Dengue was showing up as far north as Massachusetts.

The mosquitos that transmitted the Dengue virus were migrating north, while the bats who could combat the mosquitos were dying off from loss of habitat and white nose disease, a fungus that is lethal for hibernating bats. In some regions, bat populations were being decimated. Yet it seemed that Ingrid, like so many others, was blaming the poor maligned bats for Dengue's spread. Why couldn't she appreciate that bats know how to resist the Dengue virus, and so many other viruses to which humans are vulnerable?

Then again, if Ingrid wasn't even respectful towards people, it seemed unlikely that she could learn to respect bats.

19

With two interns and two residents out sick, Doctor Thea Baccay felt obliged to help cover in the hospital, so she converted her meeting with transplant coordinator Julie Jacobs from an in-person format to remote.

Julie Jacobs had met with Darius several times during his early recovery in rehab, but this was the first consult since he'd started living a somewhat normal life again. It was supposed to be in-person. Thea and Julie connected online and made small talk while waiting for Darius to arrive in Julie's office. After ten minutes elapsed, Thea became concerned. Darius was normally very punctual. She texted him, but he didn't respond.

"So how do *you* think Darius is doing?" Julie asked while they waited.

"I see so little of him, it's hard to say. When is he going to be able to move away from the transplant center?"

For a second, Julie was surprised by Thea's question, but she quickly realized what was implied. The transplant center wasn't holding Darius back. He still needed his biopsies once a month for another two months, but he could live further away in between.

"Darius can move as soon as he feels ready. Some patients never want to be too far away from the transplant center, especially if they're experiencing rejection," Julie counseled. "Do you and Darius Zoom or facetime with each other?"

"We do whenever I'm not on call and not so tired that I just collapse. Sometimes, he's too tired and we just say hi and bye. I knew internship would be like this for me, but we didn't really know what our lives would be like if Darius got saved by a transplant."

"So, in terms of how little you two see each other, how do you think Darius is doing?"

"I think he's doing amazingly well. He's regaining his strength and muscle mass. When he was wheelchair bound, he wasted away. He barely had a butt to sit on. Now he has glutes again and he's taking long walks. He's also razor focused on stuff going on in his lab that he had trouble attending to when he was dying." Thea closed her eyes for a second. "He's even getting his libido back. His recovery has just been miraculous."

Thea tried so hard to sound upbeat that it was painful to guess what she was trying to hide. Even on a computer screen, Julie could see that Thea was upset about Darius being a no-show for this appointment. That concerned Julie too. She had sent him a link to the online meeting, so he could have tuned in from wherever he was. To not even call to say that he'd been detained, that was not at all like the conscientious person Julie had previously known. She also worried that he had a medical emergency.

Thea texted him again, but he still didn't respond. Julie decided to confront Thea in spite of her anxiety. "Your husband's partner, Sullivan Dietz, contacted me. He said he sees concerning changes in Darius and that you do too. Am I misinformed?"

Thea appeared aggrieved. "Sullivan spends a lot more time with Darius than I do, and he's known him longer, so he's probably right. And I respect Sullivan. He's a very good friend and I'm certain he's genuinely interested in Darius's recovery. But what I'm seeing in my husband is a highly productive person who suddenly had everything taken away from him by a virus, who now, even more suddenly, has a new lease on life and a new zest for life. I can't wait to see where he's going to go with his research."

Julie tried to probe a little further, but Thea seemed determined to view her husband's transition in a positive light.

Finally, Darius returned her call. Thea put her phone on speaker so Julie could hear. "Are you okay, Darius? Where are you?"

"I'm fine. I'm managing a lab accident. A graduate student dropped a slide and got a puncture in her gloves picking it up. Sully knows how to decontaminate, but by regulation, I have to sign off on all the steps of the protocol. I have to go now." Darius abruptly hung up.

Julie's jaw dropped. "He's not in the lab, is he?"

"Oh no, no, no! He does it all remotely. At the start of the pandemic when we had COVID, a graduate student wired the entire lab for video, so Darius could supervise from home. Actually, at the onset of COVID-19, every lab in the world with the necessary biosafety level conditions was drafted into looking at coronaviruses. Labs that work with bats received considerable support, so that helped to finance the remote operation system."

It appeared that Thea wanted to talk about bat research instead of her relationship with her husband. Julie was starting to wonder if Thea and Darius weren't strangers to each other, even before COVID ravaged their lives.

Julie was also struck by the fact that she could hear a baseball game in the background of Darius's brief call. On Darius's last day in the hospital, when Julie visited to wish him well and set up his post-transplant appointments, she found him watching a baseball game. He seemed thoroughly engrossed.

Julie thought that maybe baseball could be an icebreaker. "It sounded like Darius was watching or listening to baseball. I wonder what the bats in the lab would think of humans calling the things they hit balls with bats. What team does Darius root for?"

Thea's face turned into a giant question mark. "Is that what that background noise was? I don't believe Darius has ever watched baseball. At least not since I know him. And I cannot imagine him doing it during a lab incident. When it comes to anything that could threaten his lab, Darius Amari becomes a very serious man."

20

Doctor Melinda Villarose demanded an appointment with Ingrid Smythe. James said he'd see what he could do. Melinda insisted it was urgent. James was sympathetic, but Melinda still had to wait two days to get on her boss's calendar.

It had been almost two months since Ingrid Smythe had advised Melinda that Doctor Ezra Rhea's status as the chief of surgery was under review. In that span of time, there had been three more serious incidents, including a death.

It was inconceivable to Melinda that nothing had been done. The nurses and residents were nervous about taking care of his patients. Senior residents would jokingly introduce new admissions to the hospitalists as patients suffering from E.R.S.A., Ezra Rhea Strikes Again. The hospital's failure to suspend this physician's privileges while he was supposedly under investigation, put patients and professionals at risk. The stench of malpractice suits had to be permeating the nostrils of Tazodan's attorneys.

Melinda was also concerned that young physicians were seeing such low standards of care as part of their training. It was the duty of physicians who valued the lives of their patients, to report incompetence by other physicians. But Melinda knew, most physicians were afraid to do so. If they did, any angry patient or competing provider could manufacture complaints against them. No one from the surgical services seemed to want to rat out Doctor Ezra Rhea. *Did he also have some kind of hold over the hospital's new administrators?*

Melinda wondered if it was the bond of the old boys' fraternity, or if Ezra Rhea had some kind of deal with Tazodan that benefitted physicians who were using the hospital's operating rooms. She tried to gain insight by talking to a variety of surgeons on Bandore's staff. With one exception, they all tried to avoid the topic of Doctor Ezra Rhea.

It was an orthopedist with whom Melinda had broached the subject that admitted that most everyone in the surgical department was concerned. This doctor confided in Melinda that the nurses who scrubbed in on his cases were reporting that Doctor Rhea was meticulous in following O.R. protocols. They claimed to have no idea why his patients were getting infected.

An infectious disease specialist cultured Doctor Rhea's skin and oral and nasal membranes for bacteria. Some healthy people harbor Staph, Strep, or other germs, without getting sick themselves. These people and their doctors usually do not know that they are carriers. Doctor Rhea's cultures didn't produce any significant bacteria. Why his patients were getting infected remained a mystery.

In one instance, intern and former surgeon Dayo Igwe, diagnosed peritoneal infection in the case of a man whose gall bladder had been removed by Doctor Rhea. The ill-looking man showed up in the E.R. with fever and abdominal pain, two days after his surgery. While the E.R. doctor waited more than three hours for the results of imaging and lab tests to make the diagnosis, Igwe correctly diagnosed the problem in about thirty seconds by the sounds generated by tapping his finger over the man's belly.

Then, there was the case of the fifty-nine-year-old cancer patient sent by his oncologist for a new intravenous portal. Most of his peripheral veins had too much scar tissue to be useful anymore. He'd been fighting chronic leukemia for years. Currently, his oncologist needed access to a large bore vein for large volumes of chemo.

Doctor Rhea decided that instead of doing a new cutdown to get to a big vein, he'd try to unblock the line that was already in the patient's ankle vein. When that didn't work, he pulled out the old-clotted line and put in a new one on the other side. That was at eight o'clock in the morning. At eight o'clock the next morning, the patient spiked a fever and was brought back to the hospital. He was immediately started on powerful antibiotics for sepsis, but even before he could be transferred from the E.R. to a hospital bed, he went into shock and had a heart attack. In spite of heroic resuscitation efforts, he died.

The night before Melinda demanded the appointment with Ingrid Smythe, another case had occurred involving a sixteen-year-old boy with severe juvenile rheumatoid arthritis. He'd been on an array of immunosuppressive drugs since he was ten years old, but wayward antibodies in his system kept attacking his joints. He was essentially crippled. Most of his young life had been about fighting a cruel disease that had also bankrupted his family.

Because he had to take immunosuppressive drugs, this unfortunate patient was frequently hospitalized for hard-to-control skin infections and pneumonias. His rheumatologist requested surgical placement of a central intravenous line, so the patient didn't have to get needled all the time. Two days after the procedure was performed by Doctor Rhea, the patient was admitted to the hospital for sepsis.

Thea Baccay was on-call at the time of the admission. She worried that the antibiotics the patient was on weren't doing the job. She took samples of blood for the lab to determine if the germ was resistant. When the patient was still febrile an hour later, she took a second set of blood specimens. Each time, she carefully labeled the culture bottles and took them to the nursing station to be transported to the lab.

Shortly after processing the second set of specimens, Thea was coming out of another patient's room when she saw the back of Doctor Ezra Rhea standing at the desk of the nursing station. He was unmistakable in his extra-long white coat and his clogs. According to hospital lore, Ezra Rhea's big, wide, aching feet found wonderful relief in rubber Crocs. Those gardening clogs had become the brunt of jokes throughout the hospital.

To her astonishment, Thea watched Doctor Rhea take the newest specimens out of the courier's basket and slip them into his coat pocket. Then he did something on the computer and quickly left the ward.

Thea was so stunned; she wasn't sure what to do. She waited two days to see if those blood culture results showed up in the computer. When they didn't, she told the director of the residency program, a flabbergasted Melinda Villarose, what she had witnessed.

21

When Melinda Villarose showed up at the office of Ingrid Smythe at the appointed time, James Dzobak informed her that Ms. Smythe had just left the office due to an emergency and they'd have to reschedule. The intense anger evident in Melinda's emerald eyes made James worry that she might start smashing things. He told Melinda how sorry he was and suggested that two old Bandore County natives should take advantage of the situation and go to lunch.

James was thinking that maybe Melinda knew something about Darius Amari's research. He'd come up with no relevant information since Ingrid had tasked him with such an investigation. Melinda seemed like she had a close relationship with Thea Baccay. Maybe he could squeeze something out of that.

Melinda was thinking that possibly, she could influence James to influence Ingrid about the problems being caused by Doctor Ezra Rhea. She thought that James might have had some input in the decision for the hospital to accept Thea Baccay outside of the resident matching program. Maybe he cared enough about the locals to not want to see patients and the hospital's reputation being put at risk by a dangerous surgeon.

Melinda suggested the Bandore Diner. She thought her meeting with Smythe would have been brief and she had scheduled herself to be away from her duties for just an hour. The diner was only a few minutes down the road.

"No way," James said. "I thought they closed that rat trap years ago."

"They did, but new owners refurbished and reopened it last summer and it's pretty good now. They have a millennial chef who's created a healthy, diverse menu. I've heard the Sunday brunch is very indulgent, but deep-fried chili dogs are no longer an option."

"Darn. I was thinking of choking down a couple of those. Hey! I feel so bad about Ms. Smythe standing you up again that I'm driving, and lunch is on me."

When James rolled his twenty-year-old ride up to the hospital portico to pick Melinda up, she realized that the custom-tailored suit that James wore to sit at Ingrid Smythe's front desk was probably worth more than his car. She wondered if he had a company expense account for the lunch tab. She wondered what James was being paid to be abused by Ingrid Smythe.

"So, what's it like working for Ms. Smythe," Melinda asked as they slid into a booth in the old eatery. Phone charging stations occupied the end of the table where a jukebox selector once sat. A young man with multiple tattoos brought them a menu.

"It's challenging," James said. "I don't normally drink alcohol at lunchtime, but if we're going to talk about the Tazodan Corporation, I need a beer."

"Then let's get some beer," Melinda said, though she actually disliked beer. But if nurturing a relationship with Smythe's right hand man could be helpful to her goals, she'd drink a pint. James seemed to be the only link she had to the top dogs that were now running the show. On the other hand, doing two doctors' jobs by herself had kept her so busy that she hadn't had time to find other inroads into the new administrative circle.

James took a giant swig from his beer mug. "I don't really know how I feel about working for Ingrid Smythe. I can tell you that I'm never bored. Every day that she's in the office, she's got another data extraction for me to do. Most of the time, I'm looking at financial spreadsheets, but then she'll give me some project related to her private businesses."

"Like what?" Melinda asked.

"Like, what are the sources of funding for research into a vaccine for Dengue fever. Apparently, she has a company that's trying to develop a vaccine. After you brought Doctor Baccay to her office, Ingrid even asked me to find out who's funding the research of Darius Amari. I've spent hours on that project, and I still don't have a handle on where the money comes from to do that kind of exotic research."

"I didn't know Amari's research was considered exotic. As little as I understand, it has to do with viruses carried by bats. Do you know what Darius does in his lab?" Melinda asked.

Once again, James's plan to get Smythe the information that she wanted had unraveled. He'd learned far more from Sullivan Dietz than Melinda seemed to know.

"Not really," James said. "I've tried researching it because I'm really interested in bats, but I've come to wonder if maybe it's confidential. I wonder if Doctor Baccay even knows what her husband does.

"Ever since the coronavirus came along, research interest in bats has exploded. However, what researchers are actually doing in their labs seems to be over the head of the average physician. I've asked a few doctors to explain Amari's research to me and they seem as overwhelmed as I am. You probably have to be an elite scientist to understand this stuff."

Melinda said that she had also looked at Darius Amari's scientific publications. She also admitted that she had minimal understanding of epigenetics, the study of how environment and behavior modify the way in which an organism's genetic code is expressed. Melinda also mentioned that she had once spent an evening with Thea who talked a lot about her husband's dedication to his research, but not about the actual research.

As the waiter delivered James's burger and Melinda's salad, James said, "by the way, I heard about Doctor Baccay's husband having a heart transplant. She came to interview when he was in critical condition. She's sure good at hiding anxiety behind that perpetual smile."

"She is very stoic," Melinda said. Her shrugged shoulders said that Thea's level of stoicism was worrisome. They turned their attention to their meals. When she was finished, Melinda pushed her mug across the table.

"I guess I wasn't in the mood for beer after all. I ordered it because I thought I needed a lift after being stood up by Ingrid Smythe again. It happens half of the times I make an appointment with her. Does she do this to everyone or just me?"

James was still working on the first mug. "It's not you, Doctor Villarose. From what I know, Ingrid Smythe is managing much more than just the revenue cycle of Tazodan's newly acquired hospitals. She owns a lot of businesses, and they seem to keep her running from one Zoom meeting to another all day, every day. What I can't figure out is how she does so much work for herself when she's employed by Tazodan."

"Well then, how does she prioritize? We have a giant nasty problem in our hospital right now that needs urgent administrative attention, so this delay is putting patients in danger.

"What kind of a problem?" James asked.

"Patients' lives are being put at risk by a physician who's not functioning well. I brought it to Ms. Smythe's attention weeks ago, but the situation has only gotten worse. I tried to get an appointment with one of the other administrators and they just referred me back to Ms. Smythe. It seems like she's the only one who makes decisions around here.

"Meanwhile, we actually lost a patient because of this doctor. There's another patient who's now at extreme risk. How can our hospital owners be indifferent to such a monstrous safety concern, not to mention a legal risk?"

"You're talking about the cancer patient who died after they put in a new line?"

"You know about that case?" Melinda wondered what else James knew about the clinical goings-on in the hospital, though probably everyone knew about that case. The human inclination to gossip supersedes privacy laws.

"That case has had the admin offices all a-buzz for the past two weeks," James said. "And Ms. Smythe has met with Doctor Ezra Rhea on several occasions."

Melinda felt the hair on her arms stand up to hear that Ezra Rhea had easy access to the hospital brass, while she had to beg to be heard. The administration wasn't ignoring the Doctor Rhea problem. It was starting to appear that they were part of it.

Melinda was also starting to think that maintaining a relationship with James might be the best way for her to try to figure out what was going on with the hospital's new management. She was also intrigued by what seemed to be James's personal interest in Thea and her husband. She was formulating more questions for him when her phone rang.

There was a crisis involving one of the interns. Melinda had to get back to the hospital immediately. She suggested that she and James meet for lunch on another occasion as she jumped out of his car and started running to the E.R.

～∿∿∿ **22** ∿∿∿

The E.R. manager gave Doctor Melinda Villarose a little more information than she had given over the phone, but it was still the short version. Doctor Suzie Nguyen was attacked in a hallway. She was knocked down hard and she has multiple injuries. Her level of consciousness was just a little better than comatose. She was being scanned at the moment.

The hospital security office was checking out tapes from the security cameras to try to identify the assailant. Officers from the county sheriff's department were on their way to the hospital to interview two teenagers who witnessed the attack.

Suzie Nguyen's employee file identified the person to be contacted in case of emergency. The E.R. manager had called and texted the number, but they hadn't yet heard back from Suzie's significant other.

The E.R. physician seemed more distressed than Melinda had ever seen her. She was highly suspicious of a brain injury. Even without x-rays, it was apparent that Suzie's jaw, cheekbone, and her right wrist were broken. She had lost some teeth. Her left hand was badly burned. An orthopedist was ready to address the wrist injury as soon as she came back from imaging, unless she needed emergency drainage of a brain bleed. The neurosurgeon was on standby.

As much as the E.R. staff sees horrors every day, seeing intern Suzie Nguyen so battered had left most of them shaken. Melinda was shaken to the core, and she had yet to even see Suzie.

The staff set the police up with the witnesses in a private cubicle, making room for Melinda to squeeze in. A hospital security officer was also present. One of the sheriff's people wore a state trooper's uniform. Another in plain clothes was introduced as a detective. The witnesses were two sisters, fifteen and seventeen years old. They were out shopping for back-to-school clothes when they decided to stop at the hospital cafeteria for lunch.

"Best deal in town," said the older sister. "We love the pizza," said the younger one. The Bandore County Hospital cafeteria was actually one of the most popular restaurants in the region and as of yet, the new hospital administration hadn't messed with the menu.

The younger sister seemed to have had the most attentive eyes and the better memory. She said she noticed the bad guy when they were walking down the hallway towards the cafeteria. She said she noticed him because he was wearing a ski hat and why would anyone be wearing a ski hat in late August when it's eighty-four degrees outside? She only saw him from the rear then. He was wearing black pants, a black tee shirt, and blue sneakers, along with the black knit cap. He was standing just outside the entrance to the cafeteria as though he was waiting for someone.

The older sister said she noticed the little Asian woman with a stethoscope around her neck come out of the cafeteria by herself. She was walking down the hallway with a steaming, insulated cup in one hand, and she was looking at her phone in her other hand.

Then, the guy in black ran up alongside of her, and with his arm stretched out, he whacked her in the back, very hard. The woman went flying forward and landed splat, face down. The man in black just kept running to the nearby exit. He was out the door before anyone got up close to the body on the floor. The woman's face was smashed into a pool of blood and coffee. Her phone was also smashed. She was out cold.

"I think he had something in his hand because of how hard he hit her," the younger sister said. "I think I saw something shiny in his hand, but I'm not sure. It all happened so fast."

Both girls described the suspect as having the ski hat pulled down over his hair, big dark sunglasses, and his tee shirt was pulled up over his mouth and nose. They could not see any part of his face or the color of his hair. There was nothing for a police sketch artist to draw.

"I saw his stomach from where the tee shirt was pulled up," the younger girl said. "It was flabby and hairy. Eww! I think he was older than my father. My father's forty and he's not in good shape, but this guy's belly looked flabbier. I also think I saw a tattoo on his arm, symbols, maybe. I couldn't tell what it was. Maybe writing."

Another hospital security officer entered the cubicle. We've got the attacker from the cafeteria hallway on tape, but he knew where all of the cameras are. He entered the hospital through the main lobby about a half-hour before the attack. He wondered around a bit, but every single time he was in the range of a camera, he managed to conceal his face very effectively by turning his head or shielding his face with his hands. We don't have a single good image of his face or his profile, but we're still looking.

"What about tattoos on his arms?" one of the policemen asked. The other policeman turned on a tablet and showed the girls some pictures of what gang tattoos looked like. The sisters looked perplexed. Gangs weren't an element of Bandore County.

The younger sister started to scroll through the images. She stopped at one that looked something like Chinese characters, but she said she couldn't be sure of what she saw or whether this image was similar. The older sister said she didn't notice the tattoo. When security reviewed the tapes again, tattoos weren't visible. The sister thought she saw it on the inside of his outstretched forearm. The tapes only showed the back of his arms.

Melinda was interrupted to take a call from someone named Mosey who identified as Suzie's domestic partner. Melinda had to deliver the devastating news. Through sobs and nose blowing,

Mosey claimed to be out of town at a dog show. Melinda learned that Suzie's partner was a highly regarded dog groomer whose clients won major canine championships all around the country. Mosey was contracted to provide services for the owners of half a dozen poodles and terriers for this show, and couldn't get back to be with Suzie for another few days.

Mosey informed Melinda that it would be difficult to contact Suzie's mother. She had recently gone through a divorce, and she had moved back to Vietnam, maybe permanently, but that hadn't yet been decided. Mosey promised to try to get in touch with the mother and also with Suzie's older brother, whose current whereabouts were unknown. He was reportedly estranged from the family. Mosey also didn't know anything about Suzie's father, except that he'd been out of her life since Suzie was very young.

It was starting to look like Suzie Nguyen's only available significant other at this tragic moment in her life, was her residency supervisor, Doctor Melinda Villarose.

$\downarrow\downarrow\downarrow\downarrow\downarrow$ **23** $\downarrow\downarrow\downarrow\downarrow$

The imaging reports were back. Suzie had managed to turn her head to the left before she hit the hard tile floor. Along with the fractures to her right jaw and cheekbone, she had also cracked her skull on that side. There was some blood pooling inside the skull. The neurosurgeon drilled a small hole in a skull bone and inserted a catheter to monitor for pressure on the brain.

Suzie was admitted to the neuro intensive care unit. Had she been more stable, the E.R. doctor would have considered Life Flighting her to University Hospital where there was more advanced care. But they were worried about the possibility of a brain bleed during transport, as well as her not having a support system there.

The orthopedist had to defer surgical repair of the wrist until they were sure the brain wasn't at risk. He splinted the hand and arm and hung it in a sling over the bed to stabilize it until he could repair it.

A plastic surgeon came to debride the burns. The hot coffee had left Suzie with serious burns on her hand and splash burns on her arm and face. Without specialized care, the fingers might have fused together. That hand was also suspended in a sling over her bed to control swelling.

An oral surgeon came to try to implant some of Suzie's smashed teeth that had been retrieved. He was able to place three of them back into their sockets. He then wired her broken jaw shut. The jaws would need immobilization for six to eight weeks for proper healing.

Another orthopedist reviewed the images of her spine. Suzie had one broken and one smashed thoracic vertebra where the attacker had whacked her. The markings on her back, suggested he may have had a wrench in his hand when he struck her.

The detective told the younger sister that her powers of observation would make her an excellent policeperson. Melinda wondered if this experience would have a profound impact on these teenagers. She told their mother, who had arrived at the hospital to support her daughters, that she'd be willing to provide counseling if they became distressed from having witnessed such a violent crime. Where she'd find the time to help them, she had no idea.

After escorting the witnesses and their mother to the cafeteria for their overdue pizza, Melinda wound up spending her overscheduled afternoon with the investigating police

Yes, there had been one complaint about the young doctor that Melinda knew of. Someone had said Doctor Nguyen was hard to understand, probably only because she was Asian. She was Texas born and bred and spoke without any traces of a foreign accent. She also spoke clearly and with empathetic facial expression.

Melinda said she'd find out from the administration if there were other complaints about this doctor about which she hadn't been informed. "Maybe it wasn't a hate crime. Maybe Suzie had cared for someone who had a bad outcome, and she was attacked out of revenge."

The police wanted to know about patients Doctor Nguyen had attended to. Extracting and analyzing those confidential records would take considerable time and effort, and Melinda didn't know where they'd find the manpower to review all of Suzie's patient encounters. The intern had spent her first rotation on the orthopedic ward where there was a high patient turnover. She was now rotating through the E.R. where she was seeing dozens of patients every day. Melinda wondered if data analyst James Dzobak could be farmed out to meet this police request. She'd look into that as soon as she got the chance.

"Yes," Melinda told the police, "there had been previous incidents of patients being hostile to foreign-looking or foreign-sounding doctors. At the height of the pandemic, it had become a serious problem, but not so much in the past year. Even during the pandemic, it was almost all verbal abuse and complaints about medical care. None of the other doctors had actually been physically attacked, though one of their doctors had been spit on, and another angry person had snatched the stethoscope off of the neck of one of the nurses.

"Yes, there were other Asian doctors on staff." Melinda told the police. The hospital also employed numerous nurses and other staff who were Asian, or who could be considered Asian. Though Bandore County was home to a Filipino community that mostly spoke Spanish, many locals didn't distinguish these people from those of Chinese, Japanese, Korean, or other Asian nationalities. All of these people experienced resentment because of a virus presumed to be of Chinese origin.

Melinda was worried about all of her residents but especially Thea Baccay. In her experience, the bigots that had been hostile to doctors of a different color were most likely to take it out on small females. Suzie Nguyen was a waif of a woman, but Thea was even tinier.

None of these bigots had the courage to come after a tall Asian guy, like David Ye. David was a senior resident who hadn't experienced any verbal abuse back when the pandemic put junior resident Jennifer Kim in the crosshairs. Jennifer, of Korean heritage, was a wonderful physician and a lovely person, but after COVID came along, she had heard just about every anti-Asian slur Americans could come up with.

Before the pandemic, the bigots mostly complained about the black and brown doctors that they didn't like receiving care from. One former resident from India had been given a lot of grief, and there had been several complaints about a resident who wore a turban, but the people of Bandore County had been more respectful before the pandemic. Melinda feared that ethnic hostility had now become even worse since the conflict between Israel and Hamas. One of her residents had given up wearing his Jewish star and another had given up wearing her Muslim head covering.

It wasn't until the ten o'clock news came on that Melinda saw a story about the attack at the hospital. The picture showing the attacker with his hand concealing his face, at least revealed his race, his body type, and his clothing. As the teenaged witnesses reported, the suspect was white, of average height, but on the pudgy side. Hopefully someone would recognize this monster.

The only thing said about the victim was that she was a new physician in the hospital, and she was in critical condition. Her Asian identity wasn't revealed, and Melinda wondered why. If the attacker was known to be prejudiced against Asians, maybe he could be more easily identified by someone who knew about his biases. Perhaps the news editors were concerned about provoking additional racial targeting.

Melinda didn't feel sleepy enough to even try to go to bed, so she stayed up reading about injuries to the temporal lobe. She finally fell asleep, only to be awakened by a call from the I.C.U. Suzie Nguyen had regained consciousness, but she didn't know who or where she was. The I.C.U. doctor was hoping a familiar face would help to orient her. They didn't know who else to call.

The request seemed ironic since Melinda had just read that one of the symptoms of right temporal lobe injury was an inability to recognize faces. But she left her townhouse at eleven p.m. and headed to the hospital with the hope that she could help.

24

It was nine-twenty on the morning after the assault. Melinda had glued herself to a chair in Ingrid Smythe's outer office while waiting for the boss. Had the assault occurred during the previous hospital administration, the CEO would have called Melinda last night to check on the status of Suzie. Melinda hadn't heard from anyone in Tazodan's administration.

Melinda didn't have an appointment, but James had told her that Ingrid was expected at nine-thirty. Melinda intended to snare her as soon as she walked in the door, and James decided that there was no reasonable way to deter her. He sensed her distress and her determination.

Melinda had explained to James about the data analysis that was needed to try to find Suzie Nguyen's attacker. Medical charts that included her name had to be gathered and reviewed. Melinda also suggested that James flag any recent chart that contained a diagnosis of substance abuse disorder. A primary reason for patients' hostility towards physicians stemmed from the doctor's unwillingness to administer or prescribe opioids.

Melinda also wanted James to flag any chart where the patient signed themselves out of the hospital against medical advice, (A.M.A.). She suggested that James should communicate with the sheriff's office directly about what other data they needed.

James said it would be easy to collect this information. He couldn't fathom why he hadn't already been put to the task by one of the higher-ups. Ingrid had been out of town for the past two days, but this morning, the story of the attack on Doctor Nguyen, and the manhunt for the attacker, had made the national news. Surely, Ingrid would know about it by now, even if the story got dropped by the next news cycle.

As Melinda would observe, the local networks would carry the story for just one more day. Patients assaulting health care workers, and racists attacking Asians, rapidly became old news that networks quickly abandoned. Like violence against women, such crimes weren't considered continually newsworthy unless the victims were attractive blondes, like Gabby Petito, murdered by her boyfriend, or Elizabeth Smart, abducted by a street preacher, or Natalee Holloway, who disappeared during a Caribbean vacation. Dark-haired Suzie Nguyen wasn't going to become a legendary victim in spite of how viciously she was attacked.

"I know why you're here," Ingrid Smythe said, as soon as she saw Doctor Villarose sitting in waiting. As though she had heard Melinda's whole conversation with James, Ingrid advised her assistant to get the sheriff's office whatever information they needed.

"How is Doctor Nguyen?" Ingrid asked as she motioned for Melinda to follow her into the inner office. Melinda was suspicious of the transformation in Ingrid's demeanor, Normally, this woman came across as a fire-breathing dragon; but at least she had asked about Suzie.

"Very seriously injured. Last night, to everyone's delight, she regained consciousness. The poor woman awoke to find her head bolted and immobilized, her face painful and swollen, her jaw wired shut, her hands bound and hanging in slings, and unimaginable pain all over. I can't even fathom the terror. Suzie became very agitated before she came to understand what had happened. She really did not know how she got there.

"The staff thought she was disoriented, so I came back to the hospital to see if I could help. By the time I arrived, the I.C.U. physician had realized that what Suzie was trying to communicate was that her vision was distorted. They took her back to the scanner and found a crack in her right eye socket, so her eye motion is compromised. They think it will heal without surgery, but for now, she has to cover that eye to avoid double vision, and that could actually be the least of her problems.

"I slept in an on-call room and checked on her again this morning. They said she became agitated again and now she's heavily sedated. She has some rib cracks along with spinal fractures, so just breathing is quite painful for her. They're also worried that she might get paradoxical agitation from pain medications. She hasn't been conscious long enough for the staff to figure out what's going on. There's no available family member who might be able to provide more history about previous drug reactions."

Ingrid Smythe sat stone-faced as Melinda described the horrific trauma that had befallen this promising young physician. Finally, she asked Melinda how they planned to come up with a replacement for Doctor Nguyen.

"Replacement?" Melinda was gobsmacked by the arrogance of this woman. They didn't even have a prognosis for Suzie at this point, and she was already being dismissed as a disabled person. Suzie was a healthy young woman. In spite of her multiple serious injuries, she could conceivably be back on the job in a few months, maybe sooner if there was no brain injury and no other complications.

Melinda didn't even want to think about Suzie being so disabled that she couldn't resume her training. She also didn't want to think about her being disabled and not having a support system. Mosey hadn't called the hospital or Melinda to check on Suzie since their initial contact.

"Our resident staff is already pitching in to cover for Doctor Nguyen, until we can get a better picture of her recovery potential. As hard as our residents work, they are willing to go an extra mile to help out. Family practice doctors tend to have generous souls. They're very caring and conscientious people. But our residents are already stretched too thin. We don't have enough of them for when circumstances cause someone to be off the schedule like this.

"We do need a substitute until we know more about Suzie's course. There are some retired physicians in our community who've helped out in the past. With your permission, I'll see if any of theme is available and willing to fill in. If not, there are agencies that rent out substitute doctors. They charge a lot, and they haven't always sent great candidates, but that's better than abusing our already overworked house staff.

"I'm increasingly concerned about the burdens being placed on our interns and residents. Between their heavy workload, the Doctor Rhea issues, and now, this horrible assault, I worry about them experiencing excessive levels of anxiety. Some may even feel too fearful to come to work. We can't burden them with extra shifts and extra patients."

Ingrid's head snapped up when Melinda mentioned Doctor Rhea. Ingrid was about to speak when Melinda put her hand up, stood up, put her hands on Ingrid's massive desk and leaned forward. "And let me tell you something about Doctor Rhea. Two days ago, Doctor Baccay drew blood specimens from a very sick patient that Doctor Rhea had managed. She was afraid the patient had an infection that wasn't being properly treated. She then witnessed Doctor Rhea pocket the specimens before the courier took them to the lab, and the results of those critical tests never showed up in the computer.

"Doctor Baccay had taken another set of cultures before that, and now they're showing bacteria in the blood. Fortunately, she'd already changed the patient's medication and the infection is coming under control. However, my physicians cannot work in an environment where they and their patients are being sabotaged. This has become an untenable situation."

Melinda sat back down in her chair and returned Ingrid's glare.

Just then, James popped into the office. He could feel the heated vibe in the room. It cooled down a bit after he interrupted them. "Sheriff's on the phone for you, Ms. Smythe. He's asking for an update on the victim." Ingrid directed James to turn the call over to Melinda and she shooed both of them out of her office.

Melinda informed the sheriff that Suzie Nguyen was expected to survive. The sheriff asked to be notified of changes that could turn assault and battery charges into murder charges. He also told Melinda that the news coverage had brought in multiple tips that were being checked out, but they hadn't yet identified a suspect.

Melinda wondered how underfunded this sheriff's office was in the low-crime-rate district of Bandore County. Perhaps the low crime rate would afford them more resources to work on this case. Melinda suspected that most of this sheriff's staff spent most of their days trying to catch speeders on the highway.

Except for some who vacationed at the lake resort, few people came to Bandore County, but many passed through it on their way to more populous places. The highway gas station/convenience store was the most profitable business in the region.

25

Several hours after Melinda had thrown her tantrum in Smythe's office, James called Doctors Villarose and Baccay and told them that Ms. Smythe wanted to meet with them at three. They were both surprised to find each other present when they arrived. After they were seated, Ingrid asked them to turn their cell phones off and put them on her desk.

As the two physicians rolled their eyes at the request, Ingrid simultaneously asked how Doctor Nguyen was doing. She addressed the question to Melinda who had just checked in with Suzie's I.C.U. physician before coming to this appointment. *Was someone reporting her activities to Smythe?* Irate to think she was being spied on; she gave Ingrid a piercing look as she placed her phone on the desk. Thea avoided the drama as she relinquished her phone.

"No bleeding in her brain so far, but it's barely been twenty-four hours," Melinda said. "Subdural bleeds can occur days later due to slow leaks from damaged blood vessels. They're keeping her sedated for another day or two, so she doesn't rattle her head.

"Her broken back and ribs make her breathing shallow and labored, so she's on oxygen. delivered through a nasal cannula. This poor woman's eyes, nose, mouth, torso, and hands are all out of commission, so it's probably better if she's not conscious. Her nurse is also observing large bruises starting to show up on her knees."

"Did someone from her family show up yet?"

"No. We understand her mother recently moved back to Vietnam and we don't have enough information to even try to find her. I've got another call into Doctor Nguyen's partner."

"And do you have a substitute physician lined up yet?"

Yet? I've only had a few hours to even consider it let alone hire some-
one. How does anyone work for this tyrant? Melinda took a deep breath
to calm herself. "I'm waiting for some call backs. Also, our intern
Doctor Igwe knows of someone who might be eligible. But I can't
have someone move here if they're only going to be employed for
a month or two unless the hospital can provide accommodations.
That's what the rent-a-doc agencies do."

"Not impossible," Ingrid responded. "I'm sure we can spare
an on-call room if we just have someone here briefly. You need to
find someone quickly. I don't want to hear about patient problems
because of holes in the schedule."

Ingrid swiveled her chair to face Thea Baccay. "How are things
going for you and your husband, Doctor Baccay? It was six months
ago when we met, just after he got his new heart."

"He's doing great. Thanks for asking. He's still not the dynamo
he used to be, but compared to how he was before the transplant,
he's a thousand percent improved. And so far, no rejection, It's a
miracle. And thank you so much for allowing my early acceptance
into the Bandore residency program."

"Of course. Is your husband back to his research?"

Thea nodded yes.

"Do you know what he's currently working on?"

Thea casually said, "the effects of thermoregulation on the syn-
thesis of the nucleotides in DNA coding for the immune response
to lyssavirus inoculation in endangered Indiana bats."

Both Ingrid Smythe and Melinda Villarose gave Thea some side
eye.

Thea lowered her chin. "In other words, one of the reasons that
bats may be able to fight off viruses is due to the fact that when they
fly, their body temperature climbs into the fever zone. Darius is trying to find out how the temperature fluctuations effect the cellular chemistry that makes bats immune to viruses that cause deadly

illness in other mammals. He's also looking at how fever effects the behavior of the viruses."

"So, are we impairing human ability to fight off germs by reducing fever?" Melinda asked.

"Theoretically, yes." Thea said. "My husband is so convinced of this that when we had COVID, he didn't want us to take any medicine that brings body temperature down. But even though Darius let his fever rage, he was unable to fight off COVID.

"After he recovered, Darius became determined to understand what in his immune system had made him so susceptible to that virus. But then, when his heart started to fail, he could barely keep up with his lyssavirus research. Lyssaviruses are the cause of rabies. Now, with his new heart, hopefully, he'll be able to tackle more research questions."

"I've got a research question for you. Are bats immune to Dengue virus?" Ingrid asked. She suspected that Thea knew a lot about her husband's research, and she'd yet to find a resource that had explained Amari's work as clearly as Thea had just done.

"I believe several South American countries and Mexico have reported instances of bats showing evidence of having had Dengue. Antibodies to Dengue have also been found in pigs, horses, cows, dogs, birds, marsupials, and rodents, if I remember correctly. And who knows how many other creatures that mosquitos feed on might also be harboring Dengue? It's a very tricky virus. It's so unique that Darius gave an entire lecture on Dengue when I took a medical school elective in immunology.

"Dengue is caused by a flavivirus. I don't think Darius has been working with flaviviruses, though we know that he himself has antibodies to Dengue. He lived in countries where most young children are exposed. That's true in the Philippines where my family is from. Some children become very ill with Dengue while others have no symptoms at all. As with any virus, the amount of the germ that enters your system and how your immune defenses respond, determines whether you fight it off or get sick from it."

"Well, I'm glad your husband is doing so well, and I hope he gets to be able to do the research he's interested in, but that's not the reason I called you in here today."

Ingrid swiveled back to face Melinda. "I called you in here to give you both some extremely confidential information. It's of the utmost importance that you do not divulge to anyone what I'm about to tell you. Do I have your word that you can keep this just between us?"

Ingrid locked eyes with each of them as they both reluctantly voiced their agreement. Neither felt like they had a choice.

"The reason Doctor Rhea pocketed the blood culture specimens that Thea drew, is because he wanted them processed in an independent lab. He believes that someone in our hospital is trying to sabotage him."

Doctors Baccay and Villarose both looked incredulous. Only a second later, Thea asked. "So, do you have the results from the other lab? Our lab is growing a pneumococcus species, a common cause of pneumonia. It should have responded to the first antibiotic that this patient was on. However, the germ needs to grow more for our lab to be able to determine what antibiotics it's sensitive and resistant to. They'll probably know by tomorrow.

"I obtained the first cultures about an hour before I drew the specimens that Doctor Rhea confiscated. I was taught to always do two sets of blood cultures if you're not sure what germ you're dealing with. If everything is legit, then the same organism should be growing in the outside lab."

"I do not have those results," Ingrid replied, "but I will find out from Doctor Rhea as soon as he gets the report."

"This is very disturbing, Ms. Smythe" Melinda interjected. "If it's true that someone is contaminating these patients or contaminating their lab specimens to make trouble for Ezra Rhea, then this hospital is guilty of not protecting patients or the health care providers who will be held accountable for bad outcomes. How is this being investigated?"

"Very secretly," Ingrid said. "If word got out about Doctor Rhea's suspicions, the sabotage would probably stop and then we'd have no way of finding out how it's happening. Then we wouldn't be able to prevent it from happening again."

"But patients' lives are being put at risk. I can't believe it's legal and it's certainly not ethical to let patients be pawns in this investigation." Melinda was totally dissatisfied with the information that Ingrid had provided. "Is law enforcement involved?" she asked.

"If the results from the outside lab confirm Doctor Rhea's suspicion, then we will call the police in on this. But in the meantime, you two are the only ones who know about this, and you'll have to serve as our eyes and ears and let us know if some other inappropriate action occurs. But, please, please, do not share with anyone else what Doctor Baccay witnessed. By the way, have you already told anyone else?"

"Just my husband," Thea said. "But he's not connected with anyone else in our hospital."

Melinda's squirmed a bit. Ingrid noticed. "And you, Doctor Villarose?"

"Well actually, shortly after Thea told me about what she witnessed, I went poking around in the hospital lab. The lab director does know I was looking to see if that patient's second set of blood cultures were somehow misplaced. Someone maybe drops a test tube. Someone uses the wrong reagent. Someone records results for the wrong patient. Humans make mistakes and the computer covers it up with remarks like 'insufficient quantity of blood.' But in this patient's case, there was no record of a second set of blood cultures ever having been received by the lab. I did not tell the lab director what Thea saw.

"The only person I told about Thea seeing Doctor Rhea pocket those specimens is you, Ms. Smythe. I'm not comfortable with any of this, but I do understand why we need to keep a lid on it at this moment. However, I won't be able to stay mum if I see another patient suffer because of someone's incompetence or someone's perverse vendetta. I hope the hospital attorneys appreciate what's at stake here."

Ingrid handed each of them back their phones to signify the meeting was over.

~~~~ **26** ~~~~

*O*utside of Smythe's office, Melinda and Thea agreed to meet
after Thea finished signing her patients over to the nightshift.

Thea was currently rotating through the pediatric service. Had
it been December, she would have been managing dozens of gasp-
ing babies with RSV, respiratory syncytial virus infections. But it
was late summer and the great germ exchange that begins with the
start of school, was still a few weeks away. Currently only twelve of
twenty pediatric beds had children in them. Besides the boy with
arthritis, occupants were mostly there for trauma: broken bones,
head injuries and a burn. There was also the cases of an infected
wound, a dehydrated baby, and two kids with hard-to-control
asthma.

After the nightshift resident was introduced to all of the patients
and their parents, he pulled Thea aside and told her to watch her
back. The mother of the asthmatic in the last room was a trouble-
maker. Her four-year old daughter had frequently been admitted to
the hospital during the previous two years.

The resident said that the mother always reeks of tobacco, and
you can smell it in her daughter's hair and clothes. Sometimes,
the mother's pupils are pinpoint as though she's taking narcot-
ics. Sometimes, her pupils are dilated as if she'd just smoked mar-
ijuana. Undoubtedly, the child wasn't being given the medications
that would keep her out of the hospital. Her symptoms always
improved once she received appropriate care.

Thea was also informed that the mother threatens to sue whenever the staff doesn't accommodate her every ridiculous demand.
The E.R. staff had repeatedly tried to hook this child up with a

pediatrician, but the mother just kept using the E.R. Perhaps, there were no doctors who wanted to deal with her.

During another hospital admission, the mother had made an enormous stink when a senior resident referred the case to child protective services. The family was investigated, but the caseworkers were unable to stake out grounds upon which they could rescue this child. The laws are weak, and the family was too manipulative. The resident wanted Thea to be aware of the issues before she found herself in the midst of them.

Thea appreciated the warnings. She had smelled the tobacco and she had sensed the mother's hostility when she first entered the room. The mother had looked at her in a disapproving way. Now, she was glad she hadn't confronted the woman about any of the evident issues. Thea could almost always see the good side of people, but she had also learned to not get into stink fights with skunks. Her instincts had warned her that this skunk had a full stink gland that was about to detonate.

While waiting for Thea to finish her rounds, Melinda tried to call Mosey. The voice mailbox was full. She sent a text asking Mosey to please call back. The I.C.U. staff also had heard nothing from Suzie Nguyen's significant other.

Melinda also tried calling potential physician substitutes. Mostly she wound up leaving messages. The one doctor that she reached wasn't available to help out.

Melinda also tried to call the medical labs that were located within a reasonable driving distance of Bandore. She found three, but they were all too far away to do pick-ups at local doctor offices. For any kind of routine lab work, most every local physician used the lab at the hospital. So, how would Ezra Rhea have even delivered those specimens to an outside lab? Had he hired an Uber or some other service, or driven the specimens there himself?

Two of the labs she called said they could only deliver culture results to the physician of record. One lab revealed that they had never processed specimens under this patient's name.

That's when Thea knocked on the door. Before Melinda said anything about having tried to check out the Doctor Rhea story, Thea told her that the meeting with Ingrid Smythe had left her perplexed and unsettled. She could not understand why Doctor Rhea would be in charge of investigating his own problem. If there was sabotage going on, why weren't other hospital staff put on alert to watch out for it?

If Doctor Rhea's handling of the specimens was legitimate, why weren't the doctors caring for the patient told to check for the culture results in an outside lab? Why did the surgeon take those specimens when it seemed there was no one else around to see him do it? The clerk at the unit desk wasn't present when Thea had left those bottles in the courier's basket. Thea said she had concealed herself behind a laundry cart that was parked in the hallway when she was watching Doctor Rhea. She thought that he had looked around before he pocketed the culture bottles, but she was certain that he didn't know she was there.

What if in his efforts to clear himself, Ezra Rhea had sent samples of his own blood to the lab? What if no samples were sent to an outside lab and Rhea just planned to submit a phony lab report? And if nothing grew or another germ grew in the blood that went to an outside lab, did that mean that they couldn't trust the results from the hospital lab? And what would it mean for the patient whose pneumonia was already improving since his medication was changed?

Thea was asking all of the questions that had been running through Melinda's mind and Melinda didn't have any good answers. She did tell Thea that she had called around to outside labs and came up with nothing besides more questions. She also advised Thea that she was going to contact an attorney outside of the hospital to see if she had any options for defending herself and her residents against an administration that didn't seem to value patient safety or appreciate the risks of physician liability. She cautioned Thea to just keep it all confidential until she could obtain some legal advice.

"I'm so sorry you got caught up in this fiasco, Thea. Internship is hard enough without these extra burdens. And then you also have the burden of your husband's situation. Is he now living here with you?"

"He's coming here this week. Sullivan is going to drive him up and set up his computers so he can interface with his lab. I think it's kind of a test run for him. He's been anxious about being so far away from the transplant team and from his research."

"Well congratulations. You must be really happy to be reuniting after being apart for so many months."

Thea was nodding and smiling in response to Melinda's words, but her blinking eyes told a different story. She seemed more apprehensive than happy about the upcoming reunion, but she just kept trying to smile.

Melinda didn't buy it.

27

Sullivan Dietz and Darius Amari pulled into a spot in the parking lot of the Bandore Diner, heading for the Sunday brunch special. By sheer coincidence, James Dzobak and his father Franz pulled into the adjacent parking spot a few seconds later. When they got out of their cars, James and Sullivan immediately recognized one another.

Introductions had barely been made when, Sullivan said, "So, why did Batman get kicked out of the hospital?"

James responded, "because his mask didn't cover his nose and mouth."

The elder Mr. Dzobak's face lit up. "Good one. So, what's the difference between Batman and a shoplifter?"

"Batman can go into a store without Robin. Old one," Sullivan said.

"How about the anti-vax woman who refused to go on a date with Batman?" James asked. Sullivan shrugged. "She didn't believe in mask(ed) man dates."

Darius was the only one in the group who didn't laugh, but the four men wound up sharing a booth amidst the Sunday crowd.

James could readily see how physically, Darius and Thea were a match. They were both of short stature and slight build. They both had features that made them not quite Caucasian, but also not quite Asian. Darius's appearance was almost mysterious. His dark hair and the olive tone of his skin made his very pale blue eyes seem kind of startling. Unlike his wife who was smiley and warm, Darius seemed serious and distant. James was also surprised by Darius's accent. He didn't know that Darius had grown up in the communities of British embassies where people spoke the king's English.

While Franz ordered the pancake platter, the other three men all went for the "garbage omelet," three eggs whipped up with sausage, ham, and vegetables. It came with a mound of home fries. Darius doused the potatoes and the omelet with ketchup and ate hungrily.

"And where's your lovely wife today?" James asked Darius when he finally stopped shoveling in the food. "I've had the pleasure of meeting her several times."

Darius scrunched up his face and shook his head. "She's covering in the hospital today. She took Suzie Nguyen's shift. As if she wasn't working hard enough already! I finally get to this God forsaken place and my wife is working every day of the week. Then, when she comes home, she's so tired she just goes to sleep. You hospital administrators sure get your money's worth out of these overworked interns. And look at the risks they're exposed to. They should be getting hazard duty pay added to their meager salaries.

"It's bloody terrifying what happened to Suzie Nguyen. Violence like this is happening all over every day now. It really sucks being brown," Darius ranted, before turning his attention to his phone. He input something and then stood the phone up against his coffee mug so that it was only visible to him.

James reminded his father that Darius was the husband of Thea Baccay, the hometown girl who was interning at the hospital. He went on to explain that Darius recently had a heart transplant and that the couple hadn't been able to live together since Thea started her internship. He also reminded Franz that Suzie Nguyen was that doctor who was attacked in the hospital, as they had seen on the TV news.

James turned back to Darius and asked if he knew how Suzie was doing. He hadn't heard any updates since leaving the hospital on Friday. She was still heavily sedated then, four days after the assault.

Darius continued to look at his phone as he spoke. "According to Thea, she's doing about as well as can be expected relative to the severity and the extent of her injuries. It sounds to me like she's a disaster, but, hey, I'm not a doctor."

"So, where do you and Thea live here in Bandore?" James continued to try to make conversation while Darius continued to look at his phone.

"On Blue Jay Drive, at Thea's mother's house, in an attached apartment that her father built for his mother. But his mother went back to the Philippines after Thea's father died. The apartment's too small for two people, but we're not investing in property here until my status becomes clearer. Cancel that. We're never investing in property here. I think there was more culture in deepest, darkest Africa where my family lived thirty years ago than there is in Bandore County."

James concluded that Darius was either angry about something or just wasn't interested in conversation, but he still had hopes that he could learn something about the man's research. "Speaking of Africa, I was wondering if you think bats are a major reservoir for Dengue virus?"

Darius abruptly turned his attention away from his phone and looked directly at James with those commanding eyes. "What's your interest in Dengue?"

"Oh, I was reading that Dengue is moving from the tropics to North America and that maybe having antibodies to COVID will make people more likely to get sick from Dengue. Is that something you study?"

"Why were you reading about this?" Darius's tone put James on the defensive.

"Because your buddy Sullivan here got me all excited about bats and now, I just read about anything that pops up on the Internet about bats. And this Dengue thing came up recently, and someone who's had it told me how horrible a Dengue infection is, so I'm just curious. I would love to know what you are studying?"

Darius sat back and stared at his phone for a while. Finally, he answered. "I try to learn about everything that everybody in the microbiology world is discovering, regardless of whether or not it's about bats or viruses.

"Humans were winning some battles against infectious diseases during the last century with drugs and vaccines. But in the ongoing war between man and microbes, the microbes may now be getting the upper hand, especially with people resisting vaccination.

"There are bacteria that are getting smarter. Some bacteria that were unable to penetrate cells have learned to literally hitch a piggyback ride on other bacteria that carry them into the cells. Some bacteria have learned how to go from cell to cell without triggering an immune response. There are bacteria that can teach other bacteria how to resist antibiotics by exchanging some of their genetic material. There are now some bacteria that are resistant to just about every antibiotic in existence. Meanwhile, increases in the incidence of bacterial infections like Anthrax and Rocky Mountain spotted fever are currently being reported in Africa and California. The U.S. rate of syphilis is skyrocketing along with the incidence of other sexually transmitted infections. Lyme Disease, tuberculosis, and meningitis are also on the rise, and so is leprosy in Florida.

"The fungi are also getting resistant to our antifungal medicines and we're now seeing human deaths from a candida species. The white nose fungus is decimating bat populations.

"Infectious agents called prions are turning deer into zombies all over the United States. Prions are little bits of protein that can act like viruses. Their purpose and behavior are poorly understood.

When they attack a mammal's nervous system, we see fatal illnesses like mad cow disease and Creutzfeldt–Jakob disease in humans. There's growing concern that prion-caused wasting disease in deer could jump to humans, and cases involving consumption of venison have been reported. We do not know how to stop prion invasion of the brain.

"We hardly have any antiviral medicines. The viruses often develop immunity to them much faster than humans can create better drugs. Viruses can also help each other by exchanging their genetic material. Viruses are essentially genetic engineers. When they get into cells, they make them do what they want, and what they want to do is replicate themselves. The bird flu (influenza) virus has managed to spread itself all over the world and it's now also attacking seals. Even the penguins in Antarctica are being infected, and the bird flu virus has also started to show up in U.S. livestock, agriculture workers, and domestic cats.

"Measles is making a comeback with people avoiding vaccination. Monkeypox and Alaska pox are nipping at humanity's heels. Perhaps polio and smallpox will resurrect themselves next. Then there are viruses on the rise for which there are no vaccines, like the chikungunya virus which leaves half of its victims with chronic arthritis, and the Marburg virus which kills about ninety percent of its victims.

"Lots of researchers are studying the connection between the Dengue virus and the COVID virus. It is known that if you have Dengue antibodies on board, and you do a home COVID test, you might get a positive result even though you don't have COVID. The same might be true if you have Zika antibodies. Zika, like Dengue is a flavivirus. Labs can do more sensitive tests which can identify these viruses independently of each other, but to confuse matters, some people are unlucky enough to get Dengue and COVID at the same time.

"We currently know little about this viral combo. In one study, children who had Dengue antibodies had less severe COVID than children who didn't have those antibodies. In another study, people who had COVID antibodies seemed to get more severe Dengue.

"Cross reacting with each other could be a brilliant strategy for these viruses. The Dengue virus needs biting mosquitos to take it from person to person. The COVID virus is highly contagious through the air, and it has mutated itself into even more transmissible forms at an astonishing rate. Of course, we pushed it to mutate by vaccinating during the pandemic. But just imagine if the COVID virus teaches the Dengue virus how to infect people without the help of mosquitos.

"What if microbes are uniting against humans? That's what keeps me up at night. Consequently, I study it all."

"That's really scary stuff, Darius. So, I take it, your research isn't just about bats and rabies."

"My lab is conducting studies of rabies transmission and host responses, amongst other immunity issues." Darius returned his focus to his phone.

James wanted to see if he could engage him further. He pointed at Sullivan who had remained quiet during the encounter. "You know, before Batman over here got me enamored with bats, I had almost never heard about rabies cases. But recently, there have been news stories about goats and foxes in Arizona having rabies, and someone in Michigan selling pet skunks that had rabies. There's also been news stories about rabid raccoons terrorizing neighborhoods in New York and Pennsylvania. In Nebraska and Alabama, health officials have been dropping food containing rabies vaccine in raccoon terrain all around those states.

"Apparently, because raccoons often interact with people's pets, there's extra concern about them as a source of rabies. Two people in Princeton, New Jersey who recently got bit by a rabid raccoon, reported that the raccoon was making chirping noises and exhibiting unprovoked aggression. So where are all of these critters getting rabies from?" James asked.

"Most likely from each other. Rabies takes over the brain and makes the infected mammal aggressive towards the next critter it encounters. Night hunters like bats, skunks, coyotes, foxes, and raccoons are most often the source. Some idiots who adopted dogs during the pandemic lockdown, released unvaccinated pets into the wild when they returned to work, creating an additional reservoir for rabies.

"If a rabid animal's saliva gets into a wound, or on a mucous membrane like an eye or tongue, then the virus is transmitted. The rabies virus is only spread by saliva. You can't get it from the blood, urine, or feces of an infected animal.

"It's quite remarkable how viruses pick their mode of transmission. Also interesting is how viruses keep evolving. What if the rabies virus is learning new tricks? What if it figures out how to transmit itself through the air? Let's hope not, but that's one of my areas of study."

James felt like a lowly student in front of an arrogant professor. He decided he wasn't going to get any insightful information no matter what he asked the master. Something about Darius's reaction to questions about Dengue gave James the feeling that Darius intended to keep the real nature of his research under wraps.

At that moment, Franz Dzobak got up to find a restroom. As he exited the booth, he noticed the baseball game on Darius's phone screen. "What's the score?" Isn't today a double header?" he asked.

Darius grimaced. "Yeah, two games and the White Sox are currently beating the Yankees five to one in the bottom of the fourth. They've got to get this pitcher out of there."

Franz Dzobak smiled. "Love those White Sox, so lunch is on me for all of you crazy batmen. And you, Professor Amari, should come visit us out on the lake before deciding that beautiful Bandore County has nothing to offer. The lake has a high copper sulfate content which makes it turquoise blue like the Caribbean. It's a very special place and I can give you the grand tour in my new boat. Come in October and the foliage is breathtaking."

"Thank you kindly, Mr. Dzobak, but having my breath taken doesn't sound all that inviting."

28

Doctor Melinda Villarose was in Ingrid Smythe's office again, but this time she had been invited. Still, she was kept waiting in the outer office.

"I met the infamous Darius Amari," James told her. "Not at all what I expected."

"How so? I've never met him, but I've been curious about him since the day I met Thea Baccay."

"Well, Darius and Thea look like they're from the same corner of the world, but they're certainly not a match in terms of temperament. Thea seems so easy-going. Her husband came across as very intense."

"Interesting," Melinda said. "We interviewed Thea three months before Darius's new heart came along. We were mystified by how she presented such a positive outlook when her husband was dying. We kind of wondered if she was for real. But then, when she requested early acceptance to the program, and we brought her back for a second interview, we saw that this was her genuine nature. Thea seems to be one of those people who sees the world through rose-colored glasses.

"Doctor Carmichael, who used to co-manage the residency program with me, saw her optimism as a bonus for her and for others, and maybe for the whole program. He thought that nothing could reduce the stress of the hard work of physician training as much as having a person who could project light into dark situations.

"As a psychiatrist, I always thought that the 'Pollyanna Syndrome' was a symptom of being naïve, and sometimes delusional. But that notion was based on my experience working with people who weren't functioning well. They were the people who really couldn't distinguish reality from wishful thinking.

"But James, I'm going to confess to you that our hometown girl, Thea Baccay, has had a major impact on my view of optimism. I don't understand where she gets it from, but her optimism can make the experience of patients and staff less stressful. There's a rhythm to her speech and movement that changes the energy in the atmosphere, like a calming effect. I don't know how else to describe it."

"Yes, I can see that, even with the brief encounters that I've had with her; but that's not at all what her husband projects. To be perfectly honest, Darius Amari gave me the creeps. He seemed like an angry, entitled, conceited nerd to me."

"Well, that's rather troubling. I've been worried about Thea having to deal with his illness, the surgery, recovery, and them being apart. She's had so much on her plate that I'm astounded at her ability to function at all.

"Here's another thing I'm worried about, and I think you could help out with this, James. I don't know if the police have honed in on any of Suzie Nguyen's patients in their attempt to identify the perpetrator, but it occurred to me that maybe the attacker confused Suzie with one of our other Asian residents. You know the old story of people of a different race all looking alike to the biased. I think all the medical records that have Thea or Jennifer Kim's name on them should also be screened. Jennifer, Suzie and Thea are all petite Asian women who could maybe be mistaken for one another by someone who doesn't actually look at faces."

James seemed eager to help. "I was planning to check in with the sheriff's office this morning, and I'll suggest that. By the way, how is Suzie doing? Did her family show up yet?"

"No, no family. Suzie's going to surgery today for her right wrist. They need to pin the fractures for functional healing. Thankfully, her brain seems to be doing okay, though it's hard to know with how sedated they've been keeping her. She still has too much pain and anxiety when they let her wake up, so for now, they'll keep the sedatives going."

"Doctor Villarose, I have a question. How do the surgeons get consent to operate in a situation like this?"

"The laws vary by state, but in this situation, where not operating would likely lead to permanent disability, physicians are protected for giving appropriate care without consent. We have no reason to believe that Suzie, or anyone who might care about her, would protest protecting the function of her dominant hand, so she's on her way to the O.R. as we speak."

Ingrid Smythe finally showed up about twenty minutes late for Melinda's appointment. She seemed slightly disheveled, but she gestured for Melinda to follow her into the inner office without further delay. Melinda got to keep her phone in her pocket this time.

"I heard they're taking Doctor Nguyen to surgery today," Ingrid said. "I guess that's a good sign. Did anyone from her family ever show up? At least the reporters have stopped bugging us. They've found fresher crimes to feast on."

Melinda said, "very disturbingly, we haven't heard anything from family or friends, but we might have a breakthrough now. Somehow, whoever picked up Suzie's smashed phone, managed to get it into the hands of Vance Kenner, one of our other interns. It turns out that Vance is very tech-savvy, and he thinks he can get it working. If we can see her contact list, maybe we can find someone who can help us with medical decision-making."

Melinda was surprised when Ingrid responded that it was sad that this young doctor seemed to be so alone in the world. But just when Melinda thought Ingrid was showing compassion, Ingrid informed her that she had called her to this meeting because there'd been a complaint about Thea Baccay. "We have a parent who's livid that a transsexual person was providing care for her young, impressionable child."

Ingrid didn't even have to give Melinda the details. Melinda instantly knew the source of the complaint. The woman had made problems every time her daughter was admitted to the hospital. Since Melinda looked at the admission notes of every one of the new interns every day, she knew the asthmatic Westerhoff girl had just spent another two days in the pediatric ward because the family did such poor care at home.

Melinda could feel the blood rising to her face until she thought about the pregnant mare, standing with its back to the storm. When she got control of her emotions, she was able to grasp how Thea Baccay could be presumed to be transsexual. It was her surprisingly deep voice, along with her boyish body.

"If the greatest physician in the world took care of that child, that mother would still find something to complain about. The gender identity of our physicians should have no bearing whatsoever on patient care. Not only should this patient's complaint be dismissed, but Mrs. Westerhoff should be counseled that if she doesn't like our doctors, she should make some effort to keep her daughter out of the hospital. How are you going to manage such an unjustified complaint?"

"Is Thea Baccay a transsexual?" was Ingrid Smythe's response.

Melinda inhaled deeply as she tried to suppress her disgust. "What difference would it make if she was, Ms. Smythe? Do we have to start pulling each other's pants down around here? Maybe we should check everyone's genetic makeup. Of course, that won't work for the cancer survivors who've had bone marrow transplants. Did you know that people who've had their bone marrow replaced may show the genetic makeup of their donors in their tissues?

"Thea Baccay is an exceptionally competent doctor. Her gender is one hundred percent irrelevant. Unless there's a legitimate complaint about mistreatment of a patient or unacceptable behavior by a physician, this discussion is a ridiculous waste of your and my time. What are you going to do with this inane complaint?"

Ingrid gave a forced smile. "I'm going to give it to you to deal with, Doctor Villarose. Mrs. Westerhoff is outraged that her young daughter has been exposed to a mixed-up person whose gender ambiguity has left her child confused. So, what are *you* going to do?"

Melinda imagined herself as a cartoon character with steam coming out of her ears. Then she imagined herself blowing cigarette smoke up Mrs. Westerhoff's nose while covering the woman's mouth, so that this mother would know what respiratory distress was like for her asthmatic daughter.

"Sure, I'll take care of this for you. I'll tell Mrs. Westerhoff that the case has been carefully reviewed, that her child received appropriate care by our physicians, and that our community educator will be glad to help her improve her home management of her daughter's asthma. There are also books that can be recommended that may help young children deal with issues regarding gender and stereotypes. That is of course, if the Tazodan Corporation hasn't already defunded our community outreach program, and if the self-righteous book banners haven't ravaged the local library."

Ingrid looked like she'd lost her edge. When she remained silent, Melinda told her that she was very glad that Ingrid had called her to this appointment because she needed the results of the blood culture specimens that Doctor Rhea had confiscated.

Ingrid didn't regain her composure as quickly as Melinda anticipated she would. She even seemed a little flummoxed. Finally, she said she was glad that Melinda brought that up because she had just learned from Doctor Rhea that the specimens never made it to the outside lab. Just before Doctor Rhea was about to drive them there, he got called in on an emergency in which an industrial metal pole had impaled a worker's chest. After that, the culture bottles which had been sitting in his hot car were no longer suitable for processing.

"And that is why physicians are not supposed to serve as couriers, Ms. Smythe. We are fortunate that another set of cultures had been drawn and that this patient didn't go the way of Doctor Rhea's other infection cases. If it can't be determined why his patients are being put at risk, the administration needs to suspend Doctor Rhea's privileges. It also needs to commend Doctor Baccay for saving this patient from death, and saving Doctor Rhea and the Tazodan Corporation from a major malpractice case.

"Now if you'll excuse me, I need to check in with twenty-four overworked doctors, check on Doctor Nguyen, and deal with Mrs. Westerhoff. I also need to orient the substitute physician that the rent-a-doc agency is sending. He's supposed to arrive later this afternoon.

"I hope we still have a health educator on staff. Thank you for your time."

29

Transplant coordinator Carlos Mackenzy had just received another letter of gratitude for the family of Zoey Collins. He hadn't wanted to forward the last one that was sent five months after Zoey's death. It was from one of the kidney recipients who was having a tough time with rejection. It could only upset Deidra Collins. Carlos told the kidney recipient's transplant coordinator that the letter didn't meet criteria for delivery.

The letter of thanks that came from the pancreas recipient was forwarded ten weeks after Zoey's death. It was a thoughtful letter from a sixteen-year-old girl whose nearly fatal juvenile diabetes was essentially cured. As far as Carlos knew, the Collins family had not responded.

Now, six months after Zoey's death, Carlos was screening a letter sent by transplant coordinator Julie Jacobs from the wife of the heart recipient. He thought this letter would be uplifting for the donor family. It just expressed what most people would describe as heartfelt thanks.

Carlos was always dumbfounded when the word "heartfelt" popped into his head. The primary argument against his own personal experience of cellular memory, (donor organ transference syndrome), was that emotions are not generated or stored by the heart.

Carlos held onto the letter in anticipation of an upcoming appointment with kidney failure patient Gavin Siddoway. He knew that Gavin's sister, policewoman Bree, had been involved with the Collins family at the time that Zoey was registered as a donor. He hoped that she might be able to give him some insight about how this donor's family would receive news from recipients. Sometimes, communications from recipients opened painful wounds.

Carlos also checked in with Julie Jacobs to find out how the heart recipient was doing. Julie was kind of evasive. She offered that the recipient had made an incredibly good recovery from a terribly debilitated state and that so far, there were no signs of rejection.

When Carlos tried to press her a little more, Julie told him that the recipient was a highly productive scientist who was so dedicated to his professional pursuits that he didn't seem to even have time to act like a transplant patient. He was off and running from the day he got out of rehab.

"Well, maybe that's why the letter came from the wife. It's a beautiful letter and I'll pass it on to the donor's loved ones."

Bree Siddoway did accompany her stepbrother to his appointment with Carlos. Gavin's kidney function had taken another nosedive after a bout of COVID that otherwise hadn't made him too ill. Except for his kidneys, he'd completely recovered. Carlos informed them that Gavin now met the criteria required for the national computer system to move him up higher on the waiting list.

When Carlos asked Bree if she remembered Zoey Collins, she refrained from telling him what she now knew about this donor and family. It was exactly the kind of information that organ recipients would be better off not knowing.

Bree had managed to get her hands on old police records about the search for Deidra's rapist. Young Deidra had been a credible witness, but she never saw the man who violated her. Her face had been covered with her winter coat for the entire ordeal. She did have the impression that the man was shorter than her. At five-foot-six, thirteen-year-old Deidra was taller than average. She also perceived her attacker as being skinny and bony. When asked if she thought he was a man or a boy, she could only say that he was very strong, much stronger than she was, and as a member of her junior high volleyball team, she had some muscle. However, she had strained her wrists and shoulders when she had unsuccessfully tried to pull and push away from her attacker.

The detective who handled Deidra's case didn't have a single lead, though the neighborhood was patrolled for suspicious types for weeks after the assault. Eight years after the rape, genetic testing results for Zoey, her mother, and her grandparents, were forwarded to the detective who'd originally handled her case, but that person had retired. The detective who took over the files took the genetic testing results to someone in their department who did forensic genetic searches. That's where the investigation ended.

Zoey's DNA profile was compatible with that of descendants from France, Scotland, England, Norway, Ukraine, Armenia, Syria, Lebanon, Uzbekistan, Egypt, Pakistan, Tibet, Saudi Arabia, Laos, and Burma. The western genes were confirmed to come from Deidra's side of the family. All that could be said of the rapist was that he was a mutt from the eastern hemisphere.

Bree thought it would be worth rerunning Zoey's DNA through the data banks, now, seven years later. There's so much more genetic information in those data banks at this juncture, and so much better software for matching crime records, that maybe a suspect would finally emerge, assuming the pervert was a serial rapist.

But maybe it had been a crime of passion. Maybe Deidra was that attractive young girl that some skinny loser was madly in love with, and he never raped again. Bree stewed about it for a week but ultimately decided that it probably wouldn't help anyone to reopen the investigation. More likely, it would cause Deidra pain.

Bree had a very clear understanding of why donor and recipient information was kept confidential. Some years before her brother had wound up on the kidney waiting list, she had handled the case of a stalker. The man who was being stalked was the recipient of a donor heart. The woman who was stalking him was a nineteen-year-old whose boyfriend was killed in a motorcycle accident. This woman became obsessed with finding out where her boyfriend's heart wound up and she decided that this man had to be the recipient. Then she came to believe that the owner of the heart had to love her like her boyfriend did. Never mind that the heart's new owner was a forty-six-year-old attorney with a wife and four kids. When restraining orders didn't work, Bree actually had to put the stalker in jail before she was finally able to let go of her fantasy.

Bree didn't want to divulge anything to Carlos about Zoey Collins's background. Some things were better left unsaid.

Gavin had gone out of the room to get some labs drawn when Carlos threw Bree a curve ball.

"The reason I'm a little reluctant to open up a channel between Zoey Collins and her organ recipients, is that there's some unsettling things in her medical file. On the day of her death, we were able to pull her medical records from her pediatrician through the portal. The computer did not flag any diagnoses in her records that would have disqualified her as a donor. Physically, she was a healthy young adolescent. However, there are some diagnoses in her records that suggest she may have been a troubled young person."

"She was that," Bree acknowledged. "Her poor mother was in agony over her daughter's behavior issues. May I ask what her diagnoses were?"

"Intermittent explosive disorder, age six. Anxiety disorder, age seven. Conduct disorder age eight. Attention deficit disorder age nine. Oppositional defiant disorder age ten. Possible bipolar disorder age eleven.

"Numerous drug trials were documented, but it appears that Zoey didn't take any of the medications for very long because they didn't work, or they caused side effects, or she just didn't want to take them. At age fourteen, the pediatrician added suspected substance abuse disorder to her problem list. At the time of her death, her drug screen was positive for cannabis, Xanax, and Adderall." Carlos looked up from his computer screen. "But she did have healthy organs."

Bree shook her head. "Based on what the mother told me, I'm not surprised, though it sounds more severe than what I imagined. As a parent, Deidra Collins was clearly suffering. It makes me wonder if letters of gratitude from organ recipients might only bring up hurtful memories of a child who caused her unimaginable stress.

"You know, Carlos. I'm really an outsider here. I was just Deidra Collins's ride to the hospital on the day of her daughter's death. I think you need to decide what to do with these letters of gratitude, and I wish you luck with that.

"Thanks so much for getting Gavin higher up on the waiting list."

30

Suzie Nguyen's I.C.U. nurse referred Doctor Vance Kenner to Doctor Melinda Villarose regarding the information he had gleaned from her phone. The nurse was way too busy trying to take care of Suzie to try to also follow-up with her elusive family.

The orthopedist had pinned her fractured wrist two days ago, and the plan for the day was to try to get her off the sedatives. Suzie had awakened in an agitated state and the I.C.U. team was trying to get her pain and anxiety under control without much success. Still unable to use her hands, Suzie was trying to move her head, and the nurses worried that she'd dislodge the catheter in her skull that was still monitoring for pressure on the brain.

Melinda Villarose was on the phone with the sheriff's department when Vance Kenner entered her office. While waiting, Doctor Kenner's attention was drawn to the painting behind her desk. He walked over to it and scrutinized the brush strokes. As a hobby artist who liked to paint animal portraits, Vance was intrigued by how out of place the horse looked.

Doctor Vance Kenner was also bothered by how exhausted Doctor Villarose looked. He knew she was now not only taking care of two dozen physicians in training, but she was also serving as next of kin for Suzie Nguyen, and she was reviewing dozens of medical charts to try to help the police. She looked upset as she told Vance that the police still didn't have a suspect. All of the tips they'd been chasing down led to nothing.

"Were you able to get into her phone?"

"Her phone was damaged both by impact and by taking a bath in the hot coffee, but I got the sim card out and installed it an old phone I had. I was able to retrieve her contact list and her messages. I didn't want to violate her privacy, so I didn't look at the messages, but last evening, I tried to call her contacts. The old phone isn't activated to send or receive calls or messages, so I left my own callback number for those persons that I couldn't reach."

"Did you find anyone in Suzie's contact list named Mosey?"

"The first person I called was from her favorites and it was someone named Moe, but the number was disconnected. There was also a listing for Mom and that number also didn't work.

"Just before I came to your office, I stopped off in the I.C.U. to see if Suzie is able to communicate. She's not, and it was devastating to see her in the state she's in. Though she's been awake to some degree this afternoon, the nurses aren't sure if she's comprehending anything. She was trying to kick her legs which is about the only body part she can move, so they had to restrain her legs too. They're going to restart the sedatives for fear she'll cause herself more injury."

"Yikes! Poor Suzie. I sure hope she turns the corner fast. It's been ten days since the assault, and I'd hoped she'd be somewhat better by now. They're going to take the catheter out of her skull and remove the burn dressings from her left hand tomorrow, so that should make a major difference in her comfort level.

"What about other contacts in her phone?"

"I was able to reach two people who identified themselves as friends from med school. Each of them is doing an internship in another part of the country. All they could offer was their well wishes.

"I also reached someone named Amy who identified herself as a childhood friend. Amy was very distraught to hear of Suzie's situation, but she lives in Key West, Florida and she's due to give birth any minute now, so she's unable to be of much help at the moment.

"I left messages at some other numbers. Some of the numbers I called connected me to doctors' office and a psychiatric clinic. I looked up the names connected to those numbers, and I think they are all psychiatrists."

"Well, that's very interesting, Doctor Kenner. You really extended yourself on Suzie's behalf. I can't thank you enough. Have you and Suzie become friends?"

"I think everyone thinks of Suzie as a friend. She and Thea Baccay are clearly the most academic of our intern class and they both always seem to be able to come up with answers to the questions the rest of us have. Suzie generously gives of her knowledge and is always willing to lend a hand. I would be honored if she considered me a friend."

"Well, I'd like to call you 'friend,' Vance. I really appreciate your efforts in this matter. You've made my job much easier. If you're willing to pass that phone to me, I'll do the follow-up and I'll let you get back to taking care of patients."

"Absolutely, Doctor Villarose. I was hoping you'd ask. I'm going to be covering Suzie's shift tonight, so I really wouldn't have the time or the energy to keep up with this task. I made a list of all the numbers I texted or called. Here's the phone and the password. If people call back on my phone, is there a number I can refer them to."

"Certainly. Give them my number. Tell them to first text me that it's about Suzie, and then leave their number and I'll call them back."

"I'll let you know if I hear from any of these people, Doctor Villarose. Before I go, though, I have a question? Do you know if someone added that pregnant horse to that painting after the original artist? It just doesn't look like it belongs there."

"That painting came with this office. That's all I know. Thanks again, Vance, and have a good shift tonight."

31

A hospital security officer called Doctor Melinda Villarose. "We have a man here who's requesting to visit Doctor Nguyen in the I.C.U. His name is Roger Andrus, and he claims to be her brother. The I.C.U. nurse said Suzie Nguyen is too out of it right now to even respond to her own name, let alone someone else's, so we're not sure who this guy is. Hopefully, he's not her assailant, here to finish her off. I was told to refer this matter to you."

Melinda arranged to meet with the man in the I.C.U. family waiting lounge. At first, she didn't comprehend that the man who was sitting on the couch alongside of the security officer, was the man she had come to meet. He bore zero resemblance to Suzie. He had light brown hair, amber eyes, and a fair and ruddy complexion. He was much taller and stockier than Suzie. With crinkles around his eyes and some gray at his temples, he also looked like he was old enough to be her father.

Roger Andrus sensed Melinda's skepticism. He raised his hand and said, "I know. Hard to believe, isn't it? Our fathers were from the opposite ends of the world."

Roger also didn't have any traces of Suzie's subtle Texas drawl. Then, he took out his phone and showed Melinda a picture of himself and Suzie standing next to another Asian woman with highly styled red hair. The picture was from Suzie's college graduation, four years ago; the last time Roger had actually seen Suzie in person. They lived far apart, but they kept in touch by phone when Mosey wasn't around. Suzie's communication with Roger was an issue for Mosey, so Suzie didn't even keep Roger's number in her phone. Most of their communication had been about managing the health issues of their mother Hazel.

Roger then showed Melinda pictures of a younger Suzie and their mother Hazel.

Melinda's doubts were erased. She asked Roger to wait while she checked on Suzie's status. She was deeply concerned about the intern's isolation from loved ones, and she hoped that seeing her brother would boost Suzie's morale.

She found Suzie's nurse taking care of her patient's hygiene. It would be the first time since they took the catheter out of her skull that they were going to shampoo her hair. After that, she was scheduled for a change of her burn dressings. The big bulky padding could finally be reduced to bandages that would leave Suzie with a somewhat functional hand, though her dominant hand would be incapacitated for at least another five weeks.

Melinda suggested that Roger and she go to the cafeteria while they waited. Over lunch, Roger explained to Melinda about having sent their mother to her family in Vietnam. Hazel's niece was a physician who was able to get Hazel the more intensive care that she needed. Roger purchased the airfare and Suzie put their mother on a flight to Vietnam shortly after her third overdose in eight months. Hazel could no longer remember to turn off the stove or keep track of her medicines.

When Roger called his family in Viet Nam to check up on Hazel, he was told that Hazel was angry that she hadn't heard from Suzie. When Roger tried to call Suzie to make sure she was okay, and found her phone out of commission, he became concerned. He knew she was interning in Bandore Hospital, and he researched this facility on the web. That's when he encountered the news story about a physician being assaulted. Roger made travel arrangements as soon as he connected the dots.

Roger explained to Melinda that his father was the first of Hazel's string of husbands. She was healthier when Roger's father married her, but Hazel was still very difficult to get along with, and he sought a divorce when Roger was barely three. He gave Hazel and his son the handsome, mortgage-free home they had all been living in. It had a great fenced yard for little Roger to play in. Daddy Andrus was an investment banker who'd made some fantastic deals in his early career, but his marriage to Hazel wasn't one of them.

After Roger's father left, Hazel brought many boyfriends into her young son's life, It was traumatic every time they left, after initially cozying up to the little boy. Finally, Roger's father was able to obtain sole custody of him. Roger was six when he went to live with his father.

After that, Roger would see his mother only occasionally, and his life became much less traumatic. Then, his father remarried, and Roger got a sobering introduction to normalcy. When Roger was seventeen and a high school senior, Hazel and her fourth husband, Tai Nguyen, gave him a half-sibling. After just one visit, Roger became enamored with baby Suzie. Thereafter, he came to see his mother more often. Holidays and birthdays and other events became reasons to nurture their connections. For Roger, it also fueled a sense of protectionism. His remembrances of his early childhood with his mother still caused him grief and he hoped Suzie's childhood would be less traumatic.

Unfortunately, Hazel's life continued to be chaotic. She attracted and lost boyfriends in rapid succession. She was exceptionally pretty and smart, and also very personable. She could be inordinately charming when she was in a good mood. When she was depressed, it was oppressive to be around her. She'd get sensitive, cynical, and morose, and if she drank more than two glasses of wine, she'd become hostile and abusive. It would be years before her severe bipolar disorder would finally get diagnosed and treated.

Suzie's father, Tai Nguyen, worked as a chemical engineer in the oil industry, and he managed to stay married to Hazel for almost five years before he reached the breaking point. Roger and his father thought Tai should have been nominated for sainthood for having lasted that long.

Tai tried to rescue Suzie after he divorced Hazel, but after losing her son, Hazel fought fiercely to keep her daughter. She also sullied Tai's reputation at the company where he worked, causing him to lose his job.

Suzie was seven when her father just disappeared. She and Hazel still don't know if Tai went back to Vietnam, or changed his identity, or if something else happened to him. Tai had been a loving father to Suzie before she lost him. Suzie had tried all through her teens to track him down, but she never succeeded. Somehow, her father had just completely vanished.

After Tai left the marriage, Suzie had to live with the chaos that Roger had escaped. Both Roger and his father became very concerned about this sweet little girl. Hazel would find all kinds of men to get into relationships with, but none stayed very long. Roger's father worried that one of Hazel's boyfriends may have sexually abused Suzie. He tried to ask her about it a few years before Mosey took possession of her, but she denied it; or maybe she'd repressed it. She was very young at the time.

One of Hazel's boyfriends convinced Hazel that they could become millionaires by breeding French bulldogs, and Hazel dove into the endeavor with all of her energy and resources, even after that boyfriend made his escape. Hazel became completely obsessed with her dogs. She had two studs and six bitches that she was breeding. Suzie was literally enslaved to help her do all the dog and puppy care, although kind-hearted Suzie loved the dogs and she made sure they were never neglected.

Hazel did not become a millionaire. Although the puppies brought her hefty prices, the vet bills were heftier. Hazel was also spending the profits by taking one of her dogs to shows, although the little stud never won a ribbon. Additionally, she had a tendency to blow her monthly budget on dog treats or some other luxury when she'd get into one of her manic phases. When she didn't have a boyfriend around to pay her bills, Roger's father often helped her out, only because she was his son's mother. When Suzie turned fourteen, she started working in a fast-food restaurant after school, just to help pay the utilities.

The situation temporarily improved when Suzie was sixteen and she came to understand her mother's mental illness. Hazel had overdosed on a combination of medicines that she was taking for anxiety and insomnia, and a physician in the hospital E.R. helped Suzie and Hazel to come to terms with what they were dealing.

After that, Suzie kind of became Hazel's mother, making her take her medicine and keep her doctor appointments. But then, Hazel got into another unsavory relationship, stopped taking her meds, and relapsed into her unstable lifestyle. Living at home was becoming increasingly impossible for Suzie, and that's when Mosey came along to rescue her.

Just when Melinda thought she was finally going to get the scoop on this Mosey person, the I.C.U. nurse texted her that Suzie was now more awake and presentable, and that she had responded to the name Roger Andrus with what appeared to be elation.

32

It would have been difficult to determine who cried the most at the initial meeting of half siblings Roger Andrus and Suzie Nguyen. With her jaw wired shut and calories limited to an intravenous solution for nearly two weeks, Roger's heart was pained to see how emaciated his sister had become.

Physical therapists had been working her legs while she was bedridden, but she'd still lost a lot of muscle. Suzie remained too disabled to do much of anything for herself with both of her hands and her mouth out of commission, but her nurses were working on getting her upright.

Relieved to be out of her bed for more than a linen change, Suzie was sitting in a chair for Roger's visit. Her injured hands rested on pillows. A nurse's aide had fashioned a flower out of a surgical cap and fastened it to her hair. Her pale hospital gown matched her pale complexion.

Roger was devastated to see his little sister so battered and frail, even beyond what he had imagined. *How could someone be so cruel and heartless?* He couldn't hold back his tears.

Suzie's tears seemed to be tears of joy. Finally, someone close to her heart had shown up when she most needed their support. She barely had enough breath to tell her brother how grateful she was that he had come, though sitting up was finally making her breathing a little easier. She still needed supplemental oxygen because of her painful spine and rib fractures.

Melinda left to give Roger and Suzie what little privacy the I.C.U. could afford. She asked Roger to try and meet with her again after the visit. Information about Suzie's medical history would be extremely valuable to the doctors who were taking care of her.

Roger wasn't sure if he could help with that kind of information. His relationship with his sister was loving but remote. Suzie's relationship with her partner had isolated her from her family for most of her young adulthood. Roger had been distraught over her situation for years.

Suzie's nurse explained to Roger that this was her first major out-of-bed moment and that she might tire very quickly. The nurse didn't want to violate her privacy, but she wanted to keep an eye on her patient. If Suzie could stay upright for more than a few minutes, it was hoped that she could start using a straw to consume some nutritional supplements. It would take practice to efficiently swallow with her jaws wired shut, but she needed the calories. Then, they hoped to get her walking.

After it took so long for her brother to get there, Suzie's nurse did not anticipate the therapeutic effect his presence would have on her patient, but what she witnessed in their reunion was amazing. It was if Roger Andrus had spread fairy dust. As the two siblings softly spoke to one another, the nurse observed her patient's demeaner go from disturbingly despondent to spirited, almost spunky.

The nurse had seen this phenomenon on a few occasions in her decades-long career. A patient who was succumbing to illness or trauma, only started to fight when someone they loved came to their bedside. Suzie's nurse had come to believe that love is *the* most powerful drug. Each time she had seen this kind of patient transformation, it provoked a sensation in her own chest that she could only describe as a warmth in her heart. In the case of her patient Suzie, it also provoked a lump in her throat and brought tears to her eyes. She'd been extremely worried that Suzie was suffering from broken heart syndrome in addition to her injuries.

The syndrome of having a broken heart due to a severe stress or loss of love has been medically validated. Pathologic changes in blood pressure, heart rhythm, and heart function can be observed. In severe cases, blood clots and heart failure may occur. While stress hormones are theorized to be responsible for these phenomena, it's still not well understood how or why this happens. The heart holds mysteries that science has yet to unravel.

The nurse was spellbound to see monitors showing immediate improvements in Suzie's heart rhythm and blood pressure, within minutes of starting to interact with her brother. Their connection was more therapeutic than all of the medications they had administered for days to try to smooth out her heart function.

Roger took Suzie's nurse aside and asked her if Mosey had visited. He wasn't surprised when the nurse said no. Susie's only visitors had been her Bandore Hospital associates. The nurse also informed Roger that Mosey's phone number had apparently been disconnected. They'd left multiple messages, but the calls stopped going through a week ago.

Whenever Suzie had been awake, she would ask if Mosey was coming. Four days before Roger showed up, Suzie had been told that Mosey's phone number no longer worked. Her cardiovascular status declined after that. Though she'd had only had brief periods of consciousness throughout her ordeal, Suzie's instincts had told her that her partner had abandoned her. Along with her physical pain, the emotional trauma hurt so badly that she'd been wishing for death.

Roger, his father, and most of Suzie's friends had repeatedly warned her. Mosey was too unstable to be a partner. There were so many red flags throughout the eight years of their tumultuous relationship. Now Suzie hated herself for ignoring them. But her more troubling concern at this moment was the fear that Mosey might have committed suicide. She asked Roger to try to find out.

33

Julie Jacobs called Carlos Mackenzy at one o'clock in the morning to tell him that a liver at her hospital was a match for a patient at his transplant center. The donor was a twenty-year-old woman who reportedly had taken just one pill at a rave, and died from a fentanyl overdose. The friend who had accompanied her to the rave thought she was just sleeping, until he realized that she wasn't breathing.

The liver recipient was a fourteen-year-old boy with congenital liver cirrhosis. Carlos said the boy's family was so discouraged that they were already planning his funeral. Carlos immediately notified the family of the recipient and activated the liver harvest team. He called Julie back and told her the team would probably arrive at her hospital in about seventy-five minutes. They agreed to talk again the next day.

Carlos called Julie in midmorning to let her know the liver transplant was under way. Of the more than two hundred fifty transplant centers across the U.S., the physicians at Carlos's center had teams for all organs, but they did more hearts and kidneys than livers. On this same day, his transplant center would also be installing a new heart in a four-year-old with congenital heart disease. The donor was a six-year-old who was shot in the head by a five-year-old sibling who was playing with an unsecured, loaded rifle. Such horrible accidents can yield healthy donor organs.

Julie asked Carlos about the case of the young boy who claimed to be transgender after receiving a new heart. Carlos said the case continued to be troubling but for entirely different reasons than how it started. The recipient was having a severe rejection reaction and the issue of gender had been completely overtaken by the issue of survival. Carlos got the impression the parents would accept whatever gender the youngster identified with if only their child might see another birthday.

Carlos asked Julie what was happening with the heart recipient whose associate had contacted her about changes in personality and preferences. He recalled that Julie was scheduled to meet with that patient shortly after they last spoke.

"Well, that's turning into an interesting case, and I have to admit, your concept of DOTS might still be on the table. That patient, let me call him X, was a no-show for his appointment. He blew it off in a discourteous way and never rescheduled, and I think that was totally out of character for him. Afterwards, I tried to contact him a few times and he didn't even return my calls. Finally, he sent me a text and said he was doing great and that he had been too busy to get to an appointment, but that I shouldn't worry about him.

"So, needless to say, I am very worried. Of all of the transplant patients I've seen over the decades, he would have been the very last person who I would have expected to become noncompliant.

"I called X's friend back; the person who had informed me of the changes he was seeing in X. This friend continues to perceive significant changes that he's worried about. Here's an example he gave. X is in charge of projects where he supervises the work of underlings. In the past, if an underling made an error, he would take that person to lunch and provide them with guidance that would relieve their anxiety and enable them to avoid making similar mistakes in the future. Recently, an underling made an error that the old X would have responded to in that supportive way. Instead, the new X lambasted the underling and kicked her off of the project. X's friend was outraged by this occurrence.

"X's friend is also worried about X's focus. Even when X was losing his battle with heart failure, he would continue to diligently work towards well-defined goals in a highly organized manner. The post-transplant X frequently moves his goal posts around and approaches tasks haphazardly. The friend says that it's hard to believe how differently X is thinking and behaving compared to his former self."

"Did you ever get to speak with the wife?" Carlos asked Julie. "I did pass along two letters of gratitude that she sent to the donor's family. They were very positive letters, but the family never responded."

Julie told Carlos about the Zoom interview she had with the wife when X failed to show up. "I don't quite know what to make of her. I have no doubt that she's seeing major changes in her husband's behavior, but she's very defensive. She seems to want to view the changes as just interesting dimensions of her husband's expansive mind.

"This woman is maybe ten to twelve years younger than X, and they weren't a couple for very long before he became a heart failure case. I think they were only married for a few months when COVID knocked him down, and I'm wondering if perhaps, the wife doesn't really know him that well. Maybe there's some hero worship coloring her perception because he was initially her medical school professor. Maybe she's just so relieved that he's still alive that she's put blinders on to the changes. But she does acknowledge changes.

"The one change that the wife seems perturbed about is that X, formerly a very intellectual person, has suddenly become inclined to spend hours watching baseball. He used to spend that time studying. His wife is one hundred percent certain that X had previously never had any interest in professional sports. I had a follow-up conversation with her when I was having trouble connecting with X. She said his interest in baseball now seems so intense that he's neglecting more important things. He used to love to play pickleball, but now that he's finally well enough to try to play again, he's too busy watching baseball.

"When the wife asked X why he's suddenly so interested in baseball, he responded that when he was in recovery from the transplant, he couldn't focus on anything too complex, and baseball was frequently on the TV where he was doing his rehab back in April. He claimed it was a great mindless distraction for him at the time, but then he found himself actually enjoying it. He didn't grow up in the United States, so it wasn't something he was familiar with for most of his life. He grew up watching people playing table tennis in the rec rooms of British embassies. Occasionally, he got to watch televised soccer or cricket matches in the embassy lounge, but he was never a devotee of any sport. He was a life-long bookworm.

"I don't know what to make of this, Carlos. I can see that watching some baseball games might have been a pastime for him when he was still very disabled, but that doesn't explain how he so quickly became such a rabid fan that he's neglecting his work. The work that X does is scientifically important. His partner told me that there are major investors funding X's research, and that the whole project could be jeopardized if X is no longer meeting expectations.

"Meanwhile, the wife is telling me that X is taking baseball so seriously that she sometimes can't get him out of the house for any reason. If they go out for a meal and there's a game on, he'll spend the whole meal looking at his phone. She also said he's now wanting to watch football on Sundays and on Monday and Thursday nights. While she's seemingly not concerned about other changes, she's clearly distressed by this new devotion to sports."

Carlos was instantly intrigued. He didn't inherit a love of sports when he got his new heart, but he was very surprised when he found himself listening to country music after his transplant. Before that, he had only listened to rock and roll, and he had looked down his nose at country. It was one of those strange changes that he didn't understand, but he didn't believe that such a radical shift in his musical taste was a side effect of cyclosporine. He was certain that his donor must have been a country music fan.

After his transplant, Carlos also developed a taste for coffee. He had previously disliked it in any form, and now he loved it. Before his transplant, Carlos had never had an iota of interest in birds. Afterwards, he became an avid birdwatcher. His wife had taken to calling him "Señor Bird Nerd." Before his transplant, Carlos disliked the color orange. Afterwards, he frequently found himself drawn to orange whenever he acquired a souvenir t-shirt or hat. He attributed all of these new preferences to his new heart.

"That kind of change does raise the question of DOTS," Carlos said. "I know it's against all the regs, but I may have a source who could verify if the donor had a passion for sports. I don't know what it means if they did, but I can't suppress my personal and professional interest in this. I'll let you know if I can find out anything relevant."

34

Bree Siddoway was disappointed when the call from Carlos Mackenzy wasn't about a kidney being available for her brother. Poor Gavin was getting dialysis three times a week for four hours a day, but he was becoming increasingly toxic. Even though he had been advanced to the top of the waiting list, a good matching kidney still hadn't come his way. People with type O blood are the hardest to match. They typically have to wait the longest.

Carlos explained to Bree why he was calling, One of the organ recipients of donor Zoey Collins had become very interested in watching professional sports, though he'd previously never paid any attention to sports. It was such a remarkable change that the family wondered if there could possibly be a connection to the donor. The family of the donor hadn't responded to letters sent by the recipient's family. They were just letters of gratitude.

Bree distinctly remembered that Zoey Collins had been described by her mother as a radical sports fan. She rooted for the New York Yankees, and she was a very avid fan of the Dallas Cowboys, even though her stepfather, or maybe it was her grandfather, liked the Green Bay Packers. That stuck in Bree's mind as she herself had grown up a New York Giants fan, though her family left New York when she was ten.

Bree's father's devotion to his football team was so profound that it almost got in the way of his second marriage because Gavin, like his deceased father, was a fan of the Baltimore Ravens. The new Mrs. Siddoway, Bree's adoptive mother, had grown up rooting for the Pittsburg Steelers. Had Gavin or his mother been fans of the Philadelphia Eagles or the Dallas Cowboys, the marriage might never have happened. That's how fanatical Bree's father was. In the rest of his life, he was an easy going, rational guy. About the only times Bree had ever seen her father in a rage was when the refs made bad calls against his beloved football team when they were playing against the Cowboys or the Eagles.

Zoey Collins on the other hand, might always have been in a rage.

Bree withheld from Carlos what she knew about Zoey being a sports fan. Having read stories about cellular memory when Gavin first became an organ transplant candidate, it bothered Bree that some organ recipient might come to think that their psycho donor's spirit had taken possession of them. The confidentiality of organ donation was too important to violate, and she didn't want to be the one to do it. Bree told Carlos that she'd see if she could find out about the donor's interests, and Carlos promised the information would not be shared unless both parties agreed to such exchange.

Bree was still wondering if it would be helpful to Deidra Collins to know that her daughter had saved so many lives, or would Deidra be better off not being reminded of her difficult daughter. Maybe that was why she wasn't responding to the thank-you letters.

Carlos's question about the heart donor being a sports fan provoked Bree's curiosity. Was sports fanaticism transmissible? And what was it about sports that could make people so irrational? As a police officer who had often been assigned to investigate domestic disputes and tavern brawls, Bree had encountered a diverse spectrum of people who had turned to violence over sports controversies. Alcohol was usually involved, but even without alcohol, she had witnessed rival sports fans turn on each other with fists, furniture, and even guns, after assembling to enjoy a game. She particularly remembered a case in which an adult male had thrown a TV at his father which killed the elderly man. They had been arguing about a penalty call in a hockey game.

Bree had also read studies that showed that domestic violence significantly increased after major sporting events in the U.S., Canada, and England. Maybe, as the saying goes, sports don't build character, they reveal character.

The police seemed to be getting more and more calls about human skirmishes, though currently, it seemed that people were more likely to maim and kill each other over political differences than sports rivalries. The constant media barrage about politics seemed to be fueling the rage.

But then, Bree reminded herself that she shouldn't be drawing conclusions about humanity based on what she sees as a policeperson. The people who need the police to resolve their conflicts aren't representative of the general population. Still, it seemed that rage had also been nurtured by the pandemic and it seemed to be getting more prevalent and more intense.

Zoey Collins sure seemed to be full of rage. With diagnoses of intermittent explosive disorder, conduct disorder, and oppositional-defiant disorder, Zoey was apparently a very angry individual. On numerous occasions, Bree had encountered children like this, and some had come from seemingly competent, loving families where other children were thriving. Some people and their families just seemed to be ill-fated. It certainly seemed that Zoey and Deidra Collins were.

Bree had repeatedly thought about Deidra Collins after Carlos revealed Zoey's list of psychiatric diagnoses. It almost seemed as though Zoey had been born with rage. Did it come from being resented because she was the offspring of a rape? Did Zoey know that she was the product of a rape? Was this girl a victim of racial hatred because of her skin tone? What had made her so angry? Did it come from the rapist's genes?

Bree was still troubled about Deidra's rape case having never been solved. Unsolved police cases often nagged at her, but her connection to Deidra had made this more personal.

That list of Zoey's psychiatric diagnoses that Carlos had disclosed seemed downright scary. Bree wondered if she would even have wanted Gavin to receive one of that troubled child's kidneys. Then again, kidneys hadn't been reported to carry cellular memory. They just needed to be able to filter out the metabolic waste. Gavin would be ecstatic to have a hooligan's kidney, if only one would come along.

Bree tracked Deidra Collins's travel from her home to her son's daycare. When she had the time, she'd station herself where Deidra passed by on her way into the building to see if Deidra recognized her and seemed receptive to some communication. As curious as she was, she didn't want to intrude.

35

Forty-eight hours after Roger Andrus had shown up at Bandore Hospital, Suzie Nguyen had improved so dramatically that she'd been transferred from the I.C.U. to a private room. When Doctor Melinda Villarose stopped by to visit, she marveled at how much better Suzie looked. She was also impressed by the bounty of beautiful bouquets and cards that her room had been decorated with.

When Melinda had heard that Suzie was being discharged from intensive care, she sent sunflowers. She was delighted to see how fresh the flowers were, and then she went around the room smelling the other arrangements and peeping at the attached notes. An elaborate bouquet was from brother Roger, and an even bigger one was from Roger's father. Another was from Suzie's I.C.U. nurses. Another was from the E.R. staff where Suzy had been doing a rotation at the time of the assault. There were also pink roses from Doctor Vance Kenner, and orange lilies from Doctor Thea Baccay. Melinda noted that there were no cards or flowers from Ingrid Smythe or the Tazodan Corporation, but there was a card from James Dzobak and family.

Being able to sit up had reduced Suzie's need for supplemental oxygen, though it was still being administered when she slept. It was refreshing to see her without the cannula taped to her nose. She was still using the eye patch. Her ability to swallow with her wired jaws was starting to come along. If she could consume enough calories through a straw, her intravenous port could be discontinued. A therapist had her taking short walks in the hallway. Her legs worked but she was weak and her balance was off, so the therapist had to support her. Her hands still couldn't manage a walker.

Suzie's doctors had been able to reduce the dosing of her pain medication which was helping to reduce her confusion. Between her bruised brain, and so many days of sedation, her cognitive function was still impaired. Only Suzie knew how much her heart was aching from not having heard from Mosey.

Roger had explained to Melinda that he had provided Suzie with a burner phone, but with her wired jaws and her hands still bandaged and casted, she was struggling to try to use it without assistance. Melinda passed along the old phone to which Vance Kenner had transferred Suzie's contacts, so she'd have her peoples' numbers.

Melinda had asked Roger if Suzie's mother knew about her situation. Seeing how helpful Roger's support had been, she wanted to round up whatever other support might be available.

Roger admitted that he hadn't told their mother about what happened to Suzie. He suspected that Hazel was still furious with Suzie for shipping her off to Vietnam, where she hadn't lived since she was three years old. She was even angrier that her beloved dogs had been put up for adoption by a French bulldog rescue organization.

But at that juncture, it was either send Hazel to her relatives or send her to a nursing home. It seemed seriously unsafe for Hazel and the dogs to be left home alone. Suzie was not about to give up her medical career to become Hazel's caretaker, and Hazel had repeatedly fired the aides that Roger and his father had hired to try to keep her safe.

Had Hazel even tried to call Suzie, she would have encountered the disconnected phone. Then she probably would have called Roger to find out what was going on, but apparently, she hadn't done any of those things. Hazel could hold a grudge for a very long time, even in her state of dementia. Roger wanted Suzie to be recovered before he shared any information about her with their impaired mother.

Hazel was already having a very bad time in the home of her aunt, where her relatives called her by her given name, Hanh. She was no longer poisoning herself on a regular basis, but she was furious about not being in charge of her own life. Roger feared that Hazel could make Suzie's recovery even more difficult if she somehow became involved.

Doctor Melinda Villarose thanked Roger for all he'd done to help and reminded him that she would still like to meet with him when they could arrange it. She told him what a good doctor Suzie was and how relieved she was to see Suzie's improvements. Hopefully, she'd be able to recover enough to resume her medical training.

Melinda was finally feeling hopeful that a search for a substitute for Suzie would stop devouring her time. When none of the local doctors had been available to temporarily fill in, Ingrid Smythe had authorized the hiring of a rental physician. The one who had arrived was competent enough that he needed little supervision. He was an older man who Melinda worried might have trouble with an intern's call schedule, but so far, Doctor Howard Blauveldt had been keeping pace with the program.

Doctor Blauveldt was a retired family practitioner who started working again after his wife's long battle with cancer had left him bankrupt. Experimental treatments had cost most of their life savings, but failed to save her. And before cancer ruined their lives, Doctor Blauveldt had encountered enormous expenses trying to help his drug-addicted son.

Doctor Blauveldt found the different assignments the rental company had farmed him out to interesting and he had enjoyed living in some new, novel places. After his wife died, his home no longer felt like home. Nonetheless, he was pretty overwhelmed to find himself as an overworked family practice intern at this stage of his life. He hoped it would be a short-term assignment and that the young doctor whose schedule he was filling in for would make a speedy recovery.

Melinda took an instant liking to Howard Blauveldt. He had a friendly demeanor and a delightful sense of humor. And, as much as she loved being around young, enthusiastic physicians all the time, she also appreciated having a colleague whose age and life experiences were closer to her own.

36

O n her day off, Bree Siddoway dressed in plain clothes and stationed herself outside the building where Deidra Collins regularly took her son Todd to daycare. She parked her police car a few blocks away, worried that a police presence near the building might unnecessarily scare the young families of these very young children.

Bree had been episodically keeping tabs on the Collins. From the arrangement of cars in their carport, she had come to know when Deidra's husband was out of town. She hoped his absence meant that Deidra was free to break out of her routine of going directly home after picking Todd up at daycare. She also hoped that this young mother would appreciate some adult companionship.

Bree pretended to be having an animated conversation on her phone when Deidra Collins walked by. She could tell from her facial expression that Deidra had both seen and recognized her, but she didn't acknowledge Bree's presence on her way to retrieve her son.

When Deidra came out of the building with her little boy, she paused as if looking for Bree. Then, she spotted the policewoman leaning against a tree and appearing to still be on the phone. Deidra stayed stalled for half a minute, as though considering her options. She spent another half a minute grooming her toddler. Then she walked right up to Bree with Todd in tow and gave a friendly wave.

Though unadorned and underdressed in olive green sweats, Deidra Collins's long copper-colored curls rendered her a striking-looking young woman. Bree waved back while also ending her pretend phone call.

"Remember me?" Deidra said. "You took me to the hospital last February when my daughter was killed in a car crash. It was under the Lincoln Avenue overpass. I so appreciate how helpful you were to me at the time. How come you're here now?"

"Hello, Mrs. Collins" Bree bowed her head. "Sadly, I remember that day very well. I hope you are making a good recovery from your bereavement. It was such a horrific accident, but you handled it so bravely.

"There's nothing to worry about here right now. Someone from the daycare center reported seeing a suspicious person hanging around yesterday afternoon. Our patrollers watched the street for several hours, but never saw anyone matching the caller's description. I'm here today to do some undercover follow-up. Fortunately, I've only seen children and parents who belong to one another.

"It was probably a false alarm. Most such calls are. Now that all of the tots seem to be safely returned to their families, and there have been no suspicious characters hanging around, I'm off to go get some dinner. If you're not on your way home to cook for your family, maybe you'd care to join me.

"I'd be very grateful to know how you're doing. I have a family member in desperate need of a kidney transplant, so I have great reverence for the families of donors such as yourself."

Deidra seemed to be seriously considering Bree's invitation. She initially stayed silent while fussing with her little boy's hair. Finally, she said "yes. Thanks. I'd love to join you, but I need to take my car so Todd can ride in his car seat. He almost always falls asleep in the car after daycare.

"The Carawaze Cafe over on Old Mill Road has the best kid's menu, and they have early bird specials. That would work for us if it would work for you, but I'm open to suggestions."

"I'd love to try the Carawaze. I've never been there. I'll meet you there."

Bree observed Deidra strapping Todd into his car seat in a shiny, new SUV. "Wow! It looks like you've got yourself a nice new set of wheels."

"Well, Zoey totaled my old one. Between the auto insurance and the life insurance policy that my husband had taken out on Zoey, we were able to purchase this car. I was very offended when Jon took that life insurance policy out for Zoey, but he seemed to have a premonition about her potential for an early demise. Jon is like that."

As they sat down in the restaurant, it almost seemed like Deidra had come along to specifically bare her soul. Bree encouraged her to just keep talking.

"I have to tell you; it was a miracle that any man would marry me after meeting my daughter. Jon not only loved me enough to tolerate Zoey, but he went out of his way to try to help her, or maybe I should say tame her. My family used to call Zoey 'The Wild Thing,'

"Jon is just a kind soul. Sometimes, I think he might have married me so he could rescue me. Sometimes I think I'm some sort of redemption for him, as though he has angst over not doing something more to help someone from his past.

"Sometimes, I wonder if I just suffer from the guilt and shame of being a rape victim. It's a pain in my heart that never goes away. That I conceived an indomitable child from such violence has been like having acid poured in my wounds on a daily basis.

"I really shouldn't fault my husband for his intuitive powers. He's so clairvoyant that he sometimes knows which team is going to win a game before he even turns on his camera. Jon Collins is an unusually sensitive man. I can't wait to see what attributes our son Todd may have inherited from him.

"The policy Jon took out on Zoey wasn't very big, but it helped to cover the cost of the funeral, as well as replacing my wrecked car. Even though it was a closed coffin, my parents insisted on having a big, formal funeral. Zoey probably would have wanted that too. She was very self-centered."

While little Todd Collins scribbled on his coloring mat, and on some of his French fries, rape victim Deidra Collins continued to share her burdens with this affable policeperson who just happened to have been present when her daughter died.

Bree learned that Deidra Collins works as a graphic artist, creating logos and catalogues for websites. She works from home and has the luxury of taking on only as much work as she feels she has the time and energy for. She frequently turns away potential clients.

Deidra perceived being a mother as her primary job, especially because her son's father is so rarely around, and because she hadn't been able to fulfill that role when Zoey was young. She was just a kid then, and her parents had confiscated the parental role in order to spare her the responsibilities of parenthood, as well as the stigma of raising the child of a rape.

In the course of their conversation, Deidra learned that Bree Siddoway had been a full-time cop-on-the-beat for most of her career. She had repeatedly been offered a detective's position, but she preferred to be out in her community where more often, there were potential remedies for people's problems.

As a detective, Bree would have to live with the frustration of working with crime victims whose cases might never get solved. Working her beat was more satisfying. It also gave her the opportunity to promote organ donation for people like her poor brother who was dying of kidney failure. Patients like Gavin who didn't get a transplant, had less than a fifty percent survival rate after five years. Those who got transplanted had an eighty percent survival rate after five years. Gavin was galloping towards his expiration date.

Deidra seemed sincerely empathetic to Bree's brother's dismal prognosis. After digesting what she had just been told, she mentioned that she had received some letters of gratitude from some of the recipients of Zoey's organs.

Then, Deidra told Bree that her parents were never going to forgive her for donating Zoey's organs. Although their family minister had assured her parents that organ donation was the Christian thing to do, Deidra's mother was repulsed by the idea, and Deidra's father was furious that Deidra had made the decision without consulting them, and without even notifying them of Zoey's death. Other family members felt strongly that Zoey herself would never have opted to be an organ donor. She cared about no one but herself.

As Deidra opened up to Bree about the rejection she was experiencing from her family, Bree sensed that the woman was racked with grief. But Deidra's misery didn't seem to stem from having lost her daughter. Bree got the impression that Deidra was suffering because she had lost everyone else who she considered family. Her grief was almost palpable, and Bree wanted to be able to do something to help.

Bree then admitted that because she was connected to the transplant community through her brother, she knew for a fact that Zoey's organs had saved at least seven lives. "Wouldn't your family take some comfort from that?" Bree asked.

Deidra remained silent as she absorbed that information. "Seven lives? Really? I had no idea," she finally said, looking somber. "I did get letters of gratitude from the recipient of the pancreas and the heart, but I didn't know that so many people benefitted from Zoey's death. I guess your poor brother wasn't one of them."

"My brother's been on the waiting list for almost three years," Bree said, wishing that she could communicate the agony of waiting for an organ to Deidra's hostile family. Only organ failure patients and their loved ones could really appreciate the torment of slow death, while most people remained indifferent to their plight.

"Oh Lord," Deidra responded. "I am so sorry to hear that. It must be so difficult for you when you see an accident like Zoey's and then the organs go to waste. My parents need to meet someone like your brother so they can come to see the other side of donation.

"I tried to share the thank you letters I received with my folks, but my father is still too angry to open up to the idea. As for my mother, she has this notion that Zoey was such an unworthy person, that her organs couldn't possibly benefit anyone. When I showed her the letter from the wife of the heart recipient, she said it was hard to believe that Zoey even had a heart."

That confession disturbed Bree Siddoway. She wondered to what extent Zoey had terrorized this family. The unsolved rape case also bothered her, compelling her to try to explore this case some more.

Just then, Todd Collins started to get restless and whiny, and Deidra said that she needed to get him home. They could meet again and talk about this some more. Bree said that she had dealt with families who were resistant to the idea of organ donations on numerous occasions. Maybe she could help Deidra develop a strategy that could mend the rift in her family.

Deidra seemed happy to have found a confident who truly appreciated her decision to donate, and the two women agreed to meet again when an opportunity presented.

37

Sunday brunch at the Bandore County Diner had become the hottest ticket in town. The new owners had figured out that offering just six extraordinary choices was more popular and profitable than breakfast and lunch menus with fifty-six ordinary options.

Melinda Villarose and Howard Blauveldt scrunched in with others in the small vestibule. Autumn had arrived with chilly winds and waves of driving rain. No one wanted to wait outside. Fortunately, the diner had efficient service and quick table turnover.

The rain intensified and two more wet people crowded into the small waiting area. When one of them lowered his rain hood, Melinda recognized James Dzobak. James introduced Melinda to his father Franz. Melinda introduced Doctor Howard Blauveldt, the physician substituting for Suzie Nguyen. With seating for four-somes more available than for twosomes, they opted to share a booth. Melinda and James had meant to meet up again anyway.

Diners had gone gaga for the garbage omelet and the seven-salad sensation. Almost as popular were the perfect pancake platter, the decadent deli dish, and the bakery buffet. Suki's surprise sandwich, with every bite featuring flavors from different ingredients, was also picking up fans.

Doctor Melinda Villarose was addicted to the salad special. She hoped that the great food would make Doctor Howard Blauveldt's assignment to Bandore Hospital just a little less distasteful. Blauveldt had quickly become an enormous asset to her overtaxed residency program. Suzie Nguyen was still weeks away from being able to function, and having this highly competent substitute doctor stay around until Suzie recovered would have multiple benefits to the program and for Melinda.

Doctor Blauveldt didn't know much about the emerging molecular and epigenetic theories of diseases and therapeutics that the younger physicians were excited about. But he knew how the course of the patient's medical problem would progress. He understood how the patients' attitudes and behaviors impacted the treatment outcomes. He had great respect for how the placebo effect cured thirty to forty percent of symptoms.

Blauveldt was also extremely cautious about using new drugs. During the course of his career, he'd seen dozens of widely prescribed medicines get pulled off the market after causing harm. The extent of side effects of new drugs is never actually known until large numbers of people have been taking them over time. The experience and the perspectives that Howie Blauveldt brought to Melinda's training program were invaluable. He also got along exceptionally well with patients and staff.

When their food came, eight eyes were on Melinda's brunch. A miniature round of fresh baked bread was cut into wedges. Surrounding it were small scoops of salads made from shrimp, chicken, tuna, eggs, pasta, vegetables, and fruit.

As they enjoyed their food, Franz Dzobak asked Melinda for an update on Doctor Nguyen. He only knew that she'd been transferred out of the I.C.U.

Melinda believed that Suzie's privacy had already been negated by local interest in her story. Besides, James apparently had clearance to look at any patient's medical record, and he and his family had even cared enough to send a get-well card.

"She's made real progress this week. They've weaned her off oxygen and pain medications. Her left hand is finally unbandaged so she can scratch her own itches. She's starting to gain some weight, but she's still being supplemented with intravenous nutrition. She's got four weeks to go before she can start to use her jaws and her right hand. She's also still having vision difficulties and now they're trying to figure out if that's due to the skull fracture or the brain injury. But she's in a much better place than she was a week ago."

"That poor woman," Franz Dzobak remarked. "Friends and neighbors have been asking my wife about her because they know James works at the hospital. A lot of locals are upset that an assault like that could happen in our community. I'm glad to hear that she's improving and now my wife can give those concerned people some good news."

"Is your wife not a fan of the Bandore Diner?" Melinda asked. She recalled that when she'd first met James, he'd said that he took the position in Bandore so he could be of some help to his parents. It looked like James's father was doing pretty well, which made Melinda wonder what might be going on with Mrs. Dzobak. *Or was it that the parents were helping James?*

Franz answered. "Oh, my wife would love this meal, but she's not up for leaving the house of late. She's been having a bad time with headaches and nausea."

"Is she getting help with that?" Melinda asked.

"Our family doctor tried her on a bunch of migraine medicines but none of them have helped. This week, she has an appointment with a new doctor that opened a practice in that old office building on Lakeview Drive. He claims to practice functional medicine, whatever that is."

The eyebrows of both Melinda Villarose and Howard Blauveldt squished downwards when Franz said, 'functional medicine.' Franz noticed.

"So maybe you can tell me, what is functional medicine? There seems to be a lot of advertising for it on the web." Franz observed that both of the physicians were looking at each other like, 'you tell him, no, you tell him.' Finally, Melinda said, "it's controversial."

"The American Academy of Family Physicians that credentials doctors doesn't think it's controversial," Doctor Blauveldt argued. "They think it's largely bogus. There's also concern that it can be harmful. The Academy has stopped awarding education credit for attendance at functional medicine training courses." Blauveldt went on to explain that most states require doctors to annually earn a certain number of "approved" education credits in order to keep their licenses.

"But what exactly is it?" Franz asked. "And why is it being widely practiced if the medical community is so divided over it?"

Doctor Blauveldt explained that proponents of functional medicine diagnose and treat conditions that they claim are the underlying causes of disease. "Functional medicine practitioners typically do highly-specialized lab tests that are suspected to have been specifically designed to indicate that many people will show nutritional or hormonal deficiencies, or toxins in their system. Then, these practitioners sell their patients supplements and detox products designed to address these deficiencies and toxicities. Wealthier patients might be induced to purchase subversion tanks, hyperbaric chambers, and other such merchandise and/or services.

"None of these tests, products, or applications tend to be covered by health insurance because there's a substantial lack of evidence of their therapeutic value. But captivating presentations by polished salespeople play well to individuals who have not been educated enough to be able to differentiate science from pseudo-science. Then the powerful placebo effect takes over."

Howard Blauveldt recounted that he had been a young, idealistic physician in the early 1990s when new pharmaceutical products were hitting the market nearly every day. When some of the most widely-prescribed drugs ultimately proved to be harmful, he and many other concerned physicians started to lose faith in pharmacology and started looking for other ways to help people.

"I attended a very persuasive lecture about functional medicine back then, and I fully embraced it, hoping it would be safer and more effective than pharmaceuticals. In theory, it had a lot of scientific foundation, and my most educated patients were also showing interest in it. But over the years, my patients who were being treated with conventional medicine seemed to do better than those who were addressing their biochemical profiles with supplements. There was a clear difference, especially for my patients suffering from high blood pressure, diabetes, asthma, eczema, sleep disorders, thyroid disorders, anxiety, headaches, infections, and cancers.

"Here we are, thirty some years later, and there's essentially no evidence of functional medicine having ever cured anything. Moreover, the people who adhere to functional medicine practices, tend to be people who are dedicated to living healthy lifestyles anyway. It's their tendency to clean eating, regular exercise, and avoidance of tobacco and other toxins, that should get credit for their good health, not the bogus supplements they take."

Melinda added: "I met people in my psychiatric practice who were taking expensive supplements for fatigue that was supposedly due to their having "tired adrenal glands." What some of them actually had was low blood pressure, fibromyalgia, depression, sleep apnea, or some other remediable condition like coronary artery disease.

"Around the millennium, I was seeing psychiatric patients who got conned into pyramid schemes and were spending a hundred dollars a week for four bottles of magic juice that was supposed to cure them of everything. Meanwhile, they couldn't afford their blood pressure pills.

"Some of these patients had seemingly been mesmerized by the alluring personalities of the doctors and the other con artists who had convinced them to spend their limited dollars on useless diagnostic tests and unproven therapies for non-existent diseases. The fact that pharmaceuticals are so flawed makes functional medicine a very successful scam. But as bad as many drugs are, there are also millions of people out there whose lives are better because of pharmaceuticals. Where would any of us be without antibiotics?"

Melinda became more animated as she spoke. "And let's not forget that the nutritional supplement industry is unregulated. Anyone can throw a bunch of chemicals or plant residues into a capsule and claim it cures whatever people are bothered by. Unless someone dies from these products, or an athlete is barred from competition because their vitamins were laced with steroids or some other banned substance that shows up on their drug screens, no one is checking to see what's actually in these products, Nor is anyone checking on whether they're actually beneficial."

Doctor Blauveldt also seemed very invested in this issue. He added that, "numerous recent studies have demonstrated that many popular products that claim to support cognitive or athletic performance, have been found to contain ingredients that significantly differ from what's on their labels. They've also commonly been found to be contaminated with Illegal drugs and potential toxins. And even when lab analysis of a particular product shows a legitimate accounting of the ingredients on the label, there's no guarantee that every capsule or container of the product has the same ingredients, or the same proportion of those ingredients. No one is monitoring for sloppy manufacturing techniques by these supplement producers.

"And then, because so many of my patients are taking all kinds of nutritional supplements from all sorts of manufacturers, I, as their physician, can't actually know what my patients might be inadvertently ingesting. Or, as in the case of a beautiful young mother in my practice, was it steroid contamination of her beauty products that caused her skin to break down? The cosmetics business is another unregulated industry that eats up gazillions of dollars from unprotected consumers."

Franz seemed to have become ruffled by the opinions of Doctors Villarose and Blauveldt, but he said that he was glad he had asked the question. Then he went back to eating his brunch more slowly than before, as did Melinda, Howard, and James. Were they all wondering if their food was contaminated with microplastics, as had just been widely publicized by the news networks? Or was the microplastics issue just another twenty-four-hour news cycle topic that they could all quickly repress?

After most of the meals had been consumed, Melinda asked Franz, "For how long has your wife been dealing with her headaches?"

"They started maybe five months ago. Her symptoms come and go. Some days she can do normal stuff and some days she says she can't move her feet?"

"Does she shuffle her feet?"

"Yeah, she kind of does that in the morning when she first gets up. She says it feels like someone glued her feet to the floor."

Melinda grimaced. "That's an unusual symptom, Franz, that's associated with an unusual condition where fluid builds up in the brain. Has your wife had a CT scan or an MRI?"

"Her doctor didn't want to radiate her head. He said it was unnecessary for migraines."

"Do you know if her doctor ever looked into the back of her eyes? Or did he send her to an eye doctor?"

Franz was only certain that his wife hadn't been referred to an eye doctor. After Melinda asked the question, Franz was reminded that his wife had recently started to complain about things looking fuzzy. In response to his mentioning this, Doctors Blauveldt and Villarose again looked at each other as though they were sharing some dark secret.

Melinda took a notepad from her purse, looked at her phone, and wrote down the name and number of the local neurosurgeon. She told Franz to get his wife an appointment immediately and to let the surgeon's office know that she had made the referral. James should let her know if they had trouble getting a timely appointment. She'd intervene if necessary. The situation was urgent.

38

*B*ree Siddoway and Deidra Collins met for a late lunch while Deidra's son was attending daycare. They sat in a quiet booth in the back of a classic old English style pub that had often served as a retreat for Bree and her police colleagues. The lunchtime crush was over; they pretty much had the place to themselves.

Bree was doing the driving so Deidra allowed herself to indulge in a cocktail. She knew she was there to tell her story to someone who seemed supportive. While everyone in her family knew about Zoey, Deidra was almost never inclined to share the particulars with outsiders. But maybe, Bree could help Deidra to break through to her parents. The fact that this woman was watching her brother slowly die for lack of a donated organ was too tragic. When Deidra had first learned about Bree's brother, it changed her dreams from nightmares about organ harvesting, to dreams about rescuing someone who was dying.

It was after she finished an expresso martini that Deidra was ready to peel away the curtain of shame that had been draped over her for the past sixteen years: She'd grown up in a peaceful suburban neighborhood in a church-going family. Her father sometimes led the Sunday services when the minister wasn't there. Professionally, her father managed a Christian radio station.

Deidra's mother taught Sunday school classes and gave painting lessons in adult education courses. She was a watercolor artist whose designs were occasionally featured on greeting cards. She also did custom floral arrangements for weddings and funerals.

At the time of Deidra's rape at age thirteen, her younger sister was ten and she had a fifteen-year-old brother. Her family was determined to keep the rape a secret, though many in the neighborhood knew about it. Secrecy became even more difficult when it was realized that Deidra was pregnant. Still, her parents wouldn't give one iota of consideration to terminating the pregnancy. The life of the unborn was their highest priority.

The Martins kept their daughter hidden after she started showing. Deidra was thin then, and her baby bump quickly became obvious. They put their house into a rental pool and relocated to another community where no one knew them. It disrupted the academic and social lives of all three of their children.

The Martins' plan was to return to their own home after the baby was born and claim that it was their child. Their plan dissolved when the baby's skin tone didn't match the rest of the family. They considered putting her up for adoption, but worried that no one would want a mixed-race baby who was the offspring of a rapist. Ultimately, they decided to keep the child and raise it as their own. They'd claim that they'd adopted Zoey.

Deidra was given no say in the matter. She's certain that she would have opted to terminate the pregnancy had she been given the choice. She couldn't fathom living with a child who would be a permanent reminder of the rape.

Throughout her pregnancy, Deidra was home-schooled, and kept hidden. She suffered from morning sickness for most of the time, and she had breakthrough bleeding in the eighth month which confined her to bed. She had a long, difficult labor and wound up having an emergency C-section when Zoey refused to leave the womb, five days after her due date.

Zoey was a bit blue when she got plucked from the uterus, but the obstetrician quickly cleared her airway. Then, she didn't just cry, she screamed. And she would continue to scream throughout her infancy. She was the most colicky baby that anyone had ever encountered.

Zoey started to walk at age thirteen months and that's when things got really difficult. Even with three teenaged siblings to run after her, she consistently managed to run amok. If they took her anywhere, they had to keep her on a leash.

Deidra recounted that, "when Zoey was told 'no,' she'd stare directly at you, and continue to do exactly what you wanted her to stop doing. If you physically restrained her, she'd let go these brain blitzing screeches until she was released or until she ran out of breath and turned blue." Her pediatrician assured the Martins that this breath holding behavior wasn't dangerous.

By the time Zoey was two, every breakable thing in the Martins' house had to be stowed away. She was a pretty little toddler, but one would only see a smile on her face if she was throwing food or destroying something. Mr. Martin's parents had taken to referring to this great granddaughter as the 'devil's spawn.'"

The Martins had always been authoritarian parents. Their three adolescent children were well-disciplined and well-behaved. But no form of discipline worked with Zoey. They wound up in counseling. Zoey's destructiveness was somewhat tamed when they learned to restrain her in a blanket and a bear hug instead of yelling at her. However, it was a rare day in the Martin household when Zoey didn't get blanketed.

Deidra and her siblings spent a lot of their teen age time and energy running after this uncontrollable gremlin who liked to break their things when she couldn't get her way. Deidra and her siblings also resented Zoey because the therapists that the Martins were consulting had demolished the family's discretionary budget. There were no more vacations or restaurant dinners. Even their grocery budget got trimmed to keep up with the expense of specialists and medications that their insurance wouldn't pay for.

Deidra said that she tried with all of her heart to love young Zoey, but she just wasn't a lovable child. Their relationship did improve when Zoey was about seven and she suddenly became enamored with team sports. She wasn't interested in watching individual sports like golf, or ice-skating, but she became obsessed with watching team sports, especially baseball and football. She'd watch hockey and basketball too, but she wasn't as obsessed with those sports as she was with baseball and football.

Zoey would go ballistic if someone else dared to change the channel during a game. She'd get furious if her team was losing, but it seemed to give her an outlet for her rage. The Martins went out and bought her a big flat screen TV with a sturdy screen protector for her new bedroom, a small attic nook that had previously served as Mrs. Martin's painting studio. Zoey hung a black shade over the south facing window. Mrs. Martin's easel and supply cart wound up taking over the dining room.

Zoey's TV, along with a subscription to a sports station, proved to be more therapeutic than any of the medications or other interventions ever advised by any of the pediatricians, psychiatrists, psychologists, spiritual advisors, and the other behavior specialists that the Martins had sought assistance from. Zoey's attic "sports den" at least spared the other family members from the heart sickness they all felt when in the presence of an angry Zoey.

Deidra was a design student in her third year of college when Zoey turned eight and started asking questions about why she didn't look like the rest of her family. That's when she was first told that she had been adopted, but she still didn't know that Deidra was her biologic mother. The Martins made considerable effort to try to convince Zoey that she had been adopted because their whole family desperately wanted to provide for a child who would otherwise not have a family.

It was also around that time when Zoey's artistic talents emerged. Both Deidra and her mother were talented at drawing. When Zoey started to sketch, she and Deidra started to draw a little closer to one another. Though Zoey mostly drew the logos of sports teams, like the scary profile of a Minnesota Viking, she was showing real talent, and Deidra and her mother were relieved to find themselves more in the role of coaches than disciplinarians. Finally, Zoey was getting some positive feedback from her family, and all of their lives became a little less traumatic.

But then, their temporarily peaceful world came crashing down.

Zoey was in second grade when she started getting into playground fights. She was being bullied because of her skin tone, and one particular boy had been going after her with venom. After the school failed to alleviate the situation, Zoey became more devious in her attempts to defend herself. One day, when this boy started pushing her around, she armed herself with a pencil and the boy wound up losing an eye.

As fate would have it, the mother of this boy had grown up in the same neighborhood as the Martins. Her family had known about the rape, and they had long speculated that when the Martins moved away and then came back with an adopted brown child, that they were covering up Deidra's pregnancy.

After the bully boy was rushed to the E.R., accompanied by his father, there was a confrontation in the school principal's office between the boy's mother, Mrs. Martin, and Zoey. In a rage, the bully's mother revealed what she believed were Zoey's real biologic origins. After it was said, there was no way for Zoey to unhear it.

The revelation had multiple impacts on Zoey. It explained the color of her skin. It gave her some comfort to know that the Martins weren't her parents and that her sister Deidra was her real mother. Deidra hadn't been punishing Zoey her whole life, so Zoey didn't hate her as much as she hated them all for lying to her.

Zoey was suspended from school while the bully was welcomed back into the classroom. His family was suing the school and the

Martins for his injury. The Martins were suing the school for failure to stop the bullying. The community at large knew about the incident, and Zoey became unwelcome everywhere she went. The whole Martin family wound up in counseling. They also wound up selling their home and trying to start over in another community where people didn't know their tragic history.

Then things got turned upside down again. That's when Jon Collins came into Deidra Martin's life and took it upon himself to try to be a friend to Zoey. The angry ten-year-old girl was uplifted by the notion that she could become the real daughter of a real family. She was always on her best behavior when Jon Collins was around. She could behave beautifully and with maturity when she wanted to. If her real mother was going to go live with this nice man, she was determined to go with her.

Zoey made an amazing turn around and Deidra's parents were starting to fantasize that they could be relieved of this burden. They were all thrilled when Jon and Deidra started to plan a wedding. Maybe their lives and Zoey's future were salvageable after all. Deidra wasn't so sure about her future, but seeing how good Zoey could be when she was motivated, gave her hope.

Deidra was continuing to reveal some more details about her husband Jon when Bree got directed by dispatch to check out another suspicious character hanging around a hospital. Her night shift was just beginning. She had the waiter put the meal on her tab. She dropped Deidra off where her car was parked at Todd's daycare, and she went back to policing.

The rest of Deidra's story would have to wait.

31

It was a few days after Darius went to the transplant center for his heart biopsy that Thea got a call from Sullivan Dietz. He would have contacted her two days previously, but he knew she was doing overnight call in the hospital in addition to the day shifts. It was going to be a difficult conversation. He wished he could spare her, but he could no longer keep his fears to himself, and there was nobody else he felt he could reveal them to. Hopefully, Thea could help him figure out what they should do.

Thea instinctively knew that the call was going to be taxing as soon as she saw Sully's number. He had called her several times in the past few weeks to express his concerns about Darius, but Darius was really good at explaining away his behaviors. Thea felt like she was being triangulated between them. She let the call go to voicemail while she pondered the situation.

Thea was becoming increasingly concerned about the changes she was seeing in her husband. At the same time, she believed that long before the transplant, Darius had suffered some psychologic trauma from being knocked down and almost killed by a virus. He had been a healthy man in his prime at the time that COVID took possession of most of his bodily functions. He didn't have any risk factors, no hypertension or diabetes. He certainly wasn't obese, he never smoked, and his doctors could not explain why the virus had hit him so hard.

Darius had spent a month physically tied down so he wouldn't pull the breathing tube out of his airway. Not only weren't his lungs functioning, but his heart, kidneys, intestines, and his brain were all failing. Throughout his weeks of being on life support, he hardly ever slept, but he was almost never fully conscience. The I.C.U. physicians had tried him on every sleeping agent available, but his addled brain could not rest.

Once he was well enough to be discharged to home care, Darius had few recollections about what had actually happened during those devastating weeks. He could only recall some twilight dreams. During his first week out of the hospital, he repeatedly recounted a dream of being tied up and forced to ingest poison by some unidentifiable monster.

Thea was disturbed by the nature of his dreams. Some of them seemed more like hallucinations. She so wished she could have supplanted his terrifying memories with better ones, not knowing that even worse illness was about to come their way.

"Darius," she would say. "Those dreams were just the drugs talking. Along with the monster waves of serotonin and norepinephrine that your inflamed nervous system and gut were spewing, your psyche was drowning in a pharmaceutical swamp. You need to let go of the dreams to replenish the dopamine in your synapses. You know the critical importance of positive thinking."

Was she really the dreamer here? Thea knew that Darius had tried to practice positive thinking throughout his ordeal. When he was finally discharged from the hospital after COVID, he then also felt like he had a new lease on life, but it showed up in unexpected ways. Thea had noticed that while the old Darius would sit back and observe people before interacting, after COVID, he no longer had that inclination to observe or listen. He seemed more self-focused and inclined to say what he wanted to say.

Then, when his heart function started failing and he was feeling lousy, his formerly cheery nature morphed into a more serious disposition. There were times when he wallowed in sadness, or he was agitated with anger. There were also still moments when his sense of humor came through. In spite of all the ups and downs, mostly downs, he never lost his focus on his research.

Now, almost three years after COVID had stolen their lives, reports about its neurologic consequences were starting to emerge. For people suffering from long COVID, symptoms could include memory loss, brain fog, involuntary movements, hearing and vision problems, sleep disorders, fainting, and occasionally, seizures.

There were also reports of the virus continuing to live in people's brains after clearing out from the rest of their systems. Blood markers for brain inflammation were showing up months after the illness had resolved. There were also reports of the virus damaging microglia, the immunologic cells in the central nervous system that help protect the brain from infection. COVID can also infect dopamine neurons which may result in depression and brain fog.

Thea was disturbed to think about how many people could be struggling with neurologic problems like these, when only a tiny few ever got to see doctors who collected and shared data about their problems. The real impact of COVID might never be fully appreciated.

Thea also knew some ominous history regarding viruses. Parkinson's disease started to surge in people who survived the "Spanish Flu" pandemic in 1918. Sometimes Parkinson's disease showed up decades later. The long-term effects of COVID might also not show up for many years. Perhaps, only a future generation will recognize the actual impact of the 2020 pandemic.

Thea was also reading reports about the COVID virus continuing to live in people's hearts. Darius's old heart was found to have traces of the virus in the walls of the arteries. This was why the virus increased the risks of heart attacks and strokes.

Darius wondered if his years of working with viruses, including corona viruses, had caused him to harbor virulent antibodies against COVID, and if it was his own antibodies that had made him so sick. When he was well enough, he planned to investigate that possibility.

In addition to his personal battle with the COVID virus, Darius, like everyone else, had experienced the impact of living through a pandemic. Fear of illness, along with the isolation of lockdowns, provoked anxiety and depression in most people. However, help was limited because mental health therapists, like nurses, were getting burned out and leaving the profession.

A lot of people tried to self-medicate their stress with alcohol. During the pandemic, American alcohol consumption increased more than it had in the previous fifty years. European countries also reported widened and accelerated alcohol use.

Thea wondered if researchers looking back at the pandemic would blame the uptick in mental illness on the virus, alcohol, or the lockdown experience. History had already shown that alcohol's neuropsychiatric effects make it the most consumed "medicine" in the world.

Ironically, it was in a lecture by Professor Darius Amari when Thea was a medical student, that she learned about the role of viruses in patients who suffered from neuropsychiatric disorders. Viruses that cause headache may impact brain function in unmeasurable ways.

No one knows why one virus goes to your airways and causes a cough, another goes to your skin and causes a rash, and another one likes to attack your gut. Then, there are viruses like polio and rabies which destroy the nerves and/or the brain and spinal cord. COVID went after the lungs primarily, but it also had the ability to infect other vital organs. Thea had little doubt that the COVID virus that destroyed Darius's heart, also did some damage to his brain.

Thea also knew that researchers had identified at least six genes that make people resilient. Maybe half the population lacks those genes, resulting in millions of people having been left psychologically scarred by the pandemic experience. Thea consoled herself by identifying Darius as a resilient person all of his life. He had survived so many tragic losses. Surely, he could recover from this as well.

Thea needed Sully to know that Darius had changed before the transplant. Sully hadn't spent much time with Darius when he was first recovering from COVID, so he hadn't seen the transition that Thea had observed. Thea believed that it was COVID that had altered her husband's brain, long before he received his new heart.

However, there was one thing that Thea couldn't attribute to COVID. Why had Darius suddenly developed an addiction to watching sports? His obsession with watching every single game had become almost as disruptive to their lives as did a failing heart.

Thea had been working for far too many hours when she saw Sully's call. She needed food, a shower, and sleep, not another problem to solve. Her mother had left a wonderful dinner for her to reheat. Darius hadn't yet returned from his trip to the transplant center, so she could fall asleep without the din of the World Series commercials. It was nice to have the space to herself, though she missed the old Darius with whom she'd once fallen in love.

She texted Sullivan that she'd return his call tomorrow after work.

40

Almost a third of the hospital staff crowded into the main lobby to cheer for Suzie Nguyen on the day she was discharged from Bandore hospital. She was on her way to the home of her brother where she could continue to recuperate. Roger's father had chartered a private plane to make her travel as easy as possible. She was still dealing with an incapacitated mouth and right hand, but her vision had improved enough for her to get around independently.

Melinda had visited Suzie almost every day that she was hospitalized. In all of that time, Suzie had never said a word about Mosey and Melinda was afraid to bring it up. Melinda knew that fellow interns Thea and Vance has also made effort to stop in to see Suzie whenever their schedules allowed, but she had never revealed anything about her former partner to them either. It had apparently become a forbidden topic for her, though her brother Roger had been more than willing to talk about it.

An hour before Suzie was discharged, Roger had stopped in to see Melinda to find out if anything had turned up from the police investigation. No solid leads had materialized as far as Melinda knew. She also didn't know if the police were even still checking out the patients whose medical charts got flagged in the investigation

Melinda took the opportunity to ask Roger how he thought Suzie was doing with respect to the collapse of her relationship with her partner. At the mere mention of Mosey, Roger's eyes narrowed, and he fisted his hands.

"Do you have an hour? Let me tell you about my sister's insane relationship," Roger responded. "Suzie told me that you're a psychiatrist, so maybe you can make sense of this. My sister's so bright. I don't know how she can be so dumb in matters of the heart."

Getting people to reveal and unload their burdens was what had made Melinda Villarose an especially successful psychiatrist. She often wished she was still practicing instead of trying to train young physicians. She closed her office door and offered Roger a beverage from her mini fridge. He sat facing her, but his eyes were frequently drawn to the picture of the golden horse in the storm.

"It started when Suzie had just turned seventeen and my mother dragged her to a dog show. A lot of those poor pooches have to stand still for hours while some maniac with scissors attacks their coat, hat, pants, and face, to make them look like a floor mop or a clown with pom-poms. That was what Mosey did for a living, although it wasn't always a living.

"My mother's French bulldogs didn't have to put up with any of that grooming stuff. Their show attire came ready-made. They could relax for a few hours while the poodles and terriers were being tortured.

"At this particular show, my mother and Suzie went to look around at all the other dogs while my mother cuddled her prize Frenchie in a baby sack. As they walked through the grooming area, Moe was working on a Bedlington terrier, sculpting the dog's curly white hair to make it look like a fleecy little lamb. Moe claimed to be a Bedlington specialist, but he could do any dog hairdo, or as he liked to call them, 'dog-dos,' Moe was grooming several terriers for this particular dog owner.

"Moe was apparently also eye candy. He had finally chiseled facial features, a buff body, luxurious expresso hair, laughing brown eyes, and perfect teeth. What he lacked in stature, he made up for in beauty and grace. He made a big fuss over my mother's dog and then hobnobbed with my mother and sister as he finished up the terriers. He asked if he could take these two beautiful ladies to dinner after the show, even though they were French bulldog fans.

"We wouldn't know until years later that Moe wasn't just this dog owner's groomer; he was her gigolo before he ultimately got out from under her yoke. It was this dog owner's hotel suite with room service in which Moe had entertained my mother Hazel and my sister Suzie. Except that one of the dog owner's terriers kept harassing Hazel's Frenchie, it had been a phenomenal evening. By the time it ended, both my mother and sister had fallen head over heels in love with the magnetic Moe Kirchlin.

"When Moe came into my family's lives, he was thirty-five, eighteen years younger than my mother, and eighteen years older than my sister. For almost a year, he had them both believing that they were very special to him. They only saw him at dog shows, but he'd email them each all kinds of endearing stuff. Neither of them knew of his relationship with the other, or with the dog owner who he worked for, and who unknowingly financed his exploits. Moe had everyone conned.

"Then came a day where Suzie had to get out of Hazel's home, just as she was about to start college. At that time, Hazel had hooked up with a lecherous old guy who made Suzie uncomfortable. Moe knew someone who could get Suzie an apartment in an old house next to the campus. Roger's father agreed to help her with the rent. It was a cute little two-room with its own entrance. That's when Moe started to pay Suzie visits when he wasn't on the dog show circuit. His business card said, "Have Scissors, Will Travel," but here and there, he'd spend a week with Suzie. She was madly in love with him.

"Then, Suzie learned that Moe would also spend an occasional week with our mother, after the lecherous old guy had moved out. Suzie had returned to Hazel's house one day when no one was there to retrieve some things she'd left behind. In our mother's bedroom, she recognized some of Moe's belongings. There was no mistaking the little leather case that contained all of his grooming scissors. His initials were embossed on it.

"My sweet, serene, sympathetic sister wanted to kill them both. Instead, she switched colleges and came to live with my wife and me. All of her energy went into studying for premed. She was determined to become a doctor.

"But then, about two years after Moe had betrayed her, he charmed his way back into Suzie's good graces and she moved into an apartment with him. I think even then, she knew that it was a mistake, but she couldn't get him out of her heart. He boosted her independence by confirming how crazy our mother was, and Suzie was in desperate need of an emotional ally.

"They lived together for a few months while Suzie finished college. For her, it was rapture. I met Moe during that time. I instantly understood his charisma. He had a way of putting you at ease by making self-depreciating jokes about how people liked to look at him. He was charming, bright, witty, and flamboyant. He had real power to pull people in. I came to understand my family's fascination with him.

"But then, Moe got hired by a top Slovenian dog breeder. He'd be spending the next few seasons touring around Europe if the dogs did well. They'd maybe even be going to shows in Thailand and Egypt. Moe was excited and once again, Suzie was devastated. She gave up on Moe and turned back to her studies, gaining acceptance to medical school. She was finishing up her second year when guess who came back into her life, the all-new androgynous version of Moe, a stunning, captivating, non-binary person named Mosey, and I hope I won't offend if I fail to use the correct pronouns.

"Moe returned claiming to just need Suzie's friendship. Up-and-coming dog groomers had taken over some of his accounts. Of course, Moe's temporary refuge with Suzie quickly morphed into dependency. Once again, this conman had managed to manipulate his way back into Suzie's heart. Estranged from our mother, missing her father who'd just completely disappeared, and scarred by multiple episodes of heartbreak, my sister was too alone and too vulnerable. She was also worried that Mosey could be suicidal. His trademark comedic tendencies had morphed into self-loathing. Suzie was extremely worried about him. However, she still couldn't get it through her head that her beloved Mosey was only a loving partner when he/she, or whoever they may be, didn't have any place else to live.

"And then again, within a few months of their reconciliation, Mosey was back on the dog grooming circuit and only keeping in touch with Suzie by phone. I think when his phone got disconnected after he was informed that Suzie was injured, my sister might have finally gotten the message that he didn't care about her at all, except as a convenient and loving place of refuge.

"If maybe something terrible did happen to him, her, whoever Mosey is or was, even suicide, so be it. My sweet sister seems to want to heal everybody of their afflictions, but it's time for her to accept that she would never have been able to fix Moe.

"My sycophant sister Suzie needs to be like the horse in that painting. She needs to learn to turn her back to the storm."

41

Thea Baccay had spent another traumatic day as an intern. She was rotating through the high-risk obstetric ward. Two patients were being managed for premature labor. One was being managed for dangerous high blood pressure. A pregnant woman who was also battling breast cancer, was admitted with pneumonia.

There were two full-term, healthy babies born that day. Thea had also been present when one of the obstetricians delivered a full-term stillborn baby to a couple who had believed that they'd finally won their infertility battle after more than a decade of failed attempts. The baby had trisomy eighteen, a rare genetic disorder that caused his heart to be too small to survive the trauma of birth. The tears shed in that room could have filled a punch bowl.

Thea had also attended the birth of a premature infant who'd be spending his early life in an incubator on a ventilator. Before this obstetric rotation would end, Thea would become one hundred per cent certain that she didn't want to be an obstetrician, and ninety-nine per cent sure that she didn't want to be pregnant anytime soon. Besides, the thought of having a child with the person that Darius had become was losing its appeal.

Still, Thea hoped that once they got past the anxiety of the first post-transplant year, the old, more affable Darius would reemerge.

As had become customary, Thea's mother left her a home-cooked meal in her fridge. Darius still hadn't come home from his recent trip to the transplant center. When he was home, he sometimes cooked, but not if there was an afternoon game on that he wanted to watch. Thea had often been left to scrounge dinner for herself after a long day in the hospital, while Darius ate a few ketchup-smothered hot dogs in front of the TV. He was flagrantly disregarding recommendations to maintain a low-salt diet.

Darius's latest heart biopsy showed some signs of rejection, and the transplant team had upped his cyclosporine dose. They wanted to observe him for a few days on the new medication regimen while he was still close to the campus, or so he claimed. Thea was grateful for how peaceful her little apartment was without blaring advertisements every few minutes. After eating and watching some news, she finally mustered up the motivation to return Sullivan's call.

After the usual pleasantries, Sully informed Thea of his most recent concern. He had a strong suspicion that Darius had snuck into the lab a few nights ago.

"But wouldn't all the security systems have gone off?"

"Not if they've been turned off, which is something only two people have the means to do, and I know I didn't turn them off. Darius is the only other person with the password. I think he even knows how to reset the system so it doesn't show that there was a gap in the tapes."

"But what about the night monitors? I thought there's always someone in attendance so the animals are never left alone."

"Almost never left alone. There's been a one-hour gap on Tuesdays in recent weeks. The graduate students leave at eleven when the monitors arrive for their night shifts. On Tuesdays, the night shift monitor's evening schedule got tweaked so that she doesn't get to our lab until midnight. She's the bioengineer for both our lab and the hospital lab, and on Tuesday nights, she calibrates a lot of the hospital lab equipment. It would be almost impossible to replace her, so we're getting one of the other night-shifters to switch schedules with her. That's supposed to happen next month. We thought the one-hour gap would be okay once a week for a few weeks.

"Recruiting, training and then retaining these people is difficult, so we try to always accommodate those individuals who are willing to do this kind of work. Cleaning up guano (bat poop) in the wee hours of the morning isn't most people's idea of a good job."

"But why would Darius even want to be in the lab at any hour? Do you have any idea what he was doing there, besides putting his immune system at risk?"

"I really don't know. It has been an interesting week in the lab though. Last weekend, we acquired a silver-haired bat. They're one of the common U.S. bat species, but unlike communal bats, they are solitary. They live alone in cavities in trees. They're also interesting because they mate in mid-air in autumn, but then, the female stores the sperm until spring and has her pup in June or July, after a two-month pregnancy.

"The silver hair we received was badly injured. She had wounds on her head and one of her wings, and she'd lost an eye, probably to a hawk or an owl who came after her in her roost. She was found on the ground by a hiker. She only weighs about a tenth of an ounce and it's amazing she survived the predator, but her prognosis was poor.

"But what was really interesting about this bat was that she was young and pregnant. No self-respecting, bug-eating bat should be pregnant in these parts at this time of year because there aren't enough bugs around to eat. She should either be hibernating or migrating to where it's warmer and where there are more bugs. Perhaps she didn't get the memo about storing the sperm. Maybe her reproductive system was immature.

"We almost always get silver-hair bats when they're dead from rabies. There's even a strain of rabies that's specific to their species. There's only a small minority of this breed that are unable to fight off a rabies infection. This bat did show antibodies to rabies, but she did not show any signs of illness. She gave birth on Tuesday morning and succumbed to her injuries shortly afterwards. Her pup was born prematurely but he seems to be healthy. The grad students named him Sergio.

"The most interesting thing about this, is that on the same day the silver-hair came to us, we also got an injured Mexican free-tailed bat. We think this one may have had a head injury. She was found on the ground near a wind turbine, Her face is bruised and there's a chunk missing out of one of her ears. She has rabies antibodies, but she doesn't appear to be ill.

"Mexican free-tails are the species that's become famous for the enormous maternity colony that lives under the Congress Avenue Bridge in Austin, Texas. In San Antonio, Texas, there's a cave that's estimated to house maybe twenty million free-tails. Besides this tendency to live in enormous colonies, free-tails are also known for their jet-like flight. They fly high and they can generate speeds of a hundred miles an hour.

"Free-tails are also known for their vocal skills. A group of foraging free-tails can change their ultrasonic vocalizations to jam the signals of rival bats when they're competing for a meal of moths, causing their rivals to be diverted away from the food.

"Mother free-tails leave their pups in the nursery at night when they go out to feed. When they return, in a nursery of hundreds of thousands of crying pups, mothers can find their own infants by the sound of their voices. The females are also known to help one another raise their pups and they will nurse another mother's hungry baby. Bats only produce one pup at a time, and they place high value on their children.

"Though the free-tail brought to us didn't have any milk, when the grad student put the baby silver-hair next to her, she took it under her wing, and it tried to nurse. These free-tails weigh about a quarter to half of an ounce; they're more than twice the size of the silver-hairs.

"We're curious to see if this silver-hair bat pup will also have rabies antibodies and if he does, will they be from the strain of rabies that his mother had, or from being licked by his surrogate mother. It's a rare opportunity to look into this.

"The pup is still being cuddled by his surrogate mom, but he's getting his nutrition from bat formula. Sergio apparently loves caresses from humans as well as kisses from his free-tail mother, so he should do okay when she's gone. His surrogate mom will probably be recovered enough to release into the wild in maybe another week, so our staff will have to take over the cuddling job. Infant bats need lots of affection, while adult free-tails need to hang with their families and friends. They're very clannish."

"Well, that's all very interesting, Sully, and I'm sure Darius really wanted to be there to see these bats, but I can't believe he'd risk his own health to do it. What is it that makes you think he was there anyway?"

"Because I set a trap. One day last month, I decided to move his hazmat suit down to the end of the decontamination chamber since he wasn't using it. The next day, I found it back in its former place in the line-up. At the time, I figured one of the grad students must have moved it back to its usual place. I moved it again, and again it got relocated. It's too small to fit anybody else, so I didn't think it was used, but just to be sure, I put some pieces of fine thread at the bottom of the sleeves. Then I moved the suit again, but this time, no one moved it back and the booby trap threads were still right where I had placed them, until Wednesday morning. When I went to put my suit on then, I found Darius's suit moved back to its original spot and the threads had been dislodged."

Thea commented that at least Darius suited up while violating his agreement with the transplant team to stay away from infectious agents. "But what was he doing there?"

"I wish I knew, Thea, but I don't have a clue. Of course, nighttime in the bat cave is when the bats are awake and busy: eating, conversing, and mating. We have some very amorous bats right now. I've tried to tell myself that Darius just wanted to be part of this again, but I have this gnawing feeling that he's got some project going on that he doesn't want me or anyone else to know about. I also suspect that this was not the first time since his transplant that he's snuck into the lab.

"Maybe he'll reveal to you what's going on, Thea. I don't feel like I have the same rapport with him that I used to."

42

Ingrid Smythe asked James to try to find some way for her to meet with Darius Amari. She seemed obsessed with finding out how this researcher had managed to obtain the high level of support and finances that were needed to operate a university-sponsored BSL-3 lab.

When Ingrid had conferred with the scientists who ran the labs she owns, they were also surprised by how this man had come to be so heavily invested in. The premises of his research papers were astute and well-developed, but they weren't unique or novel enough to have propelled him to the top of the pick list for the most endowed investors.

First, James tried to connect to Amari through Sullivan Dietz. He had texted Dietz some Batman jokes and finally got a return 'holy oleo Batman.' Then he sent Dietz a picture of a bat he had taken with an infrared camera. He asked for help identifying the species. Sullivan texted back that the photo wasn't suitable for identification.

James then invited Sullivan to come on a nightly bat spotting mission with him at his lakeside residence before the last of the bats went into seasonal hibernation. Sully texted back that he was currently too busy in the lab to get away. Maybe, he could come in the spring when they could get out on the lake. Sullivan was cordial, but a closer relationship with James appeared to rank pretty low on his priority list.

James next tried to get closer to Thea. He arranged his hospital duties around her schedule, so he'd cross paths with her a couple of times a week. She was always good for a hello, but then she was

hightailing it off to take care of the next patient. She hardly even took lunch breaks. James came to observe that she'd just wolf down a nutrition bar while inputting on the computer.

Finally, James resorted to coming into the hospital one evening while Thea was on call on the obstetric ward. He hoped she might have some down time. He showed up at the nursing station on the pretext that he was updating something in the computer system, and he found Thea sitting behind the desk and reviewing patient charts. The ward was relatively quiet.

After some ordinary conversation, James asked, "did Darius ever tell you that my dad invited him and Sullivan Dietz to our place out on the lake?"

"Darius told me that you and your father had brunch with him and Sully in the Bandore Diner some weeks ago, but he never mentioned the invitation. I'd love to come out to the lake. When I was little, my father used to trail a small sailboat to the lake when the wind was just right. But when we kids got bigger, we didn't all fit in it anymore. He wound up giving the boat to a cousin. That was before the Lake Shore housing development came along. It used to be so peaceful out there." Thea sighed.

"My family's home is on the west side of the lake. It's still pretty peaceful there, especially this time of year when hardly any one is boating. Maybe you and Darius could come out this weekend. The weather forecast is for sunny and unseasonably warm. We could take my dad's new boat out and do a little tour."

"That would be wonderful, James. Thank you so much, but I'm afraid this weekend won't work. I'm on call on Saturday, and the Cowboys are playing Sunday. I don't think there's any chance that I could drag my husband away from watching that game."

"My dad likes the Dallas Cowboys. What time are they playing? We could have the game on. He wouldn't have to miss a thing."

"Well, Darius could also tape the game and watch it at his leisure, but for reasons I can't comprehend, he insists on watching it live and listening to a hundred minutes of screaming commercials. I can't even talk to him until there's a commercial playing, and then it's so loud that he can't hear me. He takes these football games very seriously."

Thea was about to suggest that she could come out and visit by herself when she got paged away to a patient's room. The patient had been in labor for seven hours, but wasn't progressing towards delivery. A fetal heart monitor had signaled that the baby was in distress. Thea instructed the nurse to alert the obstetrician and prepare for an emergency C-section.

When Thea returned to the desk at the nursing station, James was gone. He left her a note saying he was sorry he had to go, and he hoped he could find another time in their insane schedules to do something social. Thea scrubbed up to attend the C-section.

James sensed that Thea really wanted to come for a visit, even if her husband didn't, but that wasn't going to provide Ingrid Smythe the opportunity she was seeking. He wondered if Thea had any semblance of a social life between being an intern and having a husband with serious health problems. And, after meeting the arrogant Darius Amari, James had come to perceive a mantle of misery behind Thea's perpetual smile. He felt sorry for her.

After all his networking plans fizzled, James advised his boss that he'd pretty much run out of options. He suggested that if she really wanted to meet this man, maybe she should just invite the couple to dinner. He suspected that they'd have a hard time refusing an invitation from her. At least Thea would; maybe not Darius. But perhaps, James could make Darius curious about Ingrid by telling Thea about her businesses and biolabs. Maybe Darius would want to know that she was competing for his investor dollars.

"Maybe," James suggested, "you could also include Doctor Villarose in the dinner plans. That way, the invitation to Thea and Darius would seem more like a friendly gesture than a fact-finding mission. Melinda Villarose and Thea Baccay both grew up around here, so there's more of a link between them than with the other interns. Maybe you could make it a little holiday gathering for the locals."

Ingrid appeared to be considering James's suggestion, so he added "By the way, did I tell you that Doctor Villarose recently saved my mother's life?"

Ingrid raised her eyebrows. "Please, do tell."

"So, a few Sundays ago, just by coincidence, my father and I connected with Doctor Villarose, and the rental physician Doctor Blauveldt, over at the Bandore Diner. It's a great brunch if you haven't tried it. My father mentioned that my mother was having some problems and when he said this one thing, Doctor Villarose seemed to immediately know what the diagnosis was. She told us to get my mother to a neurosurgeon immediately."

"It turns out that my mother has hydrocephalus, otherwise known as water on the brain. Apparently, the fluid that normally bathes the brain and spinal cord, can sometimes build up and become too voluminous to fit into its own space. Untreated, the fluid puts pressure on the brain causing damage. It's ultimately fatal.

"The buildup of fluid can occur because of brain injury or infection or a stroke. Sometimes a tumor blocks the drainage of the fluid into the vascular system. But sometimes, the cause of the fluid buildup cannot be identified. Fortunately, that's what my mother has, adult hydrocephalus of unknown cause, which is better than having a brain tumor.

"The neurosurgeon took my mother to surgery the next day. He put a shunting device into her head that connects to a tube that courses under her skin and empties into her abdominal cavity. It's all internal, so you can't see it. There's a little pressure valve on the device in her head. When the fluid builds up and puts pressure on the valve, the valve opens up and releases the excessive fluid down the tube until the pressure normalizes. The small amount of cerebrospinal fluid has no impact on the abdomen. The patient feels nothing."

"My poor mom. She was really suffering, and her doctor thought it was migraines. Just before she got in to see the surgeon, she was starting to lose her vision. None of her other doctors had looked in her eyes where the surgeon found obvious signs of her condition. Her optic nerves were swollen. I hate to think what might have happened if we hadn't run into Doctor Villarose that day. Now, my mom's symptoms are all resolved."

"What was the symptom that made Doctor Villarose suspect the diagnosis?"

"It was that my mother would feel like her feet were glued to the floor. I guess most doctors would ignore that clue, but it sure hit a nerve for Doctor Villarose.

"By the way, if you invite Doctor Villarose to dinner, you might also want to consider inviting Doctor Blauveldt. He's the guy who's substituting for Suzie Nguyen. I think Villarose and Blauveldt are dating."

 **43**

Melinda Villarose was just finishing up her evaluation of a problem that occurred in the cardiac care unit. Intern Sam Hornan had accidentally ordered an overdose of digitalis for a patient with heart failure, and the inexperienced nurse who administered it, hadn't caught the error.

Tiny digitalis doses can improve a weak heart's ability to pump. Bigger doses can make the heart stand still. Digitalis is normally dosed at fractional levels. Doctor Sam Hornan had put a decimal point in the wrong place and put the patient's life in danger. Fortunately, the hospitalist physician recognized digitalis toxicity when the patient reported that everything looked yellow, a side effect peculiar to this medicine. The physician immediately administered a digitalis antidote and saved the patient's life.

The patient just happened to be a nurse, so she understood the gravity of the mistake. When the hospitalist called Melinda to report the incident, they were both fearful of a malpractice lawsuit. But when Melinda arrived in the unit to evaluate the situation, she found the patient smiling while Doctor Hornan serenaded her.

Intern Sam Hornan could do a wicked impression of Tony Bennet, and when he sang, "I sent your heart to San Francisco," the elderly nurse, who was originally from San Francisco, responded with unabashed delight. *Perhaps laughter is the best medicine. Perhaps Sam Hornan can cure more people with his charm than can any doctor with a prescription pad.*

Still, Melinda was worried about a lawsuit should the patient not have a good outcome. She returned to her office to write up the incident and was stunned to find an unfamiliar person sitting in her desk chair, facing backwards, and looking at the painting of the horse in the storm.

"Um, may I help you?" Melinda asked.

When the woman spun the chair around to face Melinda, there was something vaguely familiar about her. Then, she stood up and offered her hand. "How do you do Doctor Villarose. I'm Reyna Baccay, Thea's mother. I'm sorry to have barged in on you like this, but I know that you are a psychiatrist and I need your help."

Melinda offered the woman a beverage and cancelled her next appointment. She reclaimed her desk chair while Mrs. Baccay took the visitor's chair. She was still looking at the storm painting when Melinda again asked how she could help.

"There's no chance that Thea's going to walk in here, is there? She'd be very distressed to know I'm here. That's why I didn't make an appointment in advance."

Melinda took a 'do not disturb' sign from her desk and hung it on the outer door. "Thea's really busy on the obstetric ward today and I'm confident she's doing an excellent job. She's an exceptionally gifted young physician and I'm enormously proud to have her in our program."

"I know. Thea always pours her heart into everything she does, and she always excels at whatever she does. Except at marriage. She's not doing such a good job at that. You can't become happily married by studying a textbook."

"Is a problem with Thea's marriage what brought you to me today?" Melinda asked.

"Did you ever meet her husband Darius?" Reyna asked.

"Never did," Melinda said. "But I know he's been through hell and back during the past few years, so I imagine Thea has been too. How were things for Thea and Darius before COVID changed everything?"

"That's a very good question. I will tell you; our family was initially very worried about Thea's relationship with Darius because of their age difference. After ploughing through two master's degrees, Thea was twenty-five when she started medical school, and Darius was maybe thirty-seven when she took that immunology course from him. I think just the twelve-year difference is a strike against a successful marriage, but Thea was so star-struck then, there was nothing we could say to dissuade her from pursuing the relationship.

"When we first met Darius, we were a little taken with him too. He came across as brilliant and successful and he seemed to be truly in love with my daughter."

"When you say we, who besides yourself was Darius introduced to?"

"We are a whole bunch of relatives. When Thea first brought Darius home for dinner, two of my sisters, two of Thea's siblings, and one of her cousins were all there for the occasion. We all live around here, and we all have enormous dining tables to accommodate our close-knit family. I'm sure Darius was overwhelmed by the Baccay clan. He's a man with zero family.

"Anyway, Darius seemed like a very interesting person, and you could almost feel the academic connection that he and Thea shared. There aren't too many people on the planet with minds like that."

"But?" Melinda said when Reyna seemed to pause.

"But I immediately had some misgivings about him. There weren't any red flags waving in my face, but something in my gut told me that this man wasn't who he seemed to be. Do you psychiatrists know where so-called gut feelings come from?"

"Wow is that a loaded question! Whether we call it a gut feeling or instinct or intuition or an inner voice, sometimes, an emotional reaction to someone or something is more profound than the thoughts generated by our conscious minds. There are plenty of theories about the origin of instincts, but I don't think science has really cracked that code.

"We do know that some of the powerful neurotransmitters associated with emotions, like serotonin and dopamine, are produced in the gut, but our understanding of the brain-gut interface is still pretty limited. Suffice it to say, something about Darius Amari triggered your maternal instincts to protect your child. None of us might be here if it weren't for the phenomenon we call maternal instinct.

"Mrs. Baccay, please realize that I take responsibility for the competence of the physicians in training who are serving our hospital. If your daughter is at risk, it would help me to know if you can now identify what it was that gave you that gut feeling when you first met her husband."

"I still can't define it. Perhaps I thought he was narcissistic if I had to give it a name. But so much has happened to him since, everything in the past no longer seems relevant.

"I have to admit, the marriage did seem ideal for a while because both Thea and Darius had this strong appreciation of each other's goals and need to maintain their academic edges. Thea respected Darius's commitment to his research and Darius respected Thea's need to constantly study and be on the top of her medical school class. And the two of them could talk to each other about things that few others understand. It was truly a union of brainiacs.

"But then COVID came along, and everything changed for the worse. When Darius initially came home from the hospital after being on a ventilator for a month, Thea took care of him as though she was a twenty-four-hour-a-day nurse and servant. He seemed to have no appreciation for the fact that she was also recovering from COVID and the psychologic trauma of fearing widowhood just a few months after getting married. Everything was all about him and the research projects that he had to catch up with.

"Then, when it became apparent that he was showing signs of heart failure, he became angry. He would lash out at Thea, and I understand that Sullivan, Darius's research partner and good friend, was also absorbing a lot of that abuse. Sully and Thea became very close to each other during that time.

"Meanwhile, it was Thea and Sully who were managing everything. They helped Darius prepare and tape all of the lectures for the medical students he was supposed to be teaching. Sully took over almost everything in the lab while Darius just remotely gave orders. Thea and Sully did everything possible to make Darius's life easier while he just made their lives harder.

"It was actually Sully who told me about all of this. He's a real sweetheart and he's almost become a member of our family. He calls Thea and me on a pretty regular basis just to see how we're doing. I've often wished it was Sully who's my son-in-law, instead of Darius, in spite of the fact that he's even older than Darius.

"I don't know if it's pure love for her husband or compensation for her own flaws that drives Thea, but she would never tell me about how lousy things have become. She just keeps defending Darius, even now that he's seemingly turned into someone else. Since the transplant, he's like a different person. This new passion for watching sports is so weird that I can't even begin to understand it. We're sure curious if that's something that came from the donor.

"And last week, Darius's cyclosporine got upped for some more signs of rejection. Now, in addition to all of the rest of his problems, he's become irritable and anxious and he's having trouble sleeping. He also seems to be more hearing impaired so he's playing the TV even louder. I'm almost to the point where I'd like to kick them out of the apartment I'm housing them in, but I could never do that to my daughter.

"I'm worried sick about my daughter, Doctor Villarose. She's such a perfectionist that she can't even admit that everything isn't perfect. And she's so compassionate, that I fear she can't get out from under the burden of her marriage because her conscience won't allow her to abandon this man. His health problems have turned him into a pathetic soul and the fact that he has no family to retreat to, adds a whole other measure of sadness to the situation. I know my daughter is suffering and I don't know how to help her."

"You've tried to talk to Thea about this, I'm sure. How does she respond?"

"Everyone in our family has tried, but all we get is denial. That's why I'm hoping you can get through to her. She has a great deal of respect and even affection for you, Doctor Villarose. She's said that you're what makes the whole Bandore experience worthwhile. If anyone can get through to Thea, I think it's you. I'm sorry to lay this on you, but I don't know what else to do.

"Thank you for allowing me to be here and to share this with you. And thank you for being such a positive influence on my daughter, but she's like that horse in the painting. I really fear she's just a few yards away from being swallowed up by a storm."

"Thank you for your insights, Mrs. Baccay. Thea's situation sounds very distressing. I can't make any promises, but I'll see if I can come up with some way to help."

44

Ingrid Smythe wrinkled her nose with annoyance. "I had you make dinner reservations for ten, James, and it's all prepaid. This whole thing was your idea. What do you mean, there is no Mrs. Dzobak? You were married when you interviewed for this job. I distinctly remember that you were worried that your wife wouldn't like living here. But James, I hired you anyway. I do appreciate your cyber skills."

"My wife and I had eighteen good years together, Ms. Smythe, but we've gone our separate ways. Diane was a political person who turned her volunteer campaign activities into a career as a state legislator's assistant. Then, she ran a political campaign that got her hired by a federal congressman. Now, she's headed to Washington and our dreams of having a family got sacrificed along the way. That's okay. I have real anxiety about the problems my generation has left for those who come after us. I admire Diane for trying to do something about it.

"It was a very amicable split. We're still friends and I'm glad she's achieving her goals. And I'm really glad to be back in beautiful Bandore County. I'm enjoying living in my childhood home. My family has a magnificent spot on the lake with our own private dock.

"But the only date I could bring to your dinner party might be my mother. She's finally able to be out and about again and it's been a wonderful rejuvenation of my parent's relationship. I am truly indebted to Doctor Villarose for what she's done for my family. Thank you for including her in this invite."

Ingrid had ordered James to reserve a small private dining room in Bandore's most prized resort. Set amidst magnificent, mature pine trees, it was a classic old hotel with a prime hilltop view of the jewel-colored lake. The table settings were worth designer awards. James had added to a bouquet on a side table, colorful foil bats that fluttered on thin wires when someone passed by.

It was miraculous that none of the invitees had signs of illness. They had all been warned that Darius Amari could not be exposed to even a resolving head cold. Ingrid's husband shook hands with everybody as they came into the room, but he just saluted Darius. Then he excused himself to take a phone call and he never returned.

A waiter immediately offered the guests flutes of prosecco. At first, Thea was worried that Darius had taken one. Then she hoped it might mellow him out. Alcohol wasn't totally forbidden in transplant patients, though caution was necessary. She refrained from admonishing him when he went back for a second glass. It would probably have created a scene.

Darius had only agreed to accompany Thea to this event after she had begged and pleaded. "It's going to be people who share our interests," Thea offered, but it seemed Darius could have cared less if the interests didn't include sports. He had befriended a graduate student who was maybe more fanatical about the Dallas Cowboys than even Darius was, and Darius was no longer interested in anyone who didn't share his passion for sports.

Doctors Melinda Villarose and Howard Blauveldt most certainly appeared to be in a relationship. You could see it by how they interacted with each other, and you could almost feel it in the air. James wondered if there were electrical charges that occurred along with the chemical changes known to be associated with falling in love.

If there was any electricity between Thea Baccay and Darius Amari, it had a negative charge. Amari's posture and gestures indicated he didn't want to be there. He sat slightly angled away from Thea and the table. His focus was on his glass of bubbly. Thea's glass was untouched. There was tension in her face and posture.

James's date turned out to be his ex-wife, Diane. He thought she'd find it interesting to hear what scientists were up to. The congressman she worked for was trying to legislate higher standards for labs that handle dangerous germs. Diane had remarked to James that they could legislate this matter up the wazoo, but there was no way to enforce these laws. The illegal lab in Reedley, California had proven that. But Diane's congressman represented a population that now understood that a BSL-4 lab was located in its backyard. Before the Reedley incident, neither the congressman nor the average citizen even knew that it was there.

Ingrid introduced her two other guests, both scientists in her companies, accompanied by their spouses. Hassan Kumar was a molecular biologist working on a dengue vaccine in a BSL-2 lab. Talia Levy was a molecular virologist running a company that developed serologic tests for viruses. Both expressed familiarity with Darius's work when he was introduced. Ingrid had made it seem that Darius was the star of the show with her introductions. Then she offered a toast "to science."

"I want you all to know that this gathering is also in honor of my right-hand man, James Dzobak. While my biggest dream has long been to find a way for humanity to combat the Dengue virus, a virus that took my son's life, James's passion for bats has brought me to consider new goals and new approaches. Darius, these scientists and I would really like to better understand why research with bats has become such a major focus for scientists, and for investors who support scientific research."

"What is this, an interrogation?" Darius griped. He glared at Thea. She shrugged and bowed her head. Some of the dinner guests gulped.

"We're just all fascinated by what you do, Darius," Ingrid said. "My assistant James was mesmerized by the information you shared when he met you at the Bandore Diner."

James looked pleadingly at Darius. "Bats are the most fascinating creatures on the planet. Your research partner, Sullivan Dietz, got me so excited about bats that all I want to do is learn about them and protect them. I keep reading about all the different customs that the different species have and every day, I'm more fascinated."

"I've never worked with bats," Hassan Kumar said, "but that seems to be where the money is nowadays. Ever since the COVID pandemic, bat research has become the hot ticket for getting funding. Why is that?"

Talia Levy smiled at Darius. "Forgive us, Professor Amari, for wanting to pick your brain. We all need to learn from each other in order to step up our game. If we humans don't share scientific accomplishments, artificial intelligence will take over the development of science and it will be out of our hands."

All eyes were on Darius as he sat silent. James wasn't sure if he was going to speak or throw down his napkin and storm out of the room. He wondered if Thea had kicked him under the table because Darius suddenly sat more upright. He picked up his glass and toasted, "to bats. They have more to teach us than we have the capacity to learn."

Darius's British accent made his lecture especially compelling. As a proficient wait staff unobtrusively dished out the food, Darius delivered a lecture that he had always liked to give.

"Bats are a superior species because they have had more than sixty-five million years to evolve. By comparison, modern humans have been around for about two hundred thousand years. Bats have been evolving three-hundred-twenty-five times longer than the current version of our species. Microbes have been around even longer.

"Somewhere along the way, viruses realized that bats were an ideal host for their goal of spreading themselves all over the world. Bats have greater mobility than any other mammal. Although they don't migrate as far as birds, they can cover hundreds of miles. Even in their nightly forages, Mexican free-tail bats might fly sixty miles each way from their roost to their food source. This particular species can also fly at ten thousand feet altitude to catch high-flying insect swarms. Through their excretions, they can readily disperse viruses.

"Bat species that don't migrate typically hibernate. How they slow down their metabolism and other bodily functions remains one of science's greatest mysteries. Imagine if we could all hibernate from the cold climate of January. Some bats reduce their heart rate from three hundred beats a minute to eight beats a minute when they go into a state of torpor, an almost dead state. Some bats can stay in a state of torpor for as long as six months. Viruses seem to like this state of dormancy and someday, maybe we'll understand how the low metabolic activity of dormancy supports viral survival.

"Viruses also favor bats because so many species live in close quarters. Those large, jam-packed caves housing millions of bats provide viruses with enormous opportunities to spread. Bats also like to snuggle with and groom each other which involves a lot of licking. Some bats engage in hours of oral-genital foreplay before sex, so viruses carried in their saliva have an even greater chance of being transmitted.

"Bats also have incredible longevity for such small creatures Some can live for more than forty years. Contrast that with the one to two-year life span of the typical mouse or rat. A virus's chances for life and procreation are infinitely better if its host is around for more than a few months. If we ever figure out the key to bat longevity, then maybe our species can increase its own life span."

Darius paused for a minute and blinked his eyes a few times. Then he shook his head back and forth and rubbed his eyes.

"Are you okay?" Melinda Villarose asked.

"Bloody cyclosporine blurs my vision," Darius grumbled, before returning to lecture mode.

"Bats are also favored by viruses because the germs can live in harmony with these hosts. Bats have developed immune defenses that for the most part, prevent the virus from killing its host. Dead hosts can't spread the virus, so infecting an animal that dies from the infection is a virus's dead end.

"What I study is how bats tolerate these viruses. They have several defense systems. The most appreciated is their body temperature fluctuations. It takes an enormous amount of energy to fly, and that energy also raises a bat's temperature to the equivalency of a high fever. Fever is a normal human response to being infected by a virus. Fever charges up the other immune defenses and slows down the ability of the viruses to replicate. A high enough fever can kill a virus, but at a certain level it will also kill the human who's trying to fight off the virus, so fever control can become necessary at higher temperature levels. But nightly fevers in bats seem to keep their viruses suppressed.

"Bats have also evolved to be able to control their inflammatory responses to infection. When a human gets an infection, its immune system releases cytokines and other inflammatory chemicals that not only attack the virus, but also attack the human. It's now suspected that the COVID virus didn't do nearly as much damage to human tissues as did the cytokines released to combat COVID. Bats have apparently learned how to modulate the release of cytokines so that the chemicals only attack the virus and not the bat.

"Bats also have more virus fighting proteins in their immune arsenal. Almost two decades ago, scientists discovered immunologic compounds call tetherins. These compounds can stop a virus from entering a cell, stop it from replicating, and stop it from leaving the cell if it manages to get inside. Well, now we know that humans may only have two kinds of tetherins. Vesper bats, on the other hand, like the little silver-hair bat baby we have in our lab right now, have many kinds of tetherins to inactivate viruses. They also have five times the number of genes that code for the production of tetherins.

"Some of the bat immune defenses also seem to protect these animals from cancer and diabetes. Fruit bats can consume twice their weight in sugar every day, but they don't get diabetes. We need to learn how they do this. Right now, most of the funding available for research is going towards the study of viral infections, but bat physiology has far more to offer if humans would just pay attention.

"And if humans would just stop stealing bat terrain, the bats wouldn't be moving into human terrain where they can pass their viruses to us. But that's a lecture for another day."

Darius paused again and started digging into his dinner. Then he stopped to rub his eyes again. When he finally put his utensils down, Ingrid started to ask about bats serving as a reservoir for Dengue, but she never finished the question after observing that Darius was staring off into space and his eyes were darting around. Then he began to shudder.

"He's seizing," Doctor Blauveldt said as he jumped to his feet and lowered a shaking Darius from his chair to the floor. Darius continued to convulse for another few minutes.

"Side effect of cyclosporine?" Thea said as they all stood by feeling helpless. "He had another dosage increase a few days ago."

"But seizures are a rare side effect of cyclosporine," Doctor Blauveldt said. "We need to get him to the E.R. to make sure his heart hasn't thrown a clot to his brain."

After an ambulance whisked Darius and Thea away, Ingrid's dinner guests finished their meals in relative silence.

45

It was the Tuesday after Ingrid's Saturday dinner disaster when Darius Amari was about to be transferred from Bandore Hospital to the transplant center for special perfusion studies of his heart. He was having heart rhythm issues, and he had apparently thrown a blood clot to his brain that spontaneously dislodged before he suffered permanent damage. His anticoagulation medicine was adjusted, and he was stable enough for the ambulance ride. Thea's sister Isabella, a nurse, was going to go with him so Thea could fulfill her internship duties. Thea's mother was going to watch Isabella's kids.

Melinda Villarose had visited Darius in the hospital on Sunday and Monday. He was a little more receptive on the second visit, but he was still mostly standoffish and crabby. Knowing he'd suffered one health crisis after another, she could hardly blame him. Still, he seemed cognitively okay. He also appeared to be extremely invested in a football game that was playing in his room on Sunday. Melinda had only been able to engage him for a few minutes during a commercial break. It was hardly worth her trip into the hospital, but at least she was getting a clearer picture of what Thea was dealing with.

After stopping by on Tuesday to wish Darius luck before he left, Melinda returned to her office to find Doctor Dayo Igwe waiting to see her. He had something very important to tell her that she was going to have to get involved in, but he was adamant that she couldn't reveal that he was the source of the information. He'd tell her why only after she agreed to conceal his identity and after he explained his concern.

Melinda hesitated only for a few seconds. She had come to greatly respect Doctor Igwe. He was a great clinician and a gentleman. She was pretty certain he wouldn't have approached her with this request if it wasn't legitimate. "You have my word that this is confidential."

Dayo started by reminding Melinda that he had just begun his rotation in surgery which was especially interesting for someone who had previously been performing all kinds of major operations in huts and tents in war zones in Ethiopia and Somalia. He was enthralled with all of the high-tech equipment and safety protocols in Bandore's O.R.s. He was observing how everything was done in his first case on Monday morning when he noticed something that didn't make sense.

The patient was a sixty-four-year-old man with a liver tumor. Doctor Rhea did an excellent job of excising the tumor and closing the incisions. Dayo followed the patient into the recovery area to see how things were done there. The patient's stretcher was being pushed by a person in scrubs who appeared to be an O.R. tech. He was an older man, and he didn't perceive that Dayo Igwe was following him as he pushed the stretcher down the hall.

From behind, Dayo observed the tech reach up to the patient's IV bag and circle his finger around a stem on the bottom of the bag. The stem had a rubber stopper through which medications could be injected into the intravenous solution.

At first, Dayo thought the tech was checking the seal of the stem, but the motion was too quick to check anything. After docking the stretcher, the man went to the scrub sink in the hall and diligently washed his hands.

Initially, Dayo just thought this was curious, but now he was worried that this was a deliberate act of contamination. This morning on postop rounds, the patient was noted to have spiked a fever.

His white blood cell count suggested a bacterial infection. Cultures were pending.

"Yikes," Melinda responded. "Maybe Ezra Rhea is being sabotaged. I greatly appreciate your sharing this with me. I so admire your powers of observation, Dayo. I'll take it from here. I understand why your identity needs protection. If you're right, whoever's behind this probably has unlimited power to create problems for whoever's in the way of their goals. But, please, do keep observing and let me know if you can identify this employee, and if you see anything else like this going on."

As Melinda contemplated how she'd approach the conundrum that Dayo had just loaded onto her plate, she got a phone call from Roger Andrus. It was more than three months since Suzie Nguyen's assault, and he wanted her to know that Suzie's injuries were more debilitating than was initially recognized. It was highly unlikely that she'd be able to complete her internship.

Melinda had called Suzie on a weekly basis during the preceding months, but the communication never got beyond the most superficial topics. Suzie talked a lot but seemed to not always comprehend what was said to her. Melinda was well aware that these issues were a result of injury to the right temporal lobe. If the brain contusion could heal without scarring, these problems could resolve. It was too soon to tell. Neurologic recovery could take months to years.

Suzie was receiving cognitive therapy but unfortunately, injury to this part of the brain can impair visual and auditory perception and learning ability. She was also receiving physical therapy for her hand injuries and for her slack jaw. When the wires were finally removed, the right side of Suzie's face drooped. Her facial nerve had also been traumatized.

Melinda had circled January twelfth on her calendar, the four-month mark. If Suzie hadn't turned the corner by then, there was no way she was going to be completing her internship. That put Melinda in a real quandary. Doctor Howard Blauveldt didn't plan on being an intern for more than a few weeks. He certainly wasn't going to want to complete the whole year, and the cost of his services wasn't covered by Tazodan's frugal budget for the family practice training program. Melinda was feeling increasingly positive about her budding personal relationship with this charming man. Now he'd get sent packing.

Melinda thanked Roger for the update. It was time to inform Ingrid Smythe that Suzie Nguyen wasn't coming back. They'd have to find another way to fill the gap.

As for the Doctor Rhea situation, Melinda was appalled. If what Doctor Igwe saw was deliberate sabotage, someone in the new administration was trying to get rid of this surgeon. No wonder the O.R. nurses and the other surgeons were trying to defend Ezra Rhea.

Melinda had no good ideas about how to handle this. When she had previously contacted a legal adviser about how to address the Doctor Rhea situation, she was told that having notified her superiors was all she could reasonably do, and she should otherwise stay out of it. It was the responsibility of the hospital administration to find out how and why these infections were occurring. The medical board representative she'd spoken with advised her that unless there was actual evidence of wrongdoing by this surgeon, infection control was the hospital's problem. Besides, it was implied, this particular surgeon had a stellar reputation.

But if patients were being put at risk, there was no way Melinda could stay out of it.

46

It was at the end of his Tuesday surgical shift when Doctor Dayo Igwe returned to Melinda's office and gave her the name of the person who he'd seen do something to a patient IV. The man was reportedly a scrub tech whose role was to prepare the patient and transport them to the O.R., and to make sure that everything in the O.R. was sterile. It was actually a low-paying job with a high level of responsibility.

Melinda didn't recognize the employee's name. She wondered if she could get more information about him from James Dzobak. James seemed to have access to everything in the computer, maybe even files than he wasn't entitled to see.

Melinda was just about to leave for the day when Thea Baccay appeared in her doorway. She seemed a bit agitated, which was totally unlike Thea. At first, she said she just wanted to let Melinda know that Darius had made it to the transplant center okay. But then she confessed that she also wanted to inform Melinda of something that happened this morning that Thea said was extremely disconcerting.

"Hey," Melinda said. "I'm starved. Want to tell me about it over dinner? Tonight's taco Tuesday at the Bandore Diner and the fajitas are excellent. C'mon. My treat. You look like you need some comfort food."

Thea paused. Melinda sensed she needed to urgently get something off her chest, but a few minutes of delay could sometimes help things to crystalize. "It's just seven minutes from here. Let's escape this bastion of sickness and revel in an atmosphere of sensory delight. Are you with me?"

Thea, of course, couldn't say no, if only out of reverence for her admired mentor. She also needed to communicate her fears to some wise person who she could trust.

They waited ten minutes for a table that turned out to be in the corner of the antiquated railroad car. A big Boston fern overhanging their booth conferred a sense of privacy. Melinda ordered the blue margaritas for both of them. Approximating the exquisite color of Bandore Lake, the concoction had become the restaurant's signature drink. Because it was also strong, it had become a big hit.

Thea took the opportunity to inform Melinda that the tequila in their cocktails was totally dependent on pollination of the blue agave plants by bats. "Tequila is considered the healthiest of liquors due to the benefits conferred by agavins, unique nutrients in the agave plant. Tequila is also less caloric than some other popular spirits."

Both Thea and Melinda watched some of the tension drain from each other's faces as they sipped their cocktails. *If only I could have served cocktails when I was a practicing psychiatrist,* Melinda thought. Thea was at the bottom of her glass when she got around to revealing why she was so befuddled that she needed Melinda's help.

"I have to tell you, Doctor Villarose, that little dinner party on Saturday that Ms. Smythe invited us to, was nothing but an ambush. At eight o'clock this morning, a team of federal inspectors from several different regulatory agencies barged into my husband's lab. They seemed to know all about Darius's incapacitation because of his health problems. They even seemed to know that he had just been hospitalized. There is no doubt in my mind that one of the competing scientists we met the other night reported to some authority that Darius is incapable of running a lab.

"These inspectors went over everything down to a microscopic level. Sullivan was terrified that they'd contaminate something and then claim that the lab wasn't following protocols. He followed them around like an overbearing prison guard.

"As far as Sully could tell, they didn't find any violations. There was no reason why they should have. Sullivan runs as clean a lab as could be found anywhere in the world. The technician and the graduate students that were in the lab at that time also exemplified a quality operation. So hopefully, Darius's lab isn't going to get shut down just because he's ill.

"However, there is no doubt in my mind that this inspection was triggered by our encounter with Ms. Smythe and her scientist friends. Obviously, it was a set-up by someone who wants to see Darius's lab put out of commission. So now, I feel like I'm working for an entity that wants to decapitate my husband. I don't know how to handle this, Doctor Villarose. Maybe you have some advice for me."

Melinda felt outrage. She feared that Thea's conclusions were rock solid. The limited availability of funding for research had created a cutthroat environment, and apparently, Ingrid Smythe and Darius Amaris were competitors in that business. Ingrid Smythe's ulterior motives were pathetically transparent. Melinda wondered how she could have been so naïve as to think that Ingrid was trying to be collegial. The thought of working for her now had become even more obnoxious.

Melinda could think of no helpful advice to offer Thea. How would it even be possible for her to focus on her role as a physician in training under these circumstances? As Melinda tried to come up with something helpful, she sought to better understand the risks. "So, does this Sullivan Dietz have the qualifications to run a BSL-3 lab in Darius's absence. I've just recently learned about these biosafety level lab designations."

"Sully's credentials are golden. He started out as a veterinarian technician because he couldn't afford to go to vet school. Then he got a degree in molecular biology and an advanced degree in molecular genetics. Then he worked in a variety of BSL labs.

"Sully and Darius met at a virology conference a year before the construction of Darius's lab. Darius was one hundred percent sure that Sully was the right person to bring into his research as a partner. The fact that Sully also loved bats was just a cherry on top of his Sundae. They clicked on multiple levels.

"Sully has all of the qualifications to do the kind of research that Darius does, but he never had the connections that would afford him the financial support that Darius has. Darius's adoptive mother Yasmin had been a personal stylist for a diplomat's daughters who ultimately became the wives of European royalty and political influencers. Darius got to where he is today because of the powerful people that pulled for him. And Sully, thankfully, is still pulling for him. Without Sully, all would have been lost when COVID came along.

"Did I mention that Sully lost his wife to ovarian cancer when they were both thirty-six. After that, Sully devoted himself to his research interests, and his connection to Darius was a fortuitous event in his professional life. Under Darius's name, he's getting to do exactly what he always wanted to do."

"Sully sounds like an exceptional human being. I'm glad to know you have such a friend, Thea And by the way, how are you doing with all of this going on?"

"I'm a wreck, Doctor Villarose. I'm so distressed over Darius's situation that I sometimes feel like I'm hallucinating. This is going to sound crazy, but I have this feeling that my husband has become possessed by some kind of evil spirit and that he could be doing something with his research that's related to bioterrorism. That's so crazy that I worry if I'm psychotic, but I cannot bury the feeling or the fear. I also can't shake my suspicion that the donor of Darius's heart was a dangerous person. As a psychiatrist, do you think I'm crazy?"

"Thea, I absolutely do not think you are crazy. I actually think that with your husband's ability to do something horrific, the potential needs to be evaluated. Maybe we do need to investigate the background of the donor. Do you know how we can do that?"

"Perhaps, you could do it as a physician investigating my nervous breakdown. I'll explore the possibility with Darius's transplant coordinator, Julie Jacobs. I think Julie is also worried about what's happened to Darius."

As Melinda drove them back to Thea's car at the hospital, Thea continued to lament that she was really worried that if Darius thought his lab could be shut down, he might do something terrible in retaliation. There it was again, fear that her husband was capable of causing a biologic disaster. Melinda was starting to think there could be real danger if they couldn't figure out some way to intervene.

Melinda felt about as useful as used toilet paper in her effort to try to comfort Thea. The young doctor had completely grasped the gravity of the situation and there was no way to sugar coat the theoretical threats that were plaguing her. Melinda felt Thea's pain so profoundly that her own heart was hurting. It seemed like they both needed to find someone wiser to help them deal with these issues, but Melinda didn't know who that someone could be. They needed a golden horse to carry them away from the storm.

47

Melinda had asked James if he could provide her with some background on Bandore's auxiliary surgical staff, because she wanted to find someone her teenaged nephew could interview about these kinds of jobs for his careers class.

Melinda didn't actually have a young nephew, but James got her the information anyway. He was still feeling gratitude towards Melinda for saving his mother from an awful fate.

Dayo Igwe had identified Curtis Zigby as the culprit in Doctor Rhea's infected patients. Dayo had even seen Zigby do his little contamination maneuver to the IV bag of another Rhea patient, but apparently, the infection didn't take on that occasion. The patient recovered from abdominal hernia repair without complications.

An employee file indicated that Curtis Zigby was a fifty-two-year-old scrub tech who was hired a few weeks before the Tazodan Corporation took over Bandore Hospital. Melinda recalled that around that time, a patient of Doctor Rhea's came down with a nasty wound infection, the first incident in what they then didn't know would become a series.

Curtis Zigby had previously worked at a similar job for about a year in another hospital that had also been bought by Tazodan. Before that, he had worked at several other hospitals. He had moved around a lot.

Melinda only briefly wondered how desperate Bandore's O.R. manager must have been to have filled that position with such a transient person. There was no need to wonder. Finding and retaining competent and reliable health care workers had become increasingly difficult as a result of the pandemic. Add in Bandore's rural location, and not many candidates would have been available.

Looking online at the medical community of Zigby's last hospital, Melinda recognized the name of a former colleague, Cynthia Rhodes. Cynthia had transitioned into a group practice after Tazodan had closed down the psychiatry services that her hospital used to provide.

When Melinda explained why she was calling, Cynthia knew nothing about a Curtis Zigby. But she did know that the whole surgery service of that hospital had been shaken up after Tazodan took over. There had been problems with infection control and the former surgery chief was forced to resign. After that, surgeons who wanted to continue to use the hospital operating rooms had to agree to be employees of Tazodan or lose their privileges.

Melinda could hardly believe what Cynthia was telling her. Was Tazodan also trying to get rid of Ezra Rhea this way? As she fathomed the implications, she started to feel like her own sleuthing had gone about as far it could go. This shouldn't even be her problem. She needed to turn it over to Doctor Rhea himself, but without revealing that Dayo Igwe was the source of the evidence.

Dayo Igwe still had some weeks to go in his surgery rotation and he was currently the only one who was gathering evidence. He needed protection both for the mission and for his personal safety. Melinda also worried that this exceptional doctor was not going to go down as a hero for unraveling this fiasco. She felt enormously conflicted about what she should communicate to Doctor Rhea, as she was determined to protect Dayo.

Ultimately, Melinda told Ezra Rhea that she had talked to an old friend in another Tazodan hospital who told her the story about problems with infection control. "I wonder if our new hospital owners have brought someone to our hospital who can create infections.

Maybe you should look into the files of all of the O.R. staff to see if there's someone on your service that was in that other hospital."

Doctor Rhea admitted to Melinda that he feared that Cynthia's story was precisely what was happening at Bandore. He chastised himself for not investigating Tazodan's track record when he was initially courted by this corporation. Doctor Rhea had been assured by Tazodan reps that once the surgical services were restructured, he'd become the well-rewarded chief of a greatly expanded and updated surgical facility. He'd been taken in with promises of Bandore becoming so well equipped and staffed that it would draw top surgeons from around the country and make his hospital a medical resort destination. Tazodan's presentation had amounted to a very effective con job.

Ezra Rhea was inordinately grateful for the information that Melinda passed along. He told her he had a good attorney who could investigate his predicament. He was ninety-nine percent certain that he was being sabotaged at his patients' expense, and while he now understood why, he still didn't know how.

Each of the patient's post-operative infections had proved to be related strains of pneumococcal bacteria. Every single surface in the O.R.s had been cultured and the source of these bacteria had not been found. There had to be someone bringing the germs in with them.

Melinda was hopeful that Ezra would figure it out without her having to violate Dayo's trust. Considering how compromised the futures of Suzie Nguyen and Thea Baccay now seemed; Doctor Dayo Igwe was the most promising physician in her intern class.

Melinda felt a lot lighter to have crossed this dilemma off of her to-do list. But now, like Thea Baccay, she was wondering what kind of criminals she was working for. If Tazodan would stoop so low as to infect patients in order to restructure hospital staff and revenue, what wouldn't they do?

Or, Melinda wondered, was Curtis Zigby maybe just a lone wolf who liked the power of making terrible things happen? Was he one of those psychopaths who got a new tattoo every time he killed someone? Did he change jobs every time there were a few deaths? Where would a person like Zigby even get hold of germs like that?

Melinda suddenly had a flashback to the day she had done a computer search on Ingrid Smythe and learned about the multiple companies that Ingrid and her husband owned. Didn't one of those companies provide supplies to medical laboratories? Melinda went back to the websites she had been looking at months ago when she had first met Ingrid Smythe. It wasn't called 'Germs R Us,' but the profile of one of Ingrid's companies suggested it was where researchers went to obtain purified samples of various biologic agents.

Her aha moment didn't last too long. Melinda was about to forward this company's website link to Ezra Rhea, and suggest that maybe this company provides customers with little blister packs of pneumococci, when a danger signal flashed across her psyche. *Maybe her hospital computer was being monitored.* She quickly cancelled the email and erased her entire browsing history. She'd have to pass this tidbit on to Doctor Rhea in a much more discreet manner.

Fearing that Howard Blauveldt's days at Bandore Hospital were numbered, Melinda spent the rest of her day calling physicians in her search for a replacement for Doctor Nguyen. Dayo Igwe's friend was starting to look like a good option. The woman was an anesthesiologist who grew up in England and got her medical degree in Estonia. She'd done her residency in Morocco and a fellowship in Cameroon. She would gladly serve as a family practice physician in an impoverished community if doing so would afford her and her gifted three children, opportunities in the United States. Melinda had put the credentials office onto the case to see if they could qualify her.

Melinda also thought about resurrecting the letter of resignation that she had written after her first meeting with Ingrid Smythe. After rereading it, she closed the file. Then she skipped out of the hospital to get ready for dinner with Howie Blauveldt. He was doing a rotation in the cardiac care unit, and he'd hopefully get out on time. It was also his last rotation as a lowly intern. They had lots to discuss.

48

Julie Jacobs called Carlos Mackenzy. Her week had included several sessions of listening to the spooky concerns of people related to the recipient of a heart that had come from Carlos's transplant center. These people were intent on learning more about the donor.

X, the heart recipient was doing poorly. Rejection had caught up with him and he was also experiencing arrhythmias. He threw another blood clot that caused a seizure and possibly a minor stroke. He'd been less than compliant with his anti-rejection protocol. His associates believed that he was showing a major change in his personality and his ability to function appropriately. Julie reminded Carlos that she had spoken to him previously about this heart recipient X.

Carlos remembered that X was a scientist and that his heart failure had been caused by COVID. "Isn't X the researcher who became a crazed sports fan after his transplant? I distinctly remember your telling me about him because of some changes I experienced after my transplant. And this guy also went crazy with using ketchup; am I right?"

"You've got a good memory for details, Carlos. You also have to know that I would never pressure anyone in the transplant community to violate patient confidentiality, but I think there might be a compelling reason for these people to know something more about the donor in this case."

"So lay it on me, Julie. I've never pushed a recipient-donor connection, but if you think I need to consider doing that, please tell me why."

Julie revealed that she had learned from X's wife and research partner, that X's research involves extremely dangerous viruses, the kind that can kill if mishandled. X is also very involved in the study of how viruses adapt themselves to become more transmissible. He knows how to edit genes. Just for an example, suppose a lethal virus like the one that causes rabies, which historically can only be transmitted by the bite of an infected animal, can now be modified so that it flies through the air with the greatest of ease?"

"Yowsers! Is that what this researcher is trying to do?"

"That's the problem, Carlos. His associates aren't sure of what he's trying to do, or even what he's capable of. They're worried that he could do something horrific if authorities were to threaten shutting his lab down because of his bad health.

"X's research partner suspects that some competitor researchers might be trying to sabotage X's lab or get the authorities to close it. They'd apparently love to get their hands on the funding that X procured, back when he was a healthy young scientist. Maybe they'd also like to get their hands on whatever discoveries they believe he's made. I guess scientific research is so underfunded that competition for resources has become vicious."

Carlos suddenly recalled the list of psychiatric diagnoses that went with the heart of X's donor. As he scrolled through his files to that record, he was starting to perceive why there could be a problem. The tissues of the donor and the recipient in this pairing, were exceptionally compatible.

But then, after looking back at Zoey Collins's psychiatric diagnoses, Carlos concluded that this donor's profile should never be made known to her organ recipients. "So why would connecting this scientist with his donor be of any use to anyone?"

"I'm wrestling with this too, Carlos, but here's what makes me think we have to at least give it some consideration. X's wife introduced me to a trusted associate who I will refer to as P, because she's a psychiatrist, in addition to being a friend of the family. P perceives that X is angry and extremely vengeful, and she feels that she can no longer ignore the potential of X doing something catastrophic.

"P has a rather interesting background. I've learned that she was once a psychiatric profiler for the military. She got to decide who was stable enough to be trained as a sniper, and which of the prisoners of war were most dangerous. After listening to her concerns about X's behavior, and knowing how dangerous he could be, I just don't feel right about ignoring this."

"Okay, Julie. I see why this is troubling. But just hypothetically, suppose I tell you that X's heart once belonged to a sadistic animal torturer. How will that make P stop X from doing whatever it is these people are afraid he might do?

"Maybe it's not even X who's in charge of some evil scheme. Maybe he's just a pawn and the people who fund him are actually paying him to develop a biologic weapon that they have purpose for. Maybe they'll just send the next mad scientist to run the lab if X succumbs to rejection. The lesson that some mad scientist undoubtedly learned from the pandemic was that with the right germ, you can make the whole world do what you want.

"Meanwhile, X's loved ones would have to live with the horror that X was possessed by the devil. How will that help anything? And how would the donor's family benefit from such a connection? They'd have to live with the guilt that their loved one's heart turned someone else into a demon. It could be devastating for people who are already bereaved."

"You're right, Carlos. I've told P exactly all of those things that you just told me. But now this issue is haunting me. That's me, Carlos, who doesn't even believe in DOTS. But I have witnessed a transformation in this heart recipient that's almost out of a science fiction horror movie. Even if X's significant others will never know,

I need to know if there's something I should be doing to try to prevent this possibly deranged patient from unleashing a bioterrorism disaster."

Carlos was starting to empathize with Julie's obvious unease. "Let me look into what's known about this donor, and I'll get back to you quickly. I just need to look at the files."

Carlos didn't really have to look. He had done so while he was talking to Julie. He had remembered most of it anyway, but now he needed a little time to think. The donor's profile was disheartening, if not downright frightening.

Carlos could see no value in revealing that the donor had multiple psychiatric disorders. If there really was such a thing as DOTS, and this heart contained cells that retained some of the emotions of its previous owner, then maybe this scientist had been turned into a psychopath. Julie's anxiety couldn't just be dismissed.

Carlos was starting to feel guilty about having ever publicized his own experience with Donor Organ Transference Syndrome. Maybe he had caused unnecessary anxiety in other transplant coordinators and patients. Maybe even his personal experience with what he had believed to be DOTS wasn't real.

Maybe the changes in Carlos's preferences and feelings that occurred after he received a new heart, were caused by the effects of the anesthetics on his brain during the long hours he was on the heart-lung machine during the transplant. Maybe those changes were caused by all of the many drugs, and then the many drug changes, that he went through as he transitioned from a heart failure patient to an "alien-heart" patient. Maybe the changes he experienced were the result of his self-image having had to transform from "kid with bad heart" to "man with new lease on life."

Maybe the brain of heart recipient X had also changed due to COVID, and the low oxygen levels caused by the COVID-infected lungs. Then maybe, poor X's cognitive function was further compromised by chronically deficient perfusion of his brain due to his failing heart. Maybe the changes in X had nothing to do with his donor. Carlos regretted having opened this Pandora's box.

After struggling with the conflict for almost an hour, Carlos called Julie back. "Okay, Julie. You've really challenged me. I still do not want to facilitate any connection between your heart recipient's people and the donor's people. However, I feel morally obligated to tell you that this young donor's medical records are notable for pediatric behavior disorders. I hope that helps you and P to know what to do about X."

49

It didn't take Doctor Ezra Rhea very long to conclude that Curtis Zigby was the likely suspect in the contamination of his patients. After looking at the employment files of everyone in the surgery department, Zigby's record was the most suspect.

Zigby had brief access to the patients when no one else was around when he would transport them down the hallway from an operating room to the recovery area. Doctor Rhea furtively followed Zigby down the hall after a case and saw him run his finger around the stem on the bottom of the IV bag. He also observed Zigby's hand scrubbing routine at the sink, and he came to the same conclusion that Dayo Igwe had arrived at. He'd hoped he could set up a surveillance camera to capture that hallway, but he couldn't figure out a way to do it that wouldn't alert others to his investigation.

Doctor Rhea looked at the surgical staff roster for the hospital where Zigby had last worked, and found the name of a former colleague, Russell McKeon. Ezra and Russell had done their general surgery residencies at the same hospital almost three decades ago, and they had been socially connected, although Russell was three years ahead of Ezra in the five-year program. Russell then went on to do a fellowship in thoracic surgery. He was retired now, but he had been on the staff of Zigby's last hospital for the final eight years of his career, and he had been there for the Tazodan takeover.

Russell McKeon was more than willing to divulge to Ezra Rhea what had happened at his hospital because he was still angry about it. Like Bandore, it was a medium-sized hospital located in a semi-rural area where the local population had no other options. It had always struggled financially and then the pandemic demolished its puny reserves. The trustees hoped a Tazodan takeover would save the facility from closure.

As soon as the takeover began, all of the department chairpersons found themselves in conflict with the new management whose primary goal was to streamline costs. Regardless of community needs, unprofitable services like psychiatry and pediatrics were shut down.

The local radiologists were replaced by Tazodan's staff, which viewed all the imaging studies remotely. Most of the anesthesiologists were replaced by Tazodan's squad of traveling nurse anesthetists, and the complication rate in surgery patients rose sharply.

It wasn't so easy to replace surgeons. Tazodan wanted the surgeons to become salaried staff instead of independent contractors. Naturally, there was resistance. That's when there started to be infection control problems. Russell McKeon's cases weren't affected, but the cases of some of the more vocal surgeons were. As often as twice a month, patients who had successful surgeries wound up with pneumonia or sepsis.

Russell didn't know the details for most of those cases, but he did know that a cardiac surgeon had lost a patient to a fulminant pneumococcal infection that should never have occurred and should also have been more easily treated. After about eight months of these problems, the chief of surgery was forced to resign. That put the rest of the surgical staff on notice. Those who were too rooted in the community to leave, and too young to retire, sacrificed their autonomy to take up Tazodan's demands to become hospital employees.

Russell McKeon had thought he still had a few good years of operating in his future, but he was so disgusted with Tazodan's indifference to patient safety, that he opted to retire ahead of his life plan. Meanwhile, Tazodan was providing handsome returns to its investors.

"Did you know, Ezra, that before the pandemic, about one of out of every five of some six thousand U.S. hospitals was for-profit? Now, that number has almost doubled. In states like Texas and Nevada, about half the community hospitals have become for-profit. And if some wealthy investors can't make money off of your illness or injury, then you may not be able to obtain care, especially if you live in a rural area where there's no competition.

"Just for example, in 2023, HCA Healthcare reported sixty-five billion in revenue, while some of the CEOs of these for-profit healthcare corporations take home more than twenty million in annual salary.

"Corporations also ate up private practices. When everyone was hiding during the lockdown, doctors had no way to pay their rent, employees, or other expenses. For the majority, the choice was to close their practices or sell them to corporations. Since the pandemic, more than ninety percent of private practices have been taken over by corporations. The pandemic was a great tool for transforming healthcare from a human service into a money-maker for the greedy officers and shareholders of big corporations."

"Yeesh, thanks for all the good news, Russell. I guess I haven't been paying attention to the big picture because I've been so preoccupied with the local chaos. I'm afraid Tazodan is doing to me what they did to your surgery chief. Did anyone in your hospital ever figure out what was causing the infections?"

"Oh, they looked high and low for months, but to my knowledge, the mystery was never solved. I think the issue did resolve after the surgeons became employees."

"Does the name Curtis Zigby mean anything to you? He was a scrub tech in your O.R.s and now he's working in my hospital."

"Don't recognize the name. Do you think he has something to do with the infections?"

"Well, it would be really interesting to see if the infections in your hospital correspond to the time he was working there, because the infections started here after he came on staff.

"Does the name Ingrid Smythe mean anything to you?"

"Oh yeah! Everyone around here knows that name. She came on as the chief executive officer when Tazodan took over. She was here for about a year while all of the changes were occurring and then she disappeared. Now there's another Tazodan ogre running the show. Do you think Smythe has something do with the infections?"

"I'm definitely starting to wonder. Some snooping indicates that Smythe owns numerous health care companies and one of those companies seems to provide biologic agents to research laboratories, maybe even agents like pneumococcal bacteria."

"Wow, Ezra! That's either a terrifying fact or a very presumptuous theory. What do you actually know about this guy Zigby?"

"Actually, all I know is that he's a drifter. We've got an employee file that indicates he moves from hospital to hospital pretty quickly. He quietly does his job, and he socializes with no one. I've tried to engage him in conversation, but it's like talking to cauliflower. I can't get much more out of him than a head nod.

"I've employed an attorney who's got a private eye trying to dig into his background, but I've been afraid to do much more for fear of alerting Zigby to the fact that he's a suspect. If he knew of my suspicions, and if he is the agent of Tazodan's scheme to get rid of me, and if he alerted Smythe to the fact that I'm on to their scheme, I'm afraid to think what might happen. Surely, my investigation would get quickly shut down and so might I. If what I suspect is true, Ingrid Smythe could be capable of killing people in order to achieve her goals."

"My lord, Ezra! This is too diabolical. I hope you're wrong. I will try to do some snooping at my end regarding those infections, but I see the need to not arouse anyone else's suspicions. I'll get back to you if I can find out anything relevant."

50

Gavin Siddoway had finally received a new kidney. His stepsister Bree was still right by his side when he came in for his first post-transplant appointment with Carlos Mackenzy.

The kidney had come from an anonymous living donor. Occasionally, some altruistic soul who knows of someone else whose life has been saved by a kidney transplant, becomes motivated to sacrifice a kidney for someone who is dying. Gavin's donor's kidney turned out to be an excellent match and he was doing exceptionally well after the transplant.

When Gavin got whisked off to the lab for bloodwork, Carlos mentioned to Bree that associates of Zoey Collins's heart recipient were making a concerted effort to find out more about the donor. As far as Carlos knew, the Collins hadn't even responded to letters of gratitude from the organ recipients. He was wondering if Bree might have had more contact with the family, and whether she had ever found out if the donor had been a sports fan. That seemed to be a big issue for the associates of the heart recipient.

When Carlos had first asked Bree that question, she hadn't revealed that she knew about Zoey's addiction to watching sports. She'd decided that it would be much better for everyone if she didn't divulge what she knew about this donor. Now, she was wondering if this wasn't just an innocent inquiry that could satisfy some curiosity. But then again, if this organ recipient had somehow become corrupted by the donor's heart, there could be other memories in those heart cells that wouldn't be as benign as a passion for baseball.

Bree was in a quandary. "Why, Carlos, do you think these people are so determined to find out if the donor was a sports fan? If the recipient suddenly developed this interest, why wouldn't they just assume that it's something that got passed along from the donor and that's that. There must be something else going on with this recipient that has these people anxious, and knowing what I know about the donor, their anxiety might have merit."

Bree was amplifying Carlos's concerns. "Well Bree, I do know that this donor was a troubled child, but is there something else you know about her that's even more concerning?"

"Okay, Carlos. I'm going to make a confession here. I have actually developed a relationship with Zoey Collins's mother. She's a lovely person whose life has been shaped by a number of profound tragedies. Here's what I know. Zoey was the result of an unplanned pregnancy. For about the first ten years of her life, she was parented by her maternal grandparents, and raised as though her biologic mother was her sibling.

"Because Zoey wasn't a wanted child, it appears that she may have been resented by her family. I was told that a younger sister, who had been the baby of the family, was jealous of the attention that Zoey took from her. If she thought no one was paying attention, she was mean to baby Zoey.

"Also, because Zoey's skin tone was on the brown side, she wasn't well accepted in the white enclave of a community in which her family resided. She was so bullied that the family had to eventually move.

"Zoey's biologic mother wound up assuming custody of her daughter just as Zoey was transitioning into adolescence. The anger that had built up in Zoey throughout her childhood was apparently magnified by the hormonal surges of puberty. She started hanging with a bad crowd, and I probably don't even have to tell you the rest: experimentation with drugs, risky sexual behavior, school failure, shoplifting, suicide attempts, and the other heart-wrenching problems that befall troubled teenagers and torture their parents.

"Zoey's biologic mother Deidra has also been tortured by her own parents who were furious with her for donating Zoey's organs without their knowledge. They thought the whole idea of organ donation was vile.

"I actually helped Deidra to stage an intervention with her parents. She invited her parents and siblings over for a birthday celebration for her brother, and she arranged for Gavin and me to be there too. We were introduced as friends, though it was mentioned that I was a policeperson and that Gavin had been a physical therapist before attending the dialysis clinic became his primary job.

Gavin looked like he was ready to bed down in a coffin at Deidra's family gathering, though his personality shone through. He connected well with Deidra's dad and I'm pretty sure that by the time Deidra's parents left this encounter, shall we say, they'd had a change of heart about organ donation."

"Meanwhile, my connection with Zoey Collins's family continues. The evening after I met her family, Deidra's mother called me. She said she got my number from Deidra in case she ever needed to contact the police about something. Then she told me about a crime that had impacted her family a long time ago. She asked if there was some possibility that the police could use today's more sophisticated genetic data banks to solve it. So, I'm thinking about getting even more involved with these people. I like Deidra Collins and I don't like unsolved crimes."

↲↳↲↳ **51** ↲↳↲↳

Ezra Rhea's old colleague, Doctor Russell McKeon, no longer had access to any medical records in the hospital computer system other than his own patient charts, but he did still have friends in the hospital. Someone in the lab got him a list of the dates of pneumococcal infections. A friend in the records department got him the employment dates for Curtis Zigby. The time frame coincided perfectly. Russell passed the info along to Ezra Rhea.

Russell had also had a conversation with the former chief surgeon who got squeezed out by the Tazodan takeover. She was now performing neurosurgery in a non-profit hospital, and she was glad she got pushed out. After hearing Russell's story, she admitted that when those infection issues were occurring, she had suspected that some doctors were being sabotaged for resisting Tazodan's restructuring of their services. She just didn't have the evidence to support her suspicions.

Russell had also looked into Ingrid Smythe's biologic empire, and he was alarmed by what he'd learned. All over the world, there were scientists using gene splicing techniques in the interests of conquering disease. There were also sinister labs using these techniques to create biologic weaponry, like a bacterium that's resistant to antibiotics. That could explain why initial treatment failed for some of their post-operative patients.

Maybe there was some sort of gel that the bacterium could be infused into that would protect it from topical antiseptics like alcohol or betadine, so when the stem of the IV solution bag was cleaned, the bacteria were protected. Maybe the infected gel could be packaged into a tiny bead that could be easily expressed and applied to a specific target. All Zigby had to do was squeeze a bit of the stuff onto his finger and rub it onto the rubber stopper on the stem of the IV bag. Then, when a medication was injected into the IV solution through the rubber stopper, the needle would push the bacteria into the solution which would carry the germ into the patient's bloodstream.

Pneumococcal species were legal to work with in BSL-2 labs, and there were hundreds of those labs around, legal ones anyway. Who knew how many illegal labs might be playing with pathogens like this? The possibilities were limitless. Russell admitted to Ezra that he was greatly distressed by what he was learning about the genetic manipulation of microbes.

Ezra Rhea revealed to Russell that the profile of Curtis Zigby was looking very compatible with their theories. The private eye had followed Zigby home where he parked his old clunker car behind a semi-shabby apartment complex. An hour later, Zigby came out of the building and got into a late model luxury vehicle. He then spent the rest of the night by himself at the county racetrack. He did the same thing on another night of surveillance. It appeared that he was a lone wolf with a gambling habit.

Ezra's attorney's avoided investigations at any Tazodan owned hospitals for fear it could tip off whoever was rewarding Zigby for putting patients' lives at risk. But the lawyer did obtain some data from two of the other hospitals that Zigby had formerly worked in. There were plenty of job opportunities in hospitals for transporters, so Zigby would never have trouble finding work and he could easily move around.

"Zigby's life seems boring" Ezra said. "The guy shows up and does an adequate job. He doesn't cause any problems, but he doesn't talk to anyone either. After a year or so, he gives notice that he's leaving immediately for personal reasons. His references can only say he was a reliable worker while he was there. My lawyer thinks

Zigby could be running away from gambling debts. He does seem to pay his taxes and his rent, but how is he paying for a top-of-the-line luxury automobile on the salary of a scrub tech?"

"Maybe one of his horse bets paid off big-time? Probably not. So how are you going to catch this guy?" Russell asked. "I completely understand that whatever you tell me is strictly confidential."

"I trust you, Russ. As my attorney gets some of the data he's seeking regarding Ingrid Smythe and her companies, we're planning to entrap Zigby by the placement of a special filter under the sink where he scrubs his hands after he delivers the patients to recovery. The membrane can catch and retain any bacteria that are washed off his hands and into this sink.

"Someone in my hospital who is working with me on this, knows a scientist who got us some of these membranes. These are the kinds of materials that are used in high-level biosafety labs to prevent contamination of water sources.

"The scientist will analyze what's been captured by the filter. Then we'll compare it to a pneumococcal specimen that our hospital lab processed in the case of another infected patient. We just had a case of a woman who came in for sinus surgery and wound up with pneumonia. I now know that this is the second time this ENT doctor has had a patient get a post-operative infection. The ENT is one of the old-timers around here who's been resisting the Tazodan takeover."

"And if the pneumococci from the sink filter and the patient match, then what happens?" Russell asked.

"My attorney doesn't want to approach the D.A.s office about having Zigby arrested unless he has the goods to have Smythe arrested at the same time. He thinks if he just goes for Zigby, Smythe will be sipping a strawberry daquiri on a private island where she can't be found."

"I wonder about that, Ezra. It looks to me like Smythe is way too entrenched in multiple businesses to be able to do a disappearing act like that. What I wonder is, who is behind Ingrid Smythe in this scheme? Maybe she has the wherewithal to pull it off on her own so that Tazodan thinks she's a managerial genius. Maybe Tazodan has no idea how she's bending surgical staffs around, and she's doing it for her own glory. Or maybe she's just testing biologic weapons for someone else and she's part of a dangerous cabal."

"Russell, you have a fertile imagination."

"It comes from having done my thoracic surgery fellowship in an inner-city hospital where I saw knife and gunshot wounds almost every day. At rechecks, I'd hear these victims' stories after patching up their chests, and it was sort of like a course in advanced criminology.

"Or maybe I just have a criminal mind. Anyway, I hope your attorney can figure out who all the guilty parties are here, because if just Curtis Zigby goes down, the masterminds won't have much trouble finding another patsy and more lives will be put at risk."

52

Julie Jacobs and Carlos Mackenzy continued to struggle with the case of the transplanted heart. Recipient X had worsening rejection and had now developed heart failure. He was suffering from shortness of breath, and he'd had a seizure and several fainting episodes. He was morbidly depressed and wishing he had died before this new heart came along.

Unfortunately, X's anger at his situation had morphed into outright hostility towards his supporters. X's wife was still managing to take care of other sick people every day, while X was being left in the care of home health aides. X's mother-in-law was paying for round-the-clock assistance, but X's disagreeable behavior was making the retention of nurses difficult. As his cyclosporine doses increased, everyone around him was wearing masks. For fear of bringing germs home from the hospital, his wife was sleeping in her childhood bedroom.

X was also still trying to remotely manage his research, but his partner was concerned that X's efforts had become more detrimental than helpful. X's thinking was increasingly riddled with flaws, and it sometimes seemed disturbingly unreasonable.

That's when Julie Jacobs and Carlos Mackenzy decided to put psychiatrist Melinda Villarose, an associate of the recipient, in contact with Bree Siddoway, an associate of the donor's family. Melinda and Bree would never know each other's names or phone numbers. They were connected through a portal between the transplant centers.

Melinda had worked hard to reduce her questions to just a few. Bree said she wasn't sure if she could be objective. She and the donor's mother had become friends, and she herself had a family member who was an organ recipient.

After the physician and the policeperson connected over their mutual uncertainty about the idea of cellular memory, Bree admitted that the donor had a history of antisocial behaviors. Although Bree never knew Zoey Collins, she suspected that the deceased girl had been afflicted with both genetic and environmental wickedness. But that was just a presumption she didn't care to share. She told Melinda that there were reasons to believe that the donor's antisocial behaviors were the consequence of negative life experiences.

In the course of their respective careers, both Bree and Melinda had ruminated over an age-old question. Were humans innately good but corrupted by environmental forces? Or were humans innately evil and in need of conditioning to suppress their worst instincts?

There were certainly some things that turned people bad. Back in the days when Melinda was screening military recruits for psychiatric disorders, she was always confounded by those who were galvanized by the opportunity to bomb, shoot, or otherwise destroy strangers in a foreign land. She had less concern about those whose desire to wear a soldier's uniform seemed driven by some sense of patriotism, protectionism, or paranoia.

Traumatic brain injuries can result in aggressive and antisocial behavior. Toxins can also damage the brain. Violent criminals very frequently show evidence of juvenile lead poisoning. Even mild lead exposure in young children can cause learning disabilities and behavior problems. When Flint, Michigan had its water crisis, brain damage from lead toxicity was evident on imaging studies of babies even before they were born.

Still, Melinda knew that even in the absence of toxic exposures or trauma, bad kids could come out of good homes, while good kids could come out of bad homes. In Melinda's experience, nature prevailed over nurture in most cases and some people just seemed to suffer from faulty wiring. There was also a tendency for mental illness to run in families. Melinda asked if the donor's relatives were known to have any psychiatric problems.

Bree had met Zoey's maternal family at the intervention. They all seemed quite sane. She could only imagine how much distress this unwanted child had caused them. Bree told Melinda that the donor's mother was healthy and there were no known mental health issues in her immediate family. Nothing was known about the paternal side of the family.

Bree asked Melinda for an update on the heart recipient. Melinda said his outlook was guarded. A few months previously, she would have been happy to tell the donor's family that their generosity had saved a brilliant scientist who might save humanity from lethal diseases. Now, the donor's family would be better off not knowing about the recipient's status.

"X has been fighting an uphill battle for a long time. He's an extraordinary person who has a potential for greatness. Maybe he can still muster the strength to rally," Melinda lied.

Their contrived conversation gave Melinda the impression that her counterpart was concealing the donor's true nature, and that it was much worse than anyone was going to admit. Even from what little she had just been told, she wondered if the donor was the offspring of a rape.

"Did your transplant coordinator inform you that the heart recipient is a scientist whose work is so dangerous, that it's almost like he has his finger on the button that would launch an atomic bomb? Please, I give you my word that I will not reveal anything you tell me to the recipient or his family members, not even little things, like did the donor douse her food in ketchup? But I must ask you this question. Knowing what you know, would you feel safe if this donor's heart was somehow influencing a scientist who just happens to have the capacity to unleash terror on humanity?"

Bree closed her eyes and took a long deep breath. Did her duty as an officer of the law require her to think of public safety in answering this question? Did she believe that a heart could hold memories? She did know about a rare few documented cases that gave credence to the theory of cellular memory. Most remarkable, was the story of a young child who received a transplant and then reported nightmares that included such vivid details about how her donor was murdered, that she helped the police to solve the crime. This was a widely circulated story on the Internet, but Bree didn't know if it was true or just an oft-repeated legend.

Bree wasn't sure what to believe on a cerebral level, but her own heart was compelling her to tell the truth. If there was even just a tiny fraction of a chance that this particular donor's heart could somehow influence its recipient's behavior, she would not feel safe. She reluctantly confessed that to Melinda. Based on the promise of not revealing anything to the recipient's people, and with earnest interest in protecting others, Bree also divulged to Melinda that the donor was an avid sports fan, and, that she had a penchant for ketchup.

Bree had learned about the ketchup thing at the intervention for Deidra's family. As the birthday cake was being sliced, the Martin family siblings joked that Zoey would have put ketchup on her birthday cake and on her ice cream. She especially loved ketchup with chocolate.

"I hope that helps you to decide what to do about X," Bree said. "Good luck to you and to the heart recipient and his family."

arius was fading fast. He had trouble staying awake, even for the games he really wanted to watch. In the gap between football and baseball seasons, the sounds of hockey and basketball had been reverberating throughout the Baccay household. Darius couldn't hear well, so the TV was turned up extra loud. Thea had taken to wearing earplugs though they hardly helped.

Thea had also come to believe that Darius's sports addiction was compensation for his cognitive dysfunction, Sports were much easier to follow than were the daily reports of genetic code rearrangements.

Maybe the donor's heart had nothing to do with Darius's transformation. Every other week, Thea was reading reports about emerging evidence of brain damage in COVID survivors. In one study of men who recovered from COVID Omicron, and who had previously had brain imaging for other reasons, new imaging showed that the gray matter in their brains had shrunk in areas that correlated to sleep disorders, anxiety, depression, and cognitive dysfunction. Another researcher documented six-point IQ drops in COVID survivors.

In a moment of clarity, Darius had told Sully that he was turning everything over to him: the lab, the projects, the grants, the licenses, the academic support, and whatever. Thea wondered if 'whatever' included her. But Darius was no longer cogent enough to even think about what he was saying. He was often confused. He was on oxygen again and he was rapidly declining in his physical and mental capacities.

During one of his hospitalizations for progressive heart failure, the trespassing trio of Thea, Sullivan, and Melinda wrested Darius's computers from the apartment and placed them in the hacking hands of James Dzobak. James was able to extract what Sullivan needed for legal transfer of the lab.

James also obtained for himself, a link to the lab's data banks. He hoped he could maybe come to understand this information. Besides, one of his primary guilty pleasures in life was poking holes in the most formidable of firewalls.

From the information that James had stolen, Sullivan was able to contact the investors. They knew that Sullivan had been running the lab since Darius had become ill. They had faith in him, and they were relieved that he would be taking over. They signed off on the transfers.

Thea's family's lawyer got everything legalized, including a divorce for Thea, but Darius didn't know any of this. He was either watching the Chicago Bulls or college basketball, or he was nodding off. Thea's mother was worried that Thea could wind up with a mountain of debt for loans Darius had taken without Thea's knowledge. He had unpaid education loans and he'd taken several private loans to finance his travel when he was rounding up his international investors. Thea didn't know about the loans until James plucked the numbers from Darius's personal laptop.

The university executives also welcomed the transfer of the lab, so long as it continued to bring in the dollars. They had been nervous about losing the grant that supported Darius's research. Although there would be plenty of other researchers who would be thrilled to operate such a sophisticated lab, almost none of them would come with the financial endowments that had accompanied Darius Amari.

Always reaching out for organ donors, the university's transplant center published a quarterly online newsletter read by members of the transplant community, both patients and professionals. It featured stories by donors and recipients, and it reported on new developments and controversies in the transplant world.

Because of its connection to the medical school, the spring newsletter also included a brief story about the transfer of the university biosafety lab, accompanied by old photos of molecular biologist Professor Sullivan Dietz, and virologist Professor Darius Amari, the recipient of a donor's heart.

Gavin and Bree Siddoway were recipients of that newsletter. So was Deidra Collins.

Deidra always liked to look at the work of other graphic designers, so she'd peruse the formatting and artwork of ads and publications that dropped into her mailbox. She was looking at the fonts in the transplant center newsletter when the photo of Darius Amari caught her eye. He had a swarthy complexion, but it looked like he had very pale blue eyes.

Zoey's skin tone wasn't nearly as brown as was that of the guy in the picture, but the contrast between her tan complexion and her eye color had always commanded attention. Deidra also had blue eyes, but her eyes weren't nearly as pale and compelling as Zoey's.

Darius Amari was a highly respected scientist, Deidra told herself. It was just a coincidence. He couldn't possibly be her rapist. According to the Internet, Asians and people from the Middle East could have light blue eyes. It wouldn't be so rare. She completely dismissed the possibility.

Bree Siddoway had seen some pictures of Zoey Collins. There was now a nicely framed one in the hallway of Deidra's home. Zoey's looks were striking because she had a brownish complexion, but very light blue eyes. It was a totally unexpected combination. There was something else about the picture that commanded Bree's attention. Zoey's expression seemed to communicate disdain for the photographer and the world.

When Bree had seen Zoey in her brain-dead state before her organs were harvested, she hadn't noticed the skin tone so much as she had noticed the very pale blue eyes. The rest of the face was a kind of a black and blue, bloody pancake at that time, but the eyes were still stunning.

Darius Amari was a respected scientist, Bree told herself. The light blue eyes may be uncommon, but Deidra has blue eyes too. It had to be a coincidence. Bree put it out of her mind.

The next day, Bree felt compelled to look at the photo again. Now, she couldn't put it out of her mind. What am I doing? she asked herself. "What if, just hypothetically, this virus guy was Deidra's rapist? So now, I'm going to put him in jail for what happened seventeen years ago? According to the article, 'Amari is stepping down to continue his personal battle with health issues.' How could putting him in jail help anything?

Bree was gobsmacked to have to even consider that Deidra's generous organ donation might have saved the life of her rapist. She was also repulsed by the possibility that the life of a violent rapist might have been saved by the suicide of his ostracized offspring. It tugged hard at her heartstrings to think that the rapist could have been the beneficiary of the suffering of Deidra, Zoey, and their family.

Hadn't Carlos said that the tissue match was the closest they'd ever seen between unrelated persons? Still, it was such a long shot, it couldn't be worth pursuing. Nothing in the profile of Darius Amari was compatible with his being a criminal. Again, she tried to bury the notion, but it kept invading her thoughts. Ultimately, Bree returned a call to Deidra's mother. "You told me there had been a person of interest in Deidra's rape case, but it never amounted to anything. Is there anything you can tell me about that person now?"

There were some pauses and sniffles before Deidra's mother managed to divulge her story. She used to grocery shop in an independent grocery store. The year of Deidra's rape, there had been an employee in that market who would leer at Deidra. Deidra was oblivious, but the man's ogling was offensive.

Mrs. Martin complained to the store manager about this employee. He said not to worry; the man's striking eyes made people think he was staring at them when in fact, they were staring at his eyes, and he was returning the stare. Those spectacular blue eyes almost seemed to transform the man into a bit of a freak.

One day, Deidra's mother was so incensed by how the man was looking at her daughter that she confronted him. She was embarrassed to admit it, but in her state of anger, she had used some racially charged language. The man responded with some hostile remarks, and shortly thereafter, the Martins no longer saw him stocking shelves. The manager said that he'd abruptly just stopped coming to work. His whereabouts were unknown.

After Zoey was born, her exceptionally pale blue eyes rattled Mrs. Martin. She went back to the store manager and asked about the employee again. The manager told her that the man had been a good worker, but he didn't stay long. He'd work in the store for a few hours after he worked some other job earlier in the day. He was only there for a few months. The manager couldn't remember the name, 'something not American.' But he did remember that 'blue eyes' didn't have a car. A couple of times, the manager gave him a ride in bad weather. Otherwise, he would walk to and from the store. He was living in the caretaker's apartment in the back of a laundromat. That was all the manager remembered about the man, besides his remarkable blue eyes. The police were also unable to track him down.

The grocery store had since been taken over by a chain and the manager was long gone. The laundromat had been replaced by a nail salon. Its former owner was deceased.

"Do you think you could recognize that man from a picture?" Bree asked.

Deidra's mother said she wasn't sure. It was a long time ago. But she thought his eyes would give him away. However, when Bree forwarded the photo, she couldn't really say. The only things Mrs. Martin actually remembered about him were the colors of his eyes and skin.

Bree was wishing she had never gotten involved with this. She hoped that Deidra and her family would never know that blue-eyed Darius Amari could have been the recipient of Zoey's heart. But if Deidra had seen that picture, she might be wondering too, but only because of the eye color. But having rare eye color didn't make you a rapist.

After ruminating about the case for a few days, Bree got a call from Carlos. The family of the recipient of Zoey Collins's heart had informed their transplant coordinator that X had died during the night. His failing heart had generated a fatal arrhythmia. His family was grateful that his suffering was ended. His body was donated to medical science. His COVID-damaged vital organs weren't suitable for transplantation.

Bree asked Carlos if there was any way she could obtain the genetic profile of the now deceased X. She had learned something about his background from the connection that Carlos had fostered, that could be of forensic interest for police data banks.

Carlos shared the reports after redacting all of the identifying information. The data showed that X was very much a mutt like Zoey, but his genetic heritage was even more diversified, probably because he was a chimera, a person with more than one type of DNA.

Everyone has a few cells in them that are derived from their mothers, but those cells are too scarce to show up in most tissue assays. Mothers also retain some cells from fetuses, even those lost to miscarriages. Even a blood transfusion can impart someone else's DNA.

Having a tiny bit of DNA from someone else is referred to as micro chimerism.

However, some people have a lot of cells from another being in their systems because of an organ transplant, or because in early embryonic life, one fraternal twin absorbed the other twin. That's very rare. More commonly, cancer patients who have had bone marrow transplants become chimeras.

At Darius's autopsy, the coroner expected to see genetic sequences from stem cells in Darius's heart that differed from those in his blood. What she didn't expect to find was a third set of stem cells in his bone marrow and in some of his other tissues.

Then the coroner noticed some very faint scars in the skin over Darius's hip bone. There were also old, small scars over his limb veins and his scalp. It appeared that he'd undergone some medical treatment as a baby. An oncologist on staff surmised that Darius may have been treated for infantile leukemia.

Thea then learned that India was first starting to perform bone marrow transplantation around the time that Darius was an orphan in Calcutta. Maybe he was the discarded baby who survived an experimental treatment, and neither he nor his adoptive family ever knew.

By their genetic similarities, Zoey Collins and Darius Amari could have been distantly related, but their genetic profiles were not a close enough match for them to have been father and daughter. Darius was not the blue-eyed man that Mrs. Martin had been having nightmares about for the past seventeen years. Bree assured

Deidra and her mother that they could stop wondering about the picture of the man in the newsletter. He was not Zoey's father.

However, Bree was now toying with the idea of going on a hunt for a Zoey-like pedigree with swimming pool-colored eyes. Some criminal out there had a distinct trademark glimmering between his cheeks and his forehead.

Bree only toyed with the idea for another day. Ultimately, she decided to give up her police career and pursue an education that would enable her to become a transplant coordinator. She had come to believe that helping people like Gavin would be far more satisfying than putting messed-up people in jail.

 **54**

It was almost midnight when Franz and James Dzobak brought Lily Dzobak to the Bandore Hospital E.R. She had awakened that morning with a headache, and it worsened throughout the day. She fell asleep in the early evening and woke up confused at eleven p.m. The E.R. physician diagnosed a blocked shunt and a buildup of fluid on the brain. He put in a call to the neurosurgeon.

Shunts can malfunction because of things like clumps of debris clogging them up, valve failure, or kinks in the tubing. A malfunctioning shunt needs immediate intervention to avoid brain damage, but the only neurosurgeon available to the Bandore Hospital and its patients just happened to be home with gastroenteritis, a victim of the norovirus that had been widely circulating around the region.

The neurosurgeon suggested that if Ezra Rhea was up to the challenge, he'd coach him through the procedure on a Zoom call. He knew Rhea had really good hands, the kind of steady hands that can adjust their direction and pressure to such a fine degree, that they can artfully reconnect the severed ends of a tiny blood vessel. Rhea's dexterity was remarkable considering that his hands were large. The nurses jokingly called him "Baloney Fingers." But the neurosurgeon believed that Rhea's manual sensitivity, and his engineering brain, would enable them to figure out what was wrong with the shunt.

Rhea also had the courage to try to fix whatever could be fixed. Some would say he was too brazen. As a general surgeon in a rural hospital for almost three decades, he had performed procedures that were only attempted by a smorgasbord of specialists in big city hospitals. His experience was diverse and extensive.

James Dzobak was horrified that his mother's brain was in the hands of the surgeon whose patients kept getting infected. He also understood that he had no other reasonable choice. He was greatly relieved when Lily Dzobak came out of the O.R., proclaiming that she was already feeling better. The shunt blockage had been remedied. She would be monitored in the neuro I.C.U. overnight. She was also on antibiotics to prevent shunt infection which could be extremely dangerous because it brought germs directly to the brain.

Thirty hours after Lily Dzobak's shunt procedure seemed to be entirely successful, she came down with a fever and she became confused. Within an hour, her consciousness was significantly altered. She was readmitted to the hospital for a brain infection. The neurosurgeon was able to take over her care. The next day, cultures of Lily's spinal fluid were growing pneumococcal bacteria.

As of recently, Ezra Rhea has been using the hallway scrub sink to wipe down his new camera equipment. For teaching purposes, he liked to take pictures of tumors before removing them, and his new smaller camera was too valuable to leave in the O.R. like the big old one that he'd previously used. The new one had to be sterilized every time he used it, and he'd clean the antiseptic off of it before taking it to the next O.R. where it would get sterilized again. At least that was what he told his staff he was doing at the sink between cases.

What Ezra was actually doing at the sink in the O.R. hallway, was retrieving and replacing the filters inside the sink drain. Every time that he saw Curtis Zigby on a case, he'd pretend to be wiping down his camera. He'd pass the rescued membranes from the sink drain to Melinda, who'd overnight them to Sullivan in his lab. Sully had already identified several membranes that contained a pneumococcal species, but the patients hadn't become infected. It appeared that the method of contamination wasn't foolproof. It seemed to be random as to when the germs took hold.

Thea Baccay was doing her rotation in the neurologic I.C.U. at the time of Lily Dzobak's hospitalization. She knew what antibiotics to change Lily to, even before the cultures were conclusive. By sheer coincidence, this was the third time that one of the infected patients had come under Thea's care. The neurosurgeon appreciated her experience in the matter. Thea also informed Melinda Villarose about what was going on.

Melinda learned that Curtis Zigby had been the scrub tech on call the night that Lily Dzobak had her emergency procedure for a shunt malfunction. Ezra had left the sheathed sink filter in the pocket of Melinda's lab coat which she hung in the physician lounge for just that purpose. She went to the post office on her lunch break and forwarded the filter to Sullivan.

There had been occasions where Melinda had worried that James could be part of Ingrid Smythe's toxic schemes. He always seemed to know what she was up to, and his hacking acumen was possibly greater than anyone appreciated. But when James's mother wound up a victim, Melinda's doubts about James's loyalties were erased. Melinda had met mother-killers during her military profiling days. James, an ardent lover of living things including bats, was not the type.

Like Doctor Rhea, and now like James, Melinda had been having nightmares about this potential scenario, even before Lily Dzobak became a victim. She decided it was time to act.

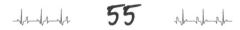

55

Shortly after hearing from Thea that Lily Dzobak was in the I.C.U. with a brain infection, Melinda managed to corral James Dzobak in the hospital cafeteria. She had become increasingly nervous about leaving any traces of her activities on her computer when it came to helping Ezra with his case. In cautious whispers, Melinda revealed to James what she and Doctor Rhea suspected was going on. She asked if he thought that Ingrid Smythe could be in on it too.

James was terrified for his mother. He had been scared by witnessing the rapid onset of cognitive impairment that his mother had exhibited when her shunt became clogged, and then again, when she developed a brain infection. He had also come to view both Melinda Villarose and Thea Baccay as allies, both medically and personally. The relationships were now beyond their local Bandore County connection, and had more to do with respect and gratitude.

James promised he'd get back to Melinda if he could find anything out. He also confirmed that she was wise to suspect that her communications might be monitored, especially since he was the techie who had been ordered to surreptitiously hack into her office desktop.

Later that night, James took Melinda's residential address from the computer and showed up at her townhouse. He believed he had found what could be incriminating evidence.

James wasn't too surprised to find Doctor Howard Blauveldt present when he arrived. Melinda and Howard weren't making any effort to conceal the relationship that had flourished between them. Howard had apparently become Melinda's personal and professional confidant, and that made James feel that he could trust them both.

James revealed that in some financial records, he had discovered some periodic payments for consulting services to a miscellaneous vendor listed as Palomino Sprints. The account was one of several in Ingrid Smythe's budget records that were separate from the Bandore Hospital general budget. The payments were each for seven thousand dollars. When James went through the hospital records looking for the patients who had been infected, it appeared in each case that Palomino Sprints received this payment within about a week of the occurrences of the infections.

There were no other vendors receiving reimbursements on a schedule like this. James had also searched widely, but he could find no other listings anywhere for a company called Palomino Sprints.

Melinda considered James's findings to be solid evidence for their theories. There was just one problem. James confessed that he wasn't actually authorized to access the information he had gleaned from being able to "get into the system." However, if this pirated information could stop a monster like Ingrid Smythe from disabling or killing people like his poor mother, James said he would be willing to face the consequences of his hacking skills becoming exposed. As much as he had tried to use this special talent of his judiciously, he'd always known that it had a serious potential to get him into trouble.

James had been thinking of quitting his current career anyway. He'd been acquiring the kind of knowledge that he hoped would make him employable in a bat lab, while he was simultaneously working to develop a relationship with Sullivan Dietz. Since hacking into Darius's computer, James had figured out that Sullivan wasn't as computer savvy as had been Darius. James hoped the knowledge he was gaining about Darius's research, along with his exceptional cyber skills, would make him a valuable asset to Sullivan.

James also hoped that Ezra Rhea's lawyer could bail him out if his clandestine hacking ability became a legal issue. Knowing that his more devious inclinations had actually saved lives, and maybe many more potential lives, incentivized James to face the consequences of his cyber espionage. He had used it only for noble purposes.

After Lily's readmission to the hospital, James and Franz had to wait the entire day before they got into the I.C.U. to spend a brief few minutes with her. She was finally awake enough to realize that they were there. The brain infection had rendered her barely conscience before the antibiotics started to work. Doctor Baccay had made the right choices. Lily seemed significantly improved and Franz and James were greatly relieved.

Doctor Howard Blauveldt intercepted James and Franz as they were leaving the hospital. There was something important that James needed to know about, and he wanted them to come with him to hear the bigger story.

Howard drove the Dzobaks to Melinda's townhouse. On the way, he explained to James that he had terminated his contract with the rent-a-doc agency, and he was now filling in at Bandore Hospital directly on an as-needed basis, while Dayo Igwe's anesthesiology friend was being incorporated into the intern class to take Suzie Nguyen's place. Like Doctor Igwe, his friend's extensive clinical experience made her a valuable asset to the training of all of the resident physicians.

Melinda contacted Ezra Rhea and told him to bring his attorney to the meeting as well. While waiting for Ezra and a take-out dinner order, Melinda also texted Thea Baccay and asked her to join them when she got out of the neuro I.C.U. They were all part of the plan.

⌇⌇⌇ 56 ⌇⌇⌇

As soon as Sullivan confirmed that the pneumococcus species in the filter was exactly the same bug that Bandore Hospital's lab was growing from Lily Dzobak's cultures, James put the plan into action.

Doctor Ezra Rhea and Thea Baccay barged into Ingrid Smythe's office when James gave them the signal. Ezra was wearing a wire. Two plain clothes law enforcement officers wearing ear buds were nearby. Ezra and Thea walked right past James and into Ingrid's inner sanctum.

Behind a closed door, and as if James was ignorant of it all, Ezra Rhea told Ingrid Smythe that James's mother was now another innocent victim of a dangerous infection, and that Bandore Hospital employee Curtis Zigby had been caught "red-handed" contaminating her.

"Who's Curtis Zigby?" Ingrid calmly asked. Thea noticed Ingrid starting to blink a lot.

Ezra leaned forward. "He's a scrub tech in the O.R. He's been infecting patients by contaminating their intravenous solution equipment. It's a very clever scheme. When he's transporting the patient, he rubs a compound containing nasty bacteria onto the stems of the bags that contain the patients' intravenous fluids. Then, when tubing is connected to the IV bag or when a nurse injects a medication into the patient's intravenous solution, the bacteria get pushed into the solution and consequently into the patient's bloodstream."

"I have no idea what or who you are talking about, Doctor Rhea.

"James," Ingrid shouted into her intercom, "pull up a file on someone in the surgical department named Curtis Zigby."

As they waited for James to respond, Thea told Ingrid Smythe how sick James's mother was because of this contamination. They'd be lucky if she recovered without brain damage.

James came into the room and told Ingrid where she could look in the computer to find auxiliary surgical staff. He also told his boss that there was still a scrub tech position open and that Zigby came on staff last June after responding to an ad by a Tazodan recruiter. "He's one of five scrub techs who cover the O.R. during regular hours. The full-timers also have some night and weekend call. What about him?" James asked, as if not knowing what was going on.

Ezra Rhea responded. "We have reason to believe that Zigby has been causing infections in people like your mother. Do you know this Zigby?"

"What?" James said. "I've seen the man's file, but I've never seen the man. Why is this guy still here if he's so incompetent?" James directed his outrage at Doctor Rhea.

"We don't believe the infections are the results of carelessness or accidental contamination. We believe that Zigby is doing this deliberately and that he's being paid to do it," Ezra responded.

"No! Oh my God! Paid by who? Why? My poor, sweet mother has never hurt anyone in her entire life. Seriously! My mother uses a have-a-heart trap to get mice out of the house. Who would do such a thing to a wonderful, kind human being like my mother, and why?"

James redirected his fury at his boss who was struggling to maintain her composure. "What's going on here, Ms. Smythe?" Thea noticed Ingrid's breathing rate increase.

Ingrid focused on her computer screen. Thea observed the blood vessels in Ingrid's neck becoming more prominent. There was a bit of quiver in her voice as Ingrid said, "okay, I see here that Curtis Zigby is on the Tazodan payroll. Where do you get off insinuating that he's being paid to hurt people?" Ingrid glowered at Ezra Rhea.

Ezra Rhea stood up, walked around Ingrid's massive desk, and planted his huge frame in front of her as she shrank back into her high-tech office chair. "Because," Ezra lied, "a law firm that cracked into Zigby's bank account, found that he receives a nice fat deposit shortly after every mysterious infection that shows up in patients undergoing surgery in Tazodan owned hospitals. The deposits are being made into the account of Palomino Sprints. Your accounting records wouldn't by any chance show that a vendor named Palomino Sprints is receiving payments from Tazodan, would it?"

Ingrid was trying to say, "That's preposterous," when the law enforcement officers burst into her office with a subpoena and ordered James to open up the computer files on payments to vendors.

Ingrid was visibly sweating now. "James," she bellowed. "Are you making payments to vendors I don't even know about?"

One of the law enforcement persons turned out to be a cyber cop. With only a few cues from James, the payments to Palomino Sprints were quickly identified on Ingrid's desktop.

Ingrid was allowed to call her lawyer before she was led away in handcuffs. She got to ride to jail in the back seat of the police car alongside of Curtis Zigby.

A few more Tazodan execs also got caught up in the sting when they tried to alter what was in the computer regarding Ingrid Smythe's discretionary budget. James had set a trap for them too. When Melinda asked him how he did that, James just sheepishly smiled.

James also informed Melinda that he would be leaving the Tazodan corporation to take a position in Sullivan Dietz's lab. He would be Sully's chief data analyst as well as a bat caretaker. He invited Melinda and Howard for a lake expedition in the summer when he planned to visit his parents.

Against all odds, Doctor Ezra Rhea continued to serve as chief of surgery for Bandore Hospital, even while successfully suing the Tazodan Corporation for defamation, corruption, medical malpractice, and attempted homicide. He turned down a financial settlement to his personal bank account in order to make the corporation accountable, and to raise the standards by which corporations treat sick and injured people and their health care providers.

Doctor Dayo Igwe actually did become the hero of Bandore Hospital when he served as the key witness in the trials of Curtis Zigby and Ingrid Smythe. He was lauded by the community for having saved lives as well as having saved the hospital's surgical services.

Doctor Rhea also found a way to bring Doctor Dayo Igwe onto his surgical staff half-way through his family practice residency. To have wasted this gifted surgeon's exceptional talent and experience in a community that desperately needed someone of his caliber, became unthinkable after Doctor Rhea had observed Igwe's skills during the family practice resident's second-year surgery rotation.

Melinda Villarose's cherished residency program also benefitted from Doctor Igwe's influence. The vacancies in her training schedule got filled by international associates of Dayo. These residents all turned out to be highly qualified, experienced, and dedicated physicians who would never have even heard of Bandore Hospital if not for their association with Dayo Igwe. One of these residents took the place of Doctor Thea Baccay.

After completing her internship, Thea accepted a second-year position in the training program of University Hospital. She would see much sicker people and a wider spectrum of pathology in a hospital that was commonly used by the people who tended to be either the sickest or the poorest or both.

Thea was torn between wanting to personally take care of people and wanting to use her intellectual gifts to contribute to the advancement of medical science. She was even thinking of taking on the work that Darius had devoted his life to. She hoped to be able to figure out what her true calling might be after another year of training.

Thea was also torn between wanting to fall in love with or just remain good friends with James. They had become really good friends. Thea and Sully got to go boating with James on the rare occasion that all three of them weren't working.

Thea also continued to visit with Melinda and Howard whenever she visited her family back in Bandore. And when Doctor Suzie Nguyen restarted her internship at Bandore Hospital, almost two years after she was attacked, Thea would visit with Suzie too.

Tazodan Corporation relented in its criteria for staffing of the Bandore Hospital training program when Doctor Melinda Villarose threatened to quit if she couldn't get help. Doctor Howard Blauveldt wound up taking the place of the now deceased Doctor Stuart Carmichael as co-manager of the family practice residency program, alongside his personal partner, Doctor Melinda Villarose.

Unlike the academic types. Blauveldt's years of office experience enriched the training of young physicians in ways that no hospital experience could.

Melinda also got around to asking junior resident Vance Kenner if he could make an adjustment to the painting that hung in her office. The pregnant belly of the horse was concealed when Vance added a baby palomino to the picture, nuzzled up to the side of the mare.

Melinda and the golden horse would no longer be weathering the storms alone.

Epilogue

As of 2023, there were more than a hundred thousand Americans on waiting lists for vital organs. Another organ failure patient is added to the list every nine minutes. **Seventeen organ failure patients die daily because of the lack of donations.**

Learn More About Organ Transplantation at:
unos.org/transplant/
optn.transplant.hrsa.gov
transplants.org
donatelife.net
www.myast.org

Bat populations are being severely stressed by loss of habitat:
Learn More About Protecting Bats at:
batworld.org
www.batcon.org
www.fws.gov/story/bats-are-one-most-important-misunderstood-animals

Acknowledgements

I am deeply indebted to Nancy Costo, Jodyne Rosen, and Amy Schapiro for their literary advice and help in creating this story. Gratitude is also extended to Doctor Kenneth Hurwitz, my husband, for his technical advice and his patience with my writing obsession. Also greatly appreciated is the assistance, competence, and creative talents of publisher Katie Mullaly of Surrogate Press who designed the cover for this novel.

About the Author

Dr. Beverly Hurwitz, originally from Brooklyn, New York, has spent her professional life as a physician, educator, and author.

In her youth she won awards for scholastic journalism and served as copy editor for her college newspaper. Before attending medical school, she spent a decade as a health and physical education teacher in rural public schools.

As a medical fellow, Beverly specialized in the care of children with neurologic disability. After three decades of clinical practice, she spent eight years as a medical case analyst/writer for administrative law judges in federal and state court systems. In recent years, she has been writing novels and hiking books.